DEATH IN THE COVENANT

ALSO AVAILABLE BY D. A. BARTLEY

Blessed Be the Wicked

DEATH IN THE COVENANT

An Abish Taylor Mystery

D. A. Bartley

CROOKED
LANE

NEW YORK

Published in the United States by Crooked Lane Books, an imprint of The Quick Brown Fox & Company LLC.

Crooked Lane Books and its logo are trademarks of The Quick Brown Fox & Company LLC.

Library of Congress Catalog-in-Publication data available upon request.

ISBN (hardcover): 978-1-64385-119-8
ISBN (ePub): 978-1-64385-120-4
ISBN (ePDF): 978-1-64385-121-1

Cover design by Mimi Bark
Book design by Jennifer Canzone

Printed in the United States.

www.crookedlanebooks.com

Crooked Lane Books
34 West 27th St., 10th Floor
New York, NY 10001

First Edition: August 2019

10 9 8 7 6 5 4 3 2 1

To Tycho

Under this law, I and my brethren are preparing tabernacles for those spirits which have been preserved to enter into bodies of honor, and be taught the pure principles of life and salvation, and those tabernacles will grow up and become mighty in the kingdom of our God. . . . If marriage be of any benefit in the eternal world, would it not be far more consistent with the law of God that [a virtuous woman] should have the privilege, by her own free, voluntary consent, to marry a good man, though he might have a family, and claim him for her husband, not only through time, but eternity?

Remarks by President Brigham Young,
Delivered in the Bowery, Provo, July 14, 1855

ONE

Damn! Please be a wrong number.

Abbie had drifted to that critical junction between pleasant drowsiness and total unconsciousness when her phone went off. Her body craved sleep—just one night of uninterrupted rest. One night with no nightmares, one night when she didn't lie awake for hours staring into the darkness. It had been too many months to count, now. John had suggested she "see someone," his big-brother way of letting her know he was worried. He had broached the topic a couple of times in gentle, oblique ways, which made Abbie feel ungrateful for being irritated.

Her phone buzzed two more times before she could focus enough to read the numbers on the screen. It was Clarke. She swiped to the right to answer the call.

"Taylor, there's been a car accident on Route 39." Jim Clarke, Abbie's partner, sounded chipper. He probably never had trouble sleeping. "The driver's dead. An old guy. I already called the doctor working as ME tonight. The chief said we should just handle it. I don't think he wants to get out of bed for a drunk driver."

"I'll be right there."

Abbie forced her body upright, the latest Tana French falling to the ground as she shifted. She picked up the book and placed it on the coffee table next to a nearly full cup of passion flower tea. Granted, reading suspense probably hadn't been the best choice for inducing sleep, but she'd hoped the herbal tea's calming qualities would do the trick.

Abbie climbed up the stairs to her bedroom. She pulled on jeans and a T-shirt, then laced up an old pair of hiking boots. As she walked back through the kitchen to the front door, the coffee pot called to her, but there wasn't time to brew a fresh one. In an act of optimism, she picked it up. It was heavy. Abbie poured day-old coffee into a thermos, grateful for small blessings.

The end of Abbie's long driveway was Route 39. Like a lot of small canyon roads in Utah, it was treacherous and narrow. Abbie's cabin wasn't far from the crash site. It wasn't long before she saw the glow of flares and police cars on the side of the road. Nearly half of the Pleasant View City Police Department was there: Clarke and the two other full-time officers. The area had been cordoned off and the three men were searching the ground.

Abbie parked her old Range Rover next to a squad car, near cement blocks that had seen better days. It had been decades since politicians in any of the nearby towns had had either the money or political will to spend on infrastructure to prevent exactly what had happened tonight. Clarke looked up when he heard her car door open. He waved.

The narrow shoulder of the road dropped precipitously to the creek below. Streams in the canyons were fast moving with snow melt this time of year, cutting jagged edges into the mountainside. Abbie hiked down the steep embankment to where the car was crumpled. The back of the dark car was in nearly perfect condition even though the automobile had taken a nose dive into the rushing creek. Despite efforts to light the scene, the darkness made it impossible to see much of the front, let alone who or what was inside it.

"What do we know about the driver?"

"Nothing," Clarke answered. "We can't touch the body until the ME gets here and does his thing. It looks to me like he drove straight off the road."

"Anyone see anything?" Beyond the lights the officers had set around the car, there was nothing but blackness. Nobody lived anywhere near this winding stretch of the canyon.

Clarke shrugged.

"Anyone check up there?" Abbie pointed to the other side of the creek. There was an unofficial campsite just past the first ridge where local teenagers liked to hang out, drink beer, and do whatever teenagers did when left to their own devices. It hadn't been so long ago that she'd spent the occasional weekend evening up a canyon beyond the careful watch of parents and Church leaders. Abbie couldn't see light from a campfire, but if she was lucky, someone might be up there, someone who could have witnessed the crash.

Clarke kicked the dirt. "No." Abbie knew he was embarrassed he hadn't already thought of checking the site, but Clarke probably hadn't been the kind of teenager who hung out at nonsanctioned campsites. It wouldn't have occurred to him.

"No worries. You stay here to meet the ME."

Flashlight in hand, Abbie crossed the stream with dry feet, courtesy of two fairly stable rocks and some luck. From there, it was a steep but not difficult climb up a well-worn dusty path. As she stepped into the cleared area, the breeze shifted so that the pleasant smell of campfire smoke was unmistakable. A few large trunks served as benches around a firepit, deep-red embers still glowing beneath the wet, charred remains of the logs.

Abbie slowly shone her flashlight in a circle around the camping area. All she could see were trees. Aside from the sound of rushing water from the creek below, it was silent. No giggling. No nervous snickering. She hadn't interrupted a lovesick teenage couple. Abbie repeated her circle of light. This time, as she faced into a breeze, she inhaled a cloud of cannabis along with the campfire smoke.

She pointed the light toward the breeze and walked around one of the large logs. Her beam lit up a sleeping bag, backpack, and a few empty cans of beer.

"Hello!" she called. "I'm Detective Abbie Taylor of the Pleasant View City Police Department. I'm not here to enforce fire violations or drug laws. I'm interested in the car accident on Route 39." Abbie hoped her voice sounded friendly enough to persuade the source of the smoke to come forward.

There was rustling on the other side of the sleeping bag. Then a man in his early twenties stepped into the light. His dark hair fell to his shoulders and he had a scruffy beard. His fitted T-shirt revealed highly developed shoulders and arms. He was a climber.

He stepped closer to the firepit and poured water over it from a plastic milk carton. The water hissed as it hit the last of the glowing coals.

"Hi. Is there a problem?" The young man didn't wait for Abbie to answer his question before launching into his explanation for being where he was at this time of night. "I'm just up here for the night. Climbing first thing in the morning."

"Actually, there is a problem. There's been a car accident." Abbie pointed toward the road. Even in the darkness, you could see the lights at the scene clearly through the trees. "Did you see anything?"

The climber hesitated for a moment, but then must have decided cooperating with the police was his best option. "Yeah, I saw it," he said. His tone went higher at the end of the sentence instead of deepening into finality. There was more.

"Can you describe what you saw, Mister . . . ?" Abbie asked.

"Strong. Bryce Strong."

"Mr. Strong, as I said before, I'm only interested in the car accident. Not any other . . ." She cleared her throat. She didn't want to spook her eyewitness. "Minor infractions."

Her words had the desired effect. Bryce Strong exhaled

and the tension in his jaw relaxed. "Okay, so the crash was sorta weird."

"Weird?"

"Yeah. You know the place in the road where you can't see around the bend?"

"Yes." Abbie knew exactly where Bryce Strong was talking about. There were twists up much of the canyon road to Huntsville. Some of the curves were gentle. A few, though, rendered a driver essentially blind. The place where this car had gone off the road was just such a spot. Large cement blocks had been placed along the side of the road as a barrier, but that was a long time ago. They were crumbling now and served more as a warning than an effective means of preventing a car from going off the road.

Bryce Strong continued his description. "Anyway, the car that crashed wasn't going all that fast, but when it came around the bend, there was this big white car in the wrong lane. That black car swerved right into the creek."

"A white car?"

"Yeah. Something expensive and new." Bryce Strong was not a car guy.

"You didn't happen to get a license plate number, did you?" Abbie had learned it never hurt to ask.

"No," the climber answered, "but I remember the letters B, L, and S, in that order." He smiled wryly. "They're my initials."

Abbie pulled her purple notebook out of her back pocket and jotted down the letters; then she looked down at the road. From where they stood, both sides of the curve were visible.

"You said the white car was stopped on the wrong side of the road. Did you see the driver?" Abbie asked.

"Yeah, he got out of his car after the other driver went off the road." Clarke hadn't mentioned anything about another car. How was this the first she was hearing about another witness to the crash? Had everyone just assumed this was a drunk driver?

"What happened then?"

"I went down to make sure nobody was hurt. I didn't really want to call the cops—I mean, I would've if I needed to—but, you know, I'm a little . . ."

"You'd been smoking marijuana."

Bryce Strong smiled. "Anyway, by the time I got down to the car, the guy driving the fancy white car was already there. When he saw me, he yelled across the creek that he'd called 911."

"That was it?" Abbie asked.

"Uh." Bryce Strong placed his palms together, the tips of his fingers touching his lips. He looked vaguely like a yoga instructor. "Now that I think about it, I asked him if the driver was okay."

"And?"

"He said the driver was fine and everything was under control."

Abbie thought of the corpse in the mangled black car. Whoever that stranger had been, he'd been lying. Even if the driver hadn't been dead at the time, he certainly could not have been "fine."

"Can you describe the man you spoke to?"

"Short hair, you know, missionary cut, maybe shorter, but he was a little old to be a missionary."

"Anything else? Do you remember what he was wearing?"

"Oh, yeah. That was sort of odd. The car was really nice, but the guy was in old jeans and a flannel shirt. He was wearing boots. Not cowboy boots, but work boots or combat boots, ones with treads."

"And you didn't talk to him beyond asking about the driver in the crashed car?"

"Nope. He looked like he knew what to do when the police got here. I didn't have any interest in sticking around if I wasn't needed. Don't get me wrong. If I'd been the only person here, I completely would've helped, but I wasn't."

"What happened after that?"

"He walked back up to his car. He drove off and I climbed back up here and doused the fire so I wouldn't get in trouble when the ambulance and cops showed up. I tried to calm down so I could fall asleep. I was still hoping to get an early start. Seeing a car accident isn't exactly the most soothing thing to happen before going to bed."

It didn't sit well with Abbie that the driver had left before Clarke and the other officers arrived. It also didn't sit well that Clarke hadn't mentioned that no one was on the scene when he arrived. They had received a 911 call. Usually, the caller stuck around.

"Do you remember if the man in the flannel shirt drove up or down the canyon?"

"He drove up. Back the way he came."

"Thanks. Anything else happen?"

"Not that I can think of."

Abbie handed Bryce Strong her card and took down his contact information. "Please call me if you think of anything else."

"Will do," Bryce Strong said, then muttered to himself, "So much for falling asleep."

He probably wasn't going to drift off to a restful slumber anytime soon, and neither was she.

By the time Abbie climbed back down to the crash site, the ME had arrived and was almost done, which meant Abbie would be able to take a look at the body. While the ME finished up, Abbie pulled Clarke away from the other officers.

"Was there a 911 call on this?" Abbie asked Clarke.

"Yes."

"Was the caller here when you arrived?"

"No," Clarke said.

"That didn't strike you as strange?"

"You know, some people don't like to get involved."

Abbie raised her eyebrow. Clarke liked to give people the benefit of the doubt. Being neighborly and law abiding was highly valued in Utah, so it was particularly unusual for someone to call 911 and not wait for the proper authorities to arrive. Abbie had yet to see it happen since she'd moved back to her home state.

"You were up there for a while. Did you find anything out?" Clarke asked.

Abbie gave him a quick rundown of her conversation

with Bryce Strong, including a description of the fancy white car and the man in the flannel shirt.

"I'll get IT to trace the 911 call first thing in the morning," Clarke said. "This is a rough curve, though. A lot of cars crash here. Usually it's just minor injuries, but this guy is old."

"We have an ID?" Abbie asked.

"No. We didn't find a wallet, but the ME found his phone."

Abbie and Clarke headed back toward their fellow officers, who seemed to have given up on the promise of finding anything interesting. Without Bryce Strong's story about the white car, the accident looked routine: either a drunk driver had missed a turn or a reckless driver had taken the curve too quickly. Either way, there was no sense in wasting energy looking for clues that weren't there.

The ME, a new guy from Oregon, finished and gave his okay for Abbie to examine the body. Normally, Clarke would have wanted to come alone, but because he and the others thought this was just a random drunk, everyone was focused on just doing what needed to be done. Abbie walked down the embankment. Something about this crash was off. As far as she could fathom, there was no reason for Bryce Strong to make up a story about the fancy white car and the man in the flannel shirt checking on the driver and calling 911. If anything, Bryce Strong's life would have been easier if he'd said he hadn't seen anything at all. Now he was involved in a police investigation.

Abbie stepped onto a rock in the creek and opened the

driver's side door of the crushed car. The car was damaged, but it wasn't in such bad shape that you'd assume it had been a fatal crash. She'd seen people emerge unscathed from much worse. Abbie lifted the head of a white-haired man slumped over the steering wheel. Her heart tightened into a knot in the center of her chest. Of all the things she'd been prepared for, knowing the dead driver wasn't one of them. She'd known him for as long as she could remember. Heber Bentsen was family, or just about.

When Abbie was little, the Taylors and the Bentsens had spent Days of '47 picnics together, the occasional Thanksgiving, and countless summer nights. The adults would sit outside talking, and the kids would play until well after the first stars started blinking in the sky. Heber had been called to be an Apostle just before Abbie left for college, and when she'd left the Church, he had been the one to broker a cease-fire between Abbie and her dad.

She placed Heber's head back on the steering wheel with the gentleness of a mother putting a sleeping child in a crib. She didn't want to leave him there, all alone, so she stood near the open door, her hand still touching his shoulder, and raised her voice so it would carry over the rushing water. "You know this is President Heber Bentsen?"

Even in the darkness lit by flares and flashlights, Abbie could see Clarke and the two other officers on the scene lose all the color in their faces.

Clarke sprinted from the road to the car. He stepped right into the cold water next to Abbie. She lifted Heber' head again, tenderly. Clarke saw what he clearly d want to see. Every member of the Church knew the First Presidency, as the President of the Church and his two counselors were called. Heber Bentsen had been the First Counselor to the Prophet for years now. Not all Counselors were beloved. Heber was.

"It's not drunk driving then," Clarke said, to himself as much as to Abbie.

Abbie didn't need to respond. The routine car accident had become anything but routine.

"Should we contact someone in the Quorum of the Twelve or the Prophet?" Clarke asked.

"No," Abbie said. The fact that the driver was one of the most important men in the leadership of the Church was clouding his judgment about protocol. Not that Abbie could blame him. "The first person who needs to be told is his wife."

"I know, you're right. It's just, you know, I mean, this changes everything."

Clarke was right about that.

Abbie scrolled through the contacts on her phone. The Bentsen addresses were still there: the house in Provo, the condo in St. George, and the cabin in Huntsville. If Heber had been heading to Huntsville, it was a pretty safe bet that his wife, Eliza, was there waiting for him.

"Will you call Henderson and let him know what's going on? I'm going to talk to Sister Bentsen."

"You know her?" Clarke asked.

"Yes. And if this news has to come from anyone, it should come from me."

TWO

Abbie left Clarke to finish at the scene and started the drive up the canyon to Huntsville. In the dark, you couldn't see the wide valley with Pineview Reservoir at its center. Once upon a time, Huntsville and the neighboring town of Eden had both been dominated by open fields punctuated by a few houses and barns. Now, the well-heeled from around Utah and beyond had discovered the quiet beauty here. The Bentsens' place was grand, but not as grand as some.

Once Abbie made it to the part of Huntsville where the big houses were, she pulled into the circular driveway in front of the Bentsens' place. The porch light was on, but the rest of the house looked dark. For a moment, Abbie wondered if she should wait a few hours until morning, but that thought left her almost as soon as it drifted into her awareness. Eliza would want to know. Abbie got out of her car, walked up the steps to the door, and rang the bell.

Eliza must have been a light sleeper. She answered the door almost immediately, wearing a lavender nightgown that touched the top of her feet with a matching robe, belted tightly at her waist. Her gray hair was thick and cut in a chin-length bob. She didn't look like she'd aged a day since the last time Abbie had seen her.

After Abbie's mom died, Eliza, like Heber, had been one of the few people Abbie could tolerate. Eliza didn't babble on about Abbie's mother being in a better place or Heavenly Father knowing what was best. She let Abbie be heartbroken and angry, without judging her for either.

"Come in." Abbie sensed Eliza was hesitant, which was an entirely normal response to anyone visiting at this hour, even someone Eliza knew as well as she knew Abbie. Abbie followed the older woman into the formal sitting room, which during the day would have had a spectacular view of the valley.

"Let's sit down," Abbie said. "I have some difficult news."

Eliza sat down on a love seat near the fireplace and turned on a table lamp. The room was large enough to accommodate Eliza's six adult children and their spouses, but probably not big enough for all the grandchildren. A grand piano dominated one corner of the room. There were fresh flowers on the coffee table.

"I'm here in my capacity as the detective of the Pleasant View Police Department." The sentence sounded stilted to Abbie's ears, but she wasn't ready to speak the words she'd come to say: *Heber is dead.*

Eliza took a lace handkerchief from her robe pocket. The two women gazed out at the Reservoir, where the reflection of an almost full moon wobbled on the surface of the dark water.

"It's Heber, isn't it?" Eliza said. "I've been trying to get a hold of him for the past several hours."

"He swerved off the road coming up the canyon." Abbie shifted uncomfortably. "I'm afraid he didn't make it."

Eliza covered her face with her hands. When she finally lifted her head, her eyes were glistening. She pressed the handkerchief underneath one eye and then the other.

"Did he suffer?" she asked.

"No." Abbie knew no such thing, but lying seemed like the right thing to do.

"Do you have any idea how it happened?"

"I don't, but I will." Abbie knew it wasn't professional to promise Eliza anything, but this case was personal. "Do you know why he was on the road so late?"

"There was a meeting in Salt Lake." Eliza didn't need to explain. Salt Lake was shorthand for Church business.

"Was it common for him to make that drive?"

"Not really, but not uncommon either. Things come up. I'd been trying to talk him into getting a driver, but Heber was not a man who liked the idea of someone else driving him. His eyesight was good. His mind was as sharp. I couldn't argue."

The handkerchief was no longer enough. Tears were streaming down Eliza's face now even though her voice was calm. Hers was the quiet crying of someone who knew loss well. Two of her children had died, one as a toddler and one to suicide in his teens. Eliza Bentsen was at a point in her life where funerals outnumbered weddings and baptisms.

"May I call Steve or Donna?" Abbie surprised herself

that she remembered the names of Eliza's children who lived in the Ogden area, less than an hour away.

"No, thank you." Eliza placed her hand on Abbie's. "I'll call everyone myself in the morning. I'd like a little time alone." She smiled through watery eyes. "Don't worry about me. Heber and I both knew this day would come. We didn't know who would be first, but we knew our time on this earth was coming to a close."

Abbie said nothing because there was nothing to say. Eliza's pain was not something anyone else could carry for her.

Abbie gave Eliza another hug before she left. She walked into the warm moonlit night, feeling not only her own grief about Heber's death but also a gut-wrenching sadness for Eliza. Did losing a spouse get easier with age? When your body approached its more natural end, was it more normal to say good-bye?

Abbie turned back to face the house. The light shining through the living room window went dark. Abbie stood, motionless. She inhaled the scent of a distant campfire as it drifted on a cool breeze. It was a stolen moment. As soon as she climbed back into her Rover, the pressure would be on. A man who had been like her father—a man who sometimes had been there more than her own father—was gone. And even more than that: Heber was one of the three most important men in the Church. All eyes in the state of Utah, and all eyes of members of the Church, would be focused on the Pleasant View City Police Department.

THREE

By the time Abbie got home, there was enough time for either a shower or a nap, but not both. The moment Chief Henderson had been told it was not a drunk driver at the bottom of the ravine but instead the much-adored First Counselor to the President of the Church, he had shifted into full-on general mode. He'd texted Abbie while she was at Eliza's, wanting to see both her and Clarke first thing, which meant six in the morning.

Abbie opted for the shower, hoping the warm water would comfort her soul and a dousing of icy water would wake her body. She ended up clean, but her heart still ached and her body still craved sleep. She pulled her long dark hair into a wet knot before pouring coffee into a mug and sitting, for a moment, at her kitchen counter to drink it. Perhaps the caffeine could do what the shower did not.

When she got to the station, Clarke was already sitting in Henderson's office. Both men were pale. Neither looked like he had slept. Abbie sat down in the chair next to Clarke.

"Every man is at your disposal," Henderson said. "We

need to find out exactly what happened as soon as we can. The *Deseret News* and the *Trib* have already posted about the passing of President Bentsen. I'm going to make a statement later this morning. There's no way around it. I'm not going to mention details, only that we're putting all our resources into finding out exactly how this tragedy happened."

Henderson and Abbie did not always see eye to eye. She had learned the hard way that if Henderson had to choose between church and state, he chose church. In this case, though, it didn't seem like that would be a problem.

"Thank you, sir," Abbie said. "As soon as we can talk to the person who made the 911 call, I'll have a much better idea of what happened. We have a partial license plate of the caller's car from our eyewitness. There can't be—"

Henderson interrupted her. "Clarke tells me your eyewitness had been smoking marijuana at the time of the accident."

Had Abbie mentioned that to Clarke? She must have. It was true, and yet something about the way Henderson pronounced the word *marijuana* made her feel uneasy.

"Yes. Bryce Strong had been smoking, but I have no reason to believe he's an unreliable witness." Abbie had plenty of friends who smoked regularly. The caricature of an incoherent pothead was hardly accurate, but Abbie wasn't at all sure she'd be able to convince Henderson of that.

"Well, be that as it may, I'd like to have something more concrete that the word of a marijuana-smoking rock climber." Henderson then made a sort of *harrumph* sound, which signaled the end of the meeting. He had a press statement to make, something Abbie knew he hated doing.

She and Clarke both stood up. There was work to be done. A lot of it.

"We can't have any mistakes. The sad fact is President Bentsen was very old and that road is very dangerous. I'm not expecting you to find anything. Let's just make sure we dot all the *i*'s and cross all the *t*'s."

Abbie wanted to counter Henderson's leap to a conclusion. He didn't expect to find anything because he had already decided that this case was a tragic accident and that the word of a young, marijuana-smoking climber was not going to stand in the way of that.

"Sir," she said. "I know there's reason to doubt the reliability of someone who is under the influence of THC, but I feel strongly that at this point in the investigation we not rule anything out. The caller left the scene—we should at least try to find him. We can cross-reference license plate numbers with automobile makes. We can also bring in Bryce Strong to work with a sketch artist."

"Whatever, but don't waste time. You know as well as I do that in all likelihood this is exactly what it looks like: a tragic accident."

Abbie wasn't sure she agreed, but at the moment, there was no reason to antagonize her boss.

"Yes, sir," Abbie and Clarke said in unison. The two left the office and were heading down the hallway toward Abbie's when Clarke said, "I've set up the conference room.

I got here early and thought we might want to spread out more than we can in your office."

"Thanks," Abbie said. It was good thinking on his part. Abbie's office was always tidy, but it was small. Being meticulous required space, and they were going to be nothing if not meticulous.

The conference room sported a whiteboard on a cement wall. There were two long tables flanked by a half dozen metal folding chairs. The single window at the end of the room provided a lovely view of the parking lot. Luxurious it was not.

Clarke sat down at a boxy computer set at the end of the table nearest the window. A few taps on the keyboard and the screen lit up. He tapped again.

"Jeez, Bryce Strong's legit. He placed in Psicobloc for the last three years and won silver medals at IFSC Bouldering World Cup for the last two. You can do that and smoke like he does?"

"It's not exactly uncommon." Abbie was relieved Bryce Strong had some credibility as a climber. It would make it easier to convince her fellow police officers that he was a reliable witness and it would be worth their time to look for the white car.

"Where are we on the 911 call?" Abbie asked.

"It was a burner phone. No trace of it since the call last night."

"Doesn't that strike you as odd?" Abbie didn't like this new development. "Who carries a burner phone?"

"Some people can't afford normal phone service," Clarke pointed out.

"People who drive a nice car?" That was how Bryce had described the white sedan.

Clarke eyes shifted away from Abbie. He exhaled.

"Taylor," he said, "I know you think Bryce Strong is a dependable witness, but who knows what kind of car he thinks is nice? Who knows how well he really remembers everything? I just think, well, maybe we shouldn't trust his account even if you don't think he had any reason to lie."

Clarke had a point. Still, Abbie felt like Henderson and Clarke were being far less skeptical of the 911 caller than they should be. It was odd for someone to call in the accident and then leave. It was strange that Heber had died in an accident that should have caused minor injuries, at worst. Whether you believed Bryce Strong or not, his story of the phantom white car and man in the flannel shirt was just plain weird.

"I'd like to hear the 911," Abbie said. Maybe she'd be able to pick up on something in the voice of the caller.

"Hazel will have it," Clarke answered. The two walked from the conference room to the reception desk where Hazel sat. She was a grandmotherly woman in her early sixties who single-handedly kept the entire station running with mechanical efficiency. She also occasionally worked overtime and took 911 calls.

Hazel went to church every Sunday and volunteered at the temple. She was also unfailingly kind and openhearted. Surely she knew Abbie had left the Church, but that didn't seem to concern her one iota. She had been Abbie's original ally in the police department when Abbie made her move back to Utah. Even if Hazel was pretty old-fashioned about most things, she seemed to take some joy in seeing Abbie in a job that would have been closed to women back in her day.

"Hi. Can we have a listen to the 911 call?" Abbie didn't need to specify which 911 call she was asking about.

"Of course," Hazel responded. On top of her efficiency and friendliness, Hazel dressed in a style one could only describe as unfailingly happy. Her wardrobe consisted of a mind-boggling variety of bright tops with seasonal appliqués along with coordinating pants and jewelry. The look might garner derision in some circles, but Abbie found it utterly charming. Today, the theme was subdued: a pale-pink T-shirt embroidered with peonies and fuchsia pants with earrings in the shape of roses in a shade of bubble gum.

Abbie and Clarke listened to the recording. It was short. The caller refused to give a name, and when Hazel asked if anyone was injured, the caller said, "Don't think so, looks like he just sorta slipped down into the creek." The caller then hung up in the middle of Hazel's voice saying, "Thank y—"

So the caller knew the victim was a man, which lent some support to Bryce Strong's account that the caller had hiked down to the car and examined it.

"Hazel, do you remember anything unusual about the call?" Abbie asked.

Hazel shook her head. "No. I really thought it was a drunk driver in the creek. When the caller hung up, I just figured he was a friend who was drunk, too, and didn't want to get in trouble."

"He didn't sound drunk to me," Abbie said.

"I know." Hazel sighed. "He wasn't slurring his words or anything, but you can be over the legal limit and sound normal."

"True," Abbie agreed. "If you think of anything else, will you let us know?"

"Of course, Detective Taylor."

Clarke grabbed a homemade peanut butter cookie from a plate on Hazel's desk before they left. He followed Abbie back to the conference room. It hadn't even been twelve hours since Heber's crash, and already Abbie didn't feel very good about how the pieces were fitting together, or, more precisely, were not fitting together.

Abbie walked over to the window, with its scenic view of the parking lot, and watched the sun peek from behind the mountains. Why would the drop from the road be fatal? If you went through accident reports from just the last year, there would be at least a handful of cars that had crashed down into the water at or near where Heber's car had gone off the road. None of the drivers or passengers in any of those accidents had even required hospitalizations. Sure, Heber Bentsen was old, but still.

According to Bryce Strong, the driver of the white car had told him that everything was okay. Was it possible that Heber had been alive when the driver checked on him but died before Clarke arrived at the scene?

Abbie surveyed the empty tables. They needed to start

putting things together. "Let's go through everything we collected last night," Abbie suggested.

"Hang on," Clarke said, "I'll get the box from the evidence closet." The evidence closet was a windowless room near Hazel's desk with shelves and a few bankers' boxes. Clarke disappeared inside, eventually returning with a box labeled HEBER BENTSEN.

He and Abbie gathered around the conference table.

Abbie watched as Clarke began to empty the box. He placed a worn brown leather wallet on the table. Abbie picked it up. There were several credit cards, a driver's license, a temple recommend, some cash, and, two old photos. The first was a wedding photo showing Eliza and Heber in white finery in front of the Salt Lake Temple. They looked like children, but Abbie knew Heber had been twenty-two and Eliza eighteen when the picture was taken. Young, but not children, at least not by Utah standards. Heber had returned from his mission and Eliza had just graduated from high school. They were beaming in a way only possible when the years behind you were happy and you had no reason to believe the years ahead would be any different.

The second photo was from about fifteen years ago. There was a tall Christmas tree in the background. Heber and Eliza stood to one side surrounded by their children, ranging in age from adult to elementary school. On the other side was the Taylor family. Abbie's teenage self was standing next to her mom. You couldn't see from the picture, but Abbie remembered the warmth of her mom's arm wrapped around her shoulder.

Abbie pressed her tongue to the roof of her mouth. According to an article she'd read, this position made it impossible to cry.

Next, Abbie picked up the well-thumbed copy of the Book of Mormon. It had been found on the floor on the passenger's side of the car. It was an old edition, maybe even the one Heber had been given when he was baptized. Abbie flipped through the pages. Large sections had been carefully underlined in red pencil. How old had Heber been when he started marking up his scriptures?

Abbie was startled back to the present when Clarke asked, "Did you notice this?" He was pointing to one of the first pictures taken of Heber's car.

Abbie stared at the picture. Whatever Clarke was seeing was eluding Abbie's power of observation. "What am I supposed to be noticing?"

"The door," Clarke said. "The driver's door."

It was open. Not wide open, but certainly not closed.

"When was the picture taken?" Abbie asked.

"Before we even climbed down to the car. We knew we had to wait for the ME before touching the body, so I just took a bunch of pictures."

"So, either Heber was alive and tried to open the door, or our mystery driver didn't shut it completely?" The former was too terrible to contemplate. If help had been just a little faster in arriving, would Heber be alive right now? The latter gave them a reason to speak to Bryce Strong again and more reason than ever to track down the 911 caller.

"What about prints?" Abbie asked.

Getting prints from the car wouldn't take long, not with everyone at the station available and anxious to help. What would take time was matching those prints. Abbie wondered if Bryce Strong had noticed whether the man in the flannel shirt was wearing gloves. She looked over her notes. Nothing. Would he have noticed such a small detail? The only way to know would be to ask.

"I'll see where we are on that." Clarke darted from the room, leaving Abbie with the last objects Heber was near when he departed this world.

Abbie stood back from the table. Alone. This time, Abbie didn't try to suppress what she was feeling. She let the tears slip down her cheeks. She thought of Heber's car. She'd ridden in the back seat at least a dozen times. People might describe it as "vintage," but really it was just old. In a state where everyone drove and most people cared about cars, Heber was odd. He was happy to drive an old car, even a slightly run-down one. As long as it worked, he didn't seem to mind. Abbie had found Heber's lack of car pride charming, but looking at these photos, her entire chest ached knowing the car had no airbags.

Abbie sat down on one of the metal folding chairs near the window. She pulled a tissue from a box on the sill and blotted her eyes.

All right. That was enough emotion for now. She reached for Bentsen's cell phone.

An idea flickered in Abbie's brain. She pressed the small concave button at the bottom of the phone. The screen lit up. Now she needed the right six digits to open it. Abbie started typing. Her first try was a fail. She tried again. Success. The screen unlocked: CTR LDS. CTR was the acronym for "Choose the Right," sort of an LDS equivalent to "What Would Jesus Do?" It wasn't a terribly original password, but in Abbie's experience, passwords rarely were.

Abbie pressed the phone icon and scrolled through all recent and missed calls. There wasn't anything from Eliza since early on the morning of the crash.

Clarke reappeared in the conference room. "We're checking the entire car for prints right now."

"Great," Abbie said, still holding the phone. "Is this the only phone we found?"

"Yes. Once we knew it was President Bentsen, we went through everything with a fine-toothed comb. I know you can never be sure you didn't miss something, but I'm as close as I've ever been to saying we didn't. There's not a man, or woman, on this case who doesn't want this done right."

"Eliza Bentsen told me she'd been calling Heber for hours." Abbie handed the phone to Clarke. Maybe he'd find something she missed.

Clarke scrolled through the calls again until he found a call from ELIZA. It was from 7:23 the morning of the accident. When Abbie had spoken to Eliza the night Heber died, she'd been under the impression the widow had been trying to call her husband in the hours just before the accident.

"She was in shock. Maybe she just thought she'd been calling him," he suggested.

"Maybe." Abbie felt her stomach tighten. One more little thing that wasn't quite right.

FOUR

Whatever favors Chief Henderson could call in, he did. By the time the sun slipped behind the Oquirrh Mountains, someone from the Pleasant View City Police Department had looked at every inch of Heber's car. As expected, most of the prints weren't in any databases. Aside from Heber's own prints, they were able to identify only one other set, from a man named Caleb Monson. Those prints were on the driver's door, both inside and out, and on the left side of the steering wheel.

Clarke was sitting at the computer in the conference room. Abbie had scooted her chair close enough for them both to look at the screen. Caleb Monson had been in the Special Forces, but his record was sealed. No explanation. Abbie stared at his image glowing from behind the glass computer screen.

He looked familiar.

Was this their mystery caller, the driver of the white sedan?

Clarke's stomach growled, loudly, for the third time in

the past hour. Abbie and Clarke had worked through lunch without stopping, and if Clarke's stomach was any indication, they had also worked through dinner. The lights in the parking lot outside blinked on.

"Let's call it a night," Abbie said. Clarke wouldn't leave unless Abbie suggested he do so.

Clarke agreed. "See you tomorrow."

"Tomorrow," Abbie said.

After Clarke left the room, Abbie went back to look through the database. She had to be sure that her instincts weren't wrong. She typed in the name BRYCE STRONG. He had a record. When he was nineteen, he'd been arrested for possession of marijuana—two joints—and underage drinking. He'd done community service. His fingerprints were in the database. They were not anywhere on Heber's car.

Abbie had never really suspected Bryce Strong. When Abbie had spoken to him last night, he hadn't triggered any red flags. Once he was comfortable that she wasn't there to get him in trouble for the campfire or the marijuana, he'd told her the truth.

"Detective Taylor."

Abbie turned around to see Chief Henderson standing in the doorway to the conference room. Judging from the scowl on his face, he was in a thoroughly foul mood. "Heber Bentsen's funeral is scheduled for next week. The ME promised to have his report finished tomorrow. I want this entire investigation wrapped up before the burial."

"Yes, sir. I do, too."

"I know you knew President Bentsen personally." Both

counselors to the President of the Church were also referred to as President. "I'm really sorry for your loss."

"Thank you, sir."

"Good night, Detective."

"Good night."

It was late. Time had outpaced progress today. Abbie knew on an intellectual level that her body was tired, exhausted even, but her mind was jumpy. She wouldn't be able to sleep now even if she tried.

Instead of heading home, she found herself driving south. A little over an hour after she'd left the station, she pulled into the parking lot on the campus of Brigham Young University.

Abbie's dad, aka Professor Taylor, was a creature of habit. He would be in one of two places on a weeknight: his office or home. Her mom was the one who had planned social engagements. When she was alive, her parents could have been anywhere on a weekday evening: a screening for a new film, an art exhibit, a concert, or a dinner party. Now, Abbie could predict with a disturbing degree of accuracy exactly where her dad would be at any given moment. It was still early for him to be home. He'd be sitting in his cramped office, working.

She stepped onto the sidewalk in front of the Religious Studies building and walked through the front door, down the hallway to the office her dad had occupied since he got tenure decades ago.

Abbie knocked on the open door. "Hello, Professor Taylor."

Her dad jumped in his chair when Abbie walked in. "Abish?"

"Sorry, I didn't mean to startle you."

"No, no. That's quite all right. It's good to see you. I've been meaning to call you. Eliza called me early this morning. It's terrible. Just terrible."

"Yes," Abbie agreed, "it is."

"Give me a minute to finish this up." Abbie watched as her father typed something on his keyboard. He still had an old black rotary-dial phone on his desk, but it looked like it wasn't connected to anything. There was a new phone right next to it. For years, the administration had been trying to persuade him to use the same phone everyone else had upgraded to. It was easier for receptionists to use and, unlike the rotary phone, allowed for conference calls. Her dad had never been an early adopter.

He kept typing, and then he pressed the power button on his monitor. "Done."

"New phone?" Abbie asked, trying to suppress a smile.

"Not by choice," he grumbled.

"Ready?" Abbie asked.

"Just about." Her dad put some papers into a scuffed leather briefcase. Abbie would have sworn it was the one her mom had given him when he first started teaching at the Y.

"Did you walk?" she asked.

He nodded.

"I'm right outside," Abbie said. They left the deserted building and walked to the parking lot. Her dad climbed into the passenger seat. In just a few minutes, Abbie pulled into her old driveway.

The Taylor house was close to campus by design. As a kid, when her dad lost track of time, Abbie's mom would send her or one of her brothers or sisters to his office to escort him home for dinner. Most nights, he returned to campus afterward.

When Abbie's mom was alive, their house had been on the "Historic Buildings of Provo" walking tour. Hannah Taylor had meticulously restored the public rooms on the first floor. She was a gifted gardener, so their little yard off Center Street was in constant bloom from early spring through the fall. It had an English cottage-garden look that made it seem like the mass of flowers was a beautiful, messy coincidence. In fact, every delphinium, bellflower, and foxglove had been carefully planned and tended. The house still looked beautiful today, but passersby would probably describe it as "having seen better days." They would be right.

Abbie's dad opened the unlocked front door and walked in. He took an inordinate amount of time to gather the mail and find a place to set his worn briefcase.

"Have you eaten?" Abbie asked.

"Uh, no, I guess I haven't. I'm sure we can find something."

Abbie did not share her dad's optimism. He looked gaunt. His clothes were hanging on him too loosely. She headed to the kitchen and opened the fridge. There she stared down a jar of Dijon mustard, a carton of 2% milk, and a sealed package of ham that had taken on a greenish tinge. The pantry wasn't much better. Abbie found a few cans of tomatoes, a loaf of sliced white bread with a sell-by date of two weeks earlier, rice, a jar of peanut butter, some honey, and a case of black cherry Shasta.

Given the options, she toasted the stale bread, spread peanut butter and honey on top, and sliced the sandwiches into triangles. One whiff of the milk inspired her to grab two cans of Shasta.

Her dad took his plate into the dining room while Abbie poured the dark purply-brown soda into glasses. She opened the antique wood sideboard and took out two cloth napkins. They were pressed. Abbie felt heat behind her eyes. She blinked and looked at the ceiling. Unless one of Abbie's sisters or sisters-in-law had done the ironing, it was her mom who had last touched these squares of cream damask.

Abbie's dad put his arm around her shoulders. "It sometimes hits me like that, too. Out of the blue. I smell lilies of the valley or see cherry-lime rickeys on a menu." Virgin, of course.

Abbie handed her dad the napkin. They ate in silence.

Her dad popped the last bit of white bread into his mouth, swallowed, and then cleared his throat.

"I'm glad you're here. I think I need to tell you something."

Professor Taylor, Abbie's dad, was a man of few words and even fewer emotions. Unless he was lecturing, he was content to eschew conversation altogether.

"I had lunch with Heber last week." Abbie knew Heber and her dad had maintained a standing lunch date. They'd been doing it for years, off and on. Since Abbie's mom had passed away, it was always on. Heber made sure of it.

"One of my top students dropped out. She was applying to PhD programs. I'd already made phone calls to some old friends at Yale. She knew she was going to get in and get funding, too. Then, out of the blue, she told me she was leaving. I tried to convince her not to give up. She had such promise."

Abbie's dad had a tendency to meander when he told stories. You were never quite sure where the beginning, middle, or end was.

"People drop out of graduate school all the time." Abbie didn't mean to sound terse, but she didn't know why her dad was bringing this up to her now.

"I know they do. That's what I told Heber."

"Why were you telling Heber about it?" Abbie asked.

"That's just it, I didn't tell Heber. He asked me."

Now Abbie was interested.

"I'm not sure exactly when—a few years ago, maybe—Heber asked me about my students, my female graduate students, the unmarried ones. He asked if any of them had dropped out. I couldn't remember. He asked me to check my records and keep a notebook of who left."

Abbie's heart skipped a few beats. This was interesting. "And?"

"I went back and checked my records and kept a notebook, just like Heber asked me to. Last week I showed it to him."

Abbie took a few deep breaths. It probably meant nothing. After all, Provo was a tough town for a single woman. By the time you were in your early twenties, a lot of your friends not only were married but were well on their way to starting families. Being a single graduate student in religious studies at the Y could be lonely.

Her dad continued. "When he looked through my notebook, he got really quiet and he lost all the color in his cheeks."

"Did he say anything?"

"I've been trying to remember his exact words. Something like 'I can't believe he already started.'"

"Do you have any idea what he meant?" Abbie asked.

"I've been turning those words over in my head ever since Eliza called to tell me about the accident. The last student who dropped out stopped by my office to thank me before she left. Then she blurted out something about being called to serve a special mission. I don't think she meant to say it. She bolted from my office and I haven't seen her since."

"Did you tell Heber that?"

"Yes. He told me not to tell anyone."

"Any idea why?"

"No." He paused, eyes wide. "The thing is, this particular student was a returned missionary. It didn't make any sense that she would go on another mission."

Abbie leaned toward her dad and cleaned a smudge of peanut butter from his chin. Her mom would have done that if she'd been here.

Her dad had managed to live the first seventy years of his life in a bubble where he focused on the things he wanted to and the rest of his life was magically taken care of by the women around him. First, it was Abbie's grandma. Then it was her mom. Now he was on his own, sustained by peanut butter, stale bread, and black cherry Shasta. Being an absent-minded professor had not provided him with the life skills necessary to live on his own.

"Do you have the notebook?" Abbie asked.

"Yes." He pushed himself up from the dining room chair. "As a matter of fact, I do." He walked through the French doors leading from the dining room to the main hallway, crossing the hall to his office. When he returned, he handed her a slim black notebook. Abbie opened it. Her father had drawn a table with the headings NAME, DATES OF ATTENDANCE, THESIS/AREA OF STUDY, REASON FOR LEAVING, and DATE OF LEAVING.

Abbie opened her bag sitting on the chair beside her. She pulled out her phone and took pictures of each page. Then she handed the notebook back to her dad.

"Did the students have anything in common?" Abbie asked.

"Almost all of them had gone on missions, they were single, and they had extremely strong testimonies. Some of my students have crises of faith when they first encounter the more obscure parts of Church history or doctrine. They come in during office hours. We talk. We pray. We ask for guidance. These young women didn't have struggles like that. They had no doubt the Church was true.

They were grateful for the Restoration, for the Gospel. That's why it was so surprising when they left. These were the last students I'd expect to quit."

Her dad tried to stifle a yawn. Abbie glanced at her phone. It was late and it would be even later by the time she got home. This was all mildly interesting, but Abbie wasn't sure what exactly it had to do with Heber's death. It could wait for another day.

She stood up from the table. Her dad did, too, and they both walked to the door together. "Abish, you don't think there's any connection between all this, my lunches with Heber, and his crash, do you?"

There was fear in her dad's voice, not fear of some nefarious force, but fear that he somehow could have prevented his friend's death.

"No, Dad. I don't think there's anything you could possibly have done—or not done—that would have stopped Heber's crash."

She opened the door and walked into the night. She hoped she hadn't just lied.

FIVE

When her alarm went off, it seemed like she had just crawled into bed minutes earlier. Every cell in her body was exhausted. Abbie questioned whether the drive to Provo the night before had been a wise choice. She couldn't deny how tired she was, but there was something about her dad's notebook that was stuck in her brain. Why would Heber be interested in graduate school dropouts?

As she drove to the station, she imagined her dad and Heber eating lunch every month at the Nauvoo Café. The two old men telling stories from life before they were grandfathers and great-grandfathers. Eating food from another era. Looking at life through the lens only people who'd been on the planet for seven or more decades could understand. Why would Heber be interested in something happening now that had nothing to do with the two friends' shared history? Still, Abbie didn't like adding one more piece of minor information related to this "tragic accident," even if it did seem irrelevant.

Abbie pulled into the parking lot. Clarke's car was already there. As soon as Abbie walked into the station,

Clarke announced, "We have the ME's report. The chief wants to see us."

Abbie followed Clarke into Henderson's office. He was facing the window, his shoulders slumped. He turned around when they walked in. Abbie had never seen the expression she was witnessing on Henderson's face. She wasn't sure exactly how to describe it—something between hopeless and despondent.

"I've got the report on President Bentsen," he said. "Homicide."

Clarke slid into the nearest chair. *Collapsed* was probably a more accurate description.

Henderson sat down, too. He rested his elbows on the desk and dropped his head into his hands. The three of them sat in silence. Someone had killed one of the longest-serving—and possibly most beloved—Apostle in memory.

"May I see the report?" Abbie asked.

Henderson handed copies to both Abbie and Clarke. Death had been caused by a single blow to the head. Someone had smashed something, probably a rock, into his forehead with enough force to fracture his skull.

"There wasn't a bloody rock at the scene?" Abbie asked the question even though all three people sitting in Henderson's office knew the answer.

"No," Clarke said. "I'll go back and check the creek. Maybe there was something we missed. It was dark." The likelihood Clarke would find a rock with Heber's blood on it lying around the crash site was basically zero, but they would look anyway.

Clarke asked, "Who's the official ME on this?" Pleasant View, being a small town, had a rotating roster of medical professionals who served as MEs at the time of a death, but the real work was done at the state facility in Taylorsville.

"Lars Eriksen." Henderson's voice was icy. The last time he'd tangled with the state medical examiner, Dr. Eriksen's reports had vindicated Abbie's theory on a double murder. Eriksen had forced the chief to open up an investigation into deaths he'd wanted to write off as suicides. Abbie feared the goodwill that had started to warm her relationship with her boss might not last.

"You two drive out to Taylorsville. Talk to Eriksen in person."

Henderson cleared his throat, their cue to leave. Just as Abbie opened the door, Henderson said, "Jim, do you have a moment?"

Henderson was excluding her from whatever he wanted to discuss with Clarke. Abbie hadn't forgotten her initial introduction to Pleasant View. Henderson had not been exactly welcoming. Neither had Clarke, but she and her partner were on good terms now, weren't they?

Now that Bentsen's death was not some tragic car accident, but a brutal killing, it meant Henderson would be on the receiving end of pressure from everyone up the food chain, from the Governor to the President of the Church. She almost felt sorry for him.

Abbie walked outside to wait for her partner. It was a cloudless day. The green grasses covering Ben Lomond were giving way to summer's dry gold. Abbie turned to face the sun. She closed her eyes and felt the heat on her skin.

Then her phone vibrated. She looked at the screen. It was Flynn, checking in.

KNOW YOU'RE BUSY WITH HEBER'S ACCIDENT. CALL WHEN YOU CAN.

Abbie smiled despite herself, despite Heber's death, despite the fact that she had no idea who could possibly have wanted Heber dead.

WILL DO.

Abbie dropped her phone back into her bag when Clarke emerged from his tête-à-tête with Henderson.

"I'll drive," Clarke said.

Abbie was fine with that. She watched the scenery pass by as they drove south. Looking toward the Great Salt Lake and the Oquirrh Mountains, she breathed in the desert. The land was flat until it reached the Oquirrhs, covered in neat green squares of fertile fields where the ditches dug by the pioneers still irrigated the land. In some of the pastures near Tooele, enterprising ranchers were now grazing bison, destined for upscale restaurants all over the country. To the east were the Wasatch Mountains. Instead of wild grasses and bushes, the foothills were now forested with McMansions growing along roads of stark black asphalt. Each year, the asphalt climbed further up the mountains like high-water marks.

"What do you make of all this?" Clarke asked, interrupting the silence.

"You mean, Henderson having us talk to the ME?" Abbie asked.

"Yeah."

"If I were in Henderson's shoes," Abbie said, "I'd want to make sure that no one could accuse me of not going the extra mile."

Abbie had forgiven Clarke for his betrayal when they'd first started working together, but she hadn't entirely forgotten it. She knew he hadn't wanted to go along with the other officers in slowing down the investigation into Steve Smith's death, but he had. At least he had apologized for it in the end. When it came to justice, she was pretty sure Clarke would do the right thing. She wasn't so sure about Henderson.

Was Henderson hoping Clarke could persuade the ME the death was an accident? That would be a lost cause. In her experience, medical examiners tended to be a pretty independent bunch. They didn't like laypeople second-guessing them, and they certainly didn't like to be pressured into coming to a conclusion that would fit into a theory of a case.

Clarke turned off the main road. They had arrived at the glass-and-steel box that was the Utah Office of the Medical Examiner.

"Why don't you take the lead on this?" Abbie suggested as they walked toward the door. She'd been burned before by Henderson early on in an investigation. She did not want to repeat that mistake. If her boss had a hidden agenda, if he and Clarke had some kind of understanding, she would rather watch it unfold than step into the middle of it.

Inside, Clarke and Abbie found Dr. Eriksen standing over the body of a teenage girl. The ME was in his late forties, north of six feet tall with broad shoulders and an athletic build. His hair was roughly equal parts salt and pepper.

"Overdose?" Abbie asked. The body on the table was a young girl. She could have been on the junior varsity tennis team. Once upon a time, being an ME had probably been a relatively easy gig, but that had been before the epidemic of suicides and opioid overdoses.

"Wish I could say it's surprising. The kids are hard. Even on my heart, which is easily three sizes too small." Dr. Eriksen was certainly no Grinch. He set down the gleaming steal instrument he was holding and then turned to face Abbie and Clarke. "You guys here about Bentsen?"

"Yes," Clarke said.

Dr. Eriksen showed them into the hallway, and then he opened the door to another room. Heber was laid out on a stainless steel table. Abbie's stomach curdled. A wave of nausea hit her hard. She must have looked pretty bad, because both Clarke and Eriksen were incapable of hiding the concern on their faces.

"You okay, Abbie?" Eriksen asked. She was caught off guard by her own reaction. She'd seen the lifeless bodies of people she loved more times than she should have at her age. She wasn't supposed to have an emotional response to the sight of an autopsied body.

"I'm fine, thanks," she said, and added by way of explanation, "Heber Bentsen was an old family friend."

"Sit down," Eriksen ordered. "Let me get you some orange juice."

Normally, she would have felt offended—her ingrained

reflex against any whiff that she was being treated carefully because she was female—but Eriksen would have offered the same to Clarke if he had looked like he was ready to faint. She took the juice.

"Not that I don't love chatting with the police in all the free time I have on my hands, but what exactly is it about my report that warrants this special visit?" Eriksen asked.

"Well, uh," Clarke stammered, "it's just that our chief thought this was a pretty clear case of a car accident: President Bentsen was old and his eyesight wasn't what it once was." Abbie was surprised to hear Clarke mention Heber's vision. They hadn't discussed it, and Eliza had told her the opposite was true.

"Look at the forehead here." Eriksen pointed. "There would have been a lot of blood, and the most obvious conclusion would be the man slammed his forehead into the steering wheel. But I'll show you what I think did this." Eriksen reached for one of several rocks he had sitting on the counter behind him. He placed one in a wound above Heber's eye.

"Someone pulled the head back so they could get enough room to swing this. It was a tight fit, but not impossible. I tried it myself with one of my assistants. It would take some strength, but it can be done. And if you look to see where the steering wheel would have hit the head"— Eriksen pulled his finger across Heber's forehead—"it's nowhere near the fracture."

Henderson wasn't going to like this.

SIX

By the time Clark and Abbie got back to the station, it was nearly noon. Henderson wanted a full run-down. Abbie let Clarke do the talking.

Henderson rubbed his temples. In a few hours, everyone in Utah, southern Idaho, and most of Nevada would know that the First Counselor to the President of the Church of Jesus Christ of Latter-day Saints had been murdered.

"Go through the evidence again. Check the car. Check the scene. Everyone is on this until I'm confident we haven't missed even one hair."

For a moment Abbie wondered if she should mention her dad's lunch conversation with Heber or the notebook about the dropouts, but she didn't. She wasn't sure herself whether any of it was relevant. And the mood Henderson was in, she knew she'd be on the receiving end of a barrage of questions to which she had no answers.

Clarke and Abbie camped out in the conference room. Abbie had given detailed instructions to the other officers to go back to the scene and look at every rock that fell within the broad parameters of the ones Eriksen had in his office. That pretty much meant every single rock. No one was happy about the task, but no one complained. The resident IT specialist was sitting with Hazel, listening for some detail in that call they had missed before.

Clarke had taken over the search of license plate numbers, even though he shared some of Henderson's misgivings about the word of a person who smoked marijuana. Abbie had insisted they include in their search cars described as white, white metallic, cream, ivory, light brown, gold, silver, and tan. Pretty much any color that could be mistaken for white.

So far, no hits.

Abbie knew she needed to make some progress on the car quickly. Henderson had every reason to focus on the easiest solution, and the mystery car was not it. She wanted to speak to their eyewitness again. Maybe there was something he hadn't mentioned, something she hadn't asked him.

Abbie called the number Bryce Strong had given her. It went straight to voicemail. She called again. Same thing.

"I want to give Bryce Strong a visit," she said, hanging up. "Care to come along?"

"Sure." Clarke's knee had been bouncing up and down while he was sitting at the computer scrolling through pages from the Division of Motor Vehicles. He needed to get out and stretch his legs.

Clarke climbed into the passenger seat of Abbie's Rover. He loved old cars and there weren't many like Abbie's left. She would drive this car until it completely gave up the ghost, which, she had to admit to herself, was probably not too far off into the future.

Clarke navigated. Bryce Strong's apartment was just off the campus of Weber State. It wasn't exactly a high-rent neighborhood, but Abbie had seen worse. The housing complex was made up of three red brick buildings, each four stories high. There was a central staircase, exposed to the elements, giving each apartment its own exit to the outside.

Abbie and Clarke climbed to the third floor of the center building. Before they even rang the doorbell, they heard barking from the other side of the door.

"It's okay, Sir Robin." Footsteps approached. "Sit."

When the door opened, Abbie and Clarke were greeted by a Newfoundland puppy, thumping its tail against the thick tan carpet. The dog, despite its obvious youth, was enormous. The young man who opened the door was scratching Sir Robin's ears while the dog crunched on a dog treat.

"His bark is much worse than his bite," the man said. "He's really a coward." Abbie stifled a smile. Brave Sir Robin. Great name.

"Hello, I'm Detective Abish Taylor of the Pleasant View City Police Department. This is Officer Jim Clarke." They showed their badges, but Sir Robin's owner didn't seem much interested.

"How can I help?" he asked.

"We're looking for Bryce Strong," Abbie said.

"He should be back from work any second now. You can come in and wait, if you want."

"Thank you." Abbie and Clarke made their way down

a very narrow hallway that opened up into a kitchen/living/dining room. The scent of beer, fried food, and marijuana was impossible to escape. An open pizza box with half a pepperoni pizza lay on the Formica counter that separated the kitchen from the rest of the space.

The young man closed the box. "Just finished lunch."

Sir Robin nuzzled Abbie's leg.

"Sit!" The dog obeyed. Another treat. "He's a puppy. We're working on his manners." The young man patted the dog. "Oh, I guess I forgot mine. Please, sit down. Can I get you something to drink? Eat?"

"No, thank you," Clarke said, with a little more force than necessary. Abbie understood his response. She had a soft spot in her heart for dog lovers, and while this young man had at least that undeniably redeeming quality, housekeeping was not among his others.

Abbie sat down on a sagging brown couch. Clarke took the faux leather recliner. The seating was arranged around a large flat-screen TV and video console. Controllers were scattered around the room. At least four that Abbie could see.

The young man stood with Sir Robin. "Uh, so, you want to talk to Bryce?"

"Yes," Clarke said.

The awkward silence was broken when they heard the sound of a key in the lock. Sir Robin bounded to the door. A few seconds later, Bryce Strong walked into the room, followed by the puppy wagging his tail so hard Abbie was convinced Sir Robin might injure himself.

"Man." Bryce Strong exhaled the word. "Is there a problem?"

"No, we'd just like to go over everything again."

"Sure." Bryce opened the fridge and pulled out a bottle. "Kombucha?"

"No, thank you." Clarke answered.

Bryce twisted open the cap and took a drink. "If you don't mind, I'll stand. Been sitting all morning."

"We need to make sure we didn't miss anything, even something that doesn't seem related or relevant," Abbie said. "You told me that by the time you got down to the creek, the man driving the white car was near the crash site. Is that right?"

"Yup." Another swallow of fermented tea.

"This man told you the driver was fine and that he had already called 911?"

"Yup."

Abbie nodded. Now to get to the new information she'd gathered from the crime scene pictures. "Did you see the driver of the white car open the door of the crashed car?"

Bryce Strong set down the bottle of kombucha. "Hmm. I'm not sure. I mean, he must've, right? How else would he know the driver was okay?" He stopped, then asked, "The driver's okay, right?"

"No, he's not. He died."

"Damn! I mean, I know he swerved off the road, but I wouldn't have thought he was going fast enough to really get hurt, you know? That's really awful." The young man leaned against the counter. He looked a shade paler than a few minutes earlier.

"It doesn't look like he died because of the accident," Abbie said. "That's why it's so important that we know everything there is to know, and why we need to talk to the driver of the white car. Is there any detail you can think that would help us track him down?"

Bryce picked up the bottle, as though it would give him strength, and took a swallow. He scratched behind Sir Robin's ears; the dog had stopped thumping his tail. "Well, the guy was big and built, you know? He was strong, had a thick neck. He looked like someone who could've played football in college. His hair was short, really short, buzz cut. He wasn't old. I mean, when I saw that white Mercedes, I was expecting to see someone older—more, I don't know, corporate looking."

"A Mercedes." Abbie repeated the word. Clarke raised an eyebrow. "You didn't mention that when we spoke before. Are you sure?"

"Pretty sure. It could've been a Lexus. It wasn't a BMW. I think it was a Mercedes, though."

"Okay," Abbie continued, knowing this new memory would make her partner more skeptical of Bryce Strong than he already was.

"What do you mean that he didn't look like what you expected?" Clarke interjected. "What do you mean by 'corporate looking'?"

Abbie could tell that Bryce Strong didn't think "corporate looking" was a compliment, and Clarke—well, Clarke did.

"I don't know. I guess I mean I expected whoever drove a car like that would be, you know, soft. Someone who couldn't handle himself in a fight. But this guy looked tough."

"Do you think you could pick him out if you saw him again?" Abbie asked.

"Yeah. Probably."

"Do you think you could work with a sketch artist and come up with a drawing?" Abbie asked.

"Sure."

That was great news. Now Abbie shifted gears. "You mentioned that the Mercedes, the white car, was in the wrong lane. Do you mind going over that again?"

"Nope." Bryce bent down to scratch Sir Robin's ears, more for his own sake than for the dog's. "It's not like much happened. The dark car came driving up, and it looked like the Mercedes was parked in the wrong lane on purpose. I mean, like it was there to force the other driver off the road and down into the creek."

Clarke coughed, then asked, "You told Detective Taylor you remembered three letters from the license plate. That's pretty hard to believe, given that you didn't write anything down and you couldn't even identify the make of the car until today." Clarke's tone was a touch harsh. Bryce and Clarke would not have been friends in high school, Abbie thought wryly.

A broad grin spread across Bryce Strong's face. "Let me tell you, when your initials spell BS, you pay attention. Kids can be mean, so in school I learned to be vigilant and make sure that I always used my middle name, Leonard. Everything was BLS. I never leave the *L* out."

No, Abbie thought. *You wouldn't.*

Clarke's expression softened. "No idea of the numbers?"

Bryce Leonard Strong shook his head.

"Anything else you can think of?" Clarke asked.

BLS shook his head.

Abbie and Clarke each handed the climber a card. "Please call us if you think of anything. We'll want you to come down to the station to help with a sketch. A woman named Hazel will call you and set it up."

They said their good-byes.

Clarke and Abbie drove back to the station. Clarke admitted, a little begrudgingly at first, that the climber seemed to be pretty observant and had likely given them a pretty accurate description of what he saw, even with the whole I-now-think-it-was-probably-a-Mercedes memory lapse.

That left them with tracking down a tough guy driving a whitish probably Mercedes with a license plate that started with *B*. Having Clarke at least neutral when it came to Bryce Strong's interview made Abbie feel comfortable handing that search over to him completely. She could focus on other things.

She spent what was left of the afternoon reviewing every single bit of evidence neatly arranged in the conference room. She assigned every one of Pleasant View's six police officers to a specific task and headed home. Again, not a single one complained, even though they were being asked to do tedious and time-consuming work.

The sky was a shade of dusky lavender when Abbie turned off Route 39 onto the long dirt road leading to her cabin. She still sometimes debated her move back to Utah, but she had no second thoughts about the house. An early Swedish convert had built the traditional *sommarstuga* on the property in the early 1900s, deep red with white trimmed windows and doors. Inside it was bright and airy. There was a sauna, a plunge pool, and enough bedrooms to sleep sixteen. When Abbie bought the place, she'd planned to host weekend get-togethers for her family and friends like she and her late husband Phillip had done at their place in upstate New York. So far, though, the guest rooms had remained empty. Abbie was the only person who had used the sauna.

She opened her front door, turned off the alarm, and headed straight upstairs to wash her face and change into pajamas. Then she walked back downstairs and poured a glass of Domaines Ott. It was, after all, officially rosé season. Abbie liked her pink wines the same way she liked her whites: dry and crisp. Any hint of fruit had to finish off clean. Phillip used to tease her that her definition of citrus was what most people called astringent. He might have been right. As she sipped the pale-peach liquid from her glass, she tried to relax, but her mind wouldn't let go of the swirl of strange facts—the disappearing driver of an expensive white car, his mysterious 911 call, and her dad's conversation with Heber about missing BYU students.

The sound of crunching gravel interrupted her thoughts. For a moment, she felt panic rise in her throat. Clarke had updated her security system. She was safe. Still, her level of anxiety had been a little higher ever since the Smith case when she'd watched Elder Bowen, the General Authority and frequent Church spokesman, and his partner in crime rifling through her house. She had her suspicions about what they'd been looking for, but the boxes of her father's notes were still safely hidden in her attic.

The crunching stopped. Abbie took a long swallow of wine and walked to the window.

She opened the door. "John?"

Her big brother reached down and gave his sister a bear hug. "I hope you don't mind me dropping by unannounced. I was in Ogden all day, but we finished early. Couldn't pass up the opportunity."

John walked past her into the kitchen, opened the fridge, and grabbed a seltzer. "Are you eating? I'm starved. We could head up to Huntsville. I could be talked into the Ogden Valley Smokehouse." He twisted open the cap on his bottle of water and took a swallow. He looked at his sister, slumped on a kitchen stool, and added, "Or, if you're exhausted from the day, we can make something here."

He then turned back into the kitchen and started opening cabinets. He knew Abbie well enough to know she loved cooking, but large stretches of time could pass between visits to a grocery store. Beyond coffee and popcorn, it was unclear what food could be found in the house. This was as close to the opposite of John's house as could be. With four kids at home, two of those being teenagers, it was considered famine if the fridge was not stuffed to the gills. John bought milk and ice cream by the gallon.

"Here we go!" There was optimism in his voice.

Abbie took a swallow from her glass. John didn't bat an eye. No judgment on the wine, no judgment on the state of her pantry, no judgment on the coffeemaker. She was lucky to have a brother like him. Her other brothers had fallen in line with her sisters. They were cordial, but not warm. They had taken her leaving the Church as a personal affront. John hadn't. He knew she had struggled and had made the only decision she could make. It shouldn't have mattered to anyone else, but, Abbie was learning, it did.

John found some bread and cheese. He sliced both and arranged them on a plate, with a handful of dates and raw almonds. He pushed the food toward Abbie. "I heard about Heber. Are you okay?"

Abbie took a bite of cheese, then said, "I'm okay. It was awful. It caught me completely off guard. When I got the call, we thought it was a drunk driver."

"Are you going to be okay working on the case? I mean, is there any way you could step aside?" John was trying to sound casual, but he wasn't entirely successful in disguising the level of his concern about her well-being.

"I love you for worrying about me, but this is my job. This will sound corny, I know, but I feel like I owe it to Heber. He was always so good to us, to me. I'll never be able to repay him for being there with Mom. You know?" Abbie chewed on the crust of a piece of bread.

"Yeah, I know. Heber was a great man and a good man. I feel the kind of hole in my stomach I did when Mom passed away. I know that they were ready, but I wasn't. I still am not."

John believed in the elaborate Mormon afterlife. Abbie had asked him once if he'd ever had doubts. His answer had been cryptic, but Abbie would never forget that he said: "Yes, the doubts remind me that we each must walk our own path." She wasn't sure exactly what he meant, but had felt ever since that he understood her in a way no one else in the family did.

"You mind if I use up what's left in the fridge?" John asked.

"Knock yourself out." She knew she should help, but she was so exhausted that the pull of the chair, the cheese, and the wine required more strength to resist than she possessed. She watched her brother assemble something from the meager contents of her fridge.

"Great." John seasoned the lone salmon fillet. It might be enough for both of them if John ate a lot of bread. The fish sizzled when he placed it facedown on the cast-iron skillet.

"My trip to Ogden isn't the only reason I'm here." He juiced a lemon and whisked in olive oil and Dijon mustard until the pale-yellow mixture emulsified.

"I suspected as much." Abbie built herself another tiny sandwich of cheese and bread.

"I'm worried that this case is only going to make your sleep issues worse. I know how you get when you care about something. You won't eat properly, you won't work out like you normally do, and sleep will be relegated to 'optional.'"

He was right. She did do all those things when a case was intense.

John sliced red onion and cucumbers into paper-thin rings.

"As it is," he said, looking up from drizzling the lemon vinaigrette over arugula, shaved parmesan, and the circles of onion and cucumber, "you already are not sleeping." He was sounding very big brother.

"It's not a big deal." Abbie shrugged. "I don't always sleep through the night. It's hardly life or death."

"Abs, it's been going on for far too long, and 'not sleeping through the night' is an understatement. You can make it sound as trivial as you like, but I want you to see someone." He reached into his shirt pocket and pulled out an ivory card with a name embossed in black letters, followed by the initials M.D., PH.D.

This was not the first time John had hinted that he was worried about her. He had a theory that she hadn't been able to process losing both her mom and her husband in such a close time frame. John would always preface what he said with "I'm not a psychiatrist, but . . ."

Abbie took the card.

"She's supposed to be the best in the state. She's on faculty at the U." John flipped the salmon. The crust was dark brown on the outside. He sliced it in half, revealing a deep-pink center. Then he slid each half onto a dinner plate.

The two of them sat at the counter, enjoying the results of John's labor.

"You know," Abbie said, "I actually went to a farmers'

market this weekend. That red onion you just sliced: organic. The cucumber? From a lady who lives just up the road in Eden. And"—she paused for dramatic effect—"I'm getting in about twenty-five miles a week." He knew she was referring to the number of miles she ran. She was doing pretty well. She was trying to eat regularly, she ran at least four miles almost every morning, and she was back into weight training. "I even downloaded a book on mindfulness meditation," she added, to demonstrate just how mentally healthy she was.

"You downloaded a book on mindfulness?" John put his fork down. "Have you read it?"

"It got a good review in the *Times*."

"So, you haven't read it." John knew her too well. "Sometimes we all need a little help. You've had a rough few years. I know you think the move to Utah was the right choice for you. Don't get me wrong, I'm thrilled that I can jump in the car and see you whenever, but still, Abs, it was a move. Death of a loved one and moving are major triggers for depression. I'm not a doctor, but . . ."

"But you think I need to see one?" Abbie filled in.

John shrugged. "Yeah, I do." He pointed to the business card Abbie had set down on the other side of her plate. "This woman is great." He turned to face his baby sister. "Abs, we want you to be happy and healthy. Dad and I are here for you, but we're not enough."

Deep down, Abbie knew he was right. Still, she wasn't sure she was suppressing anything. After all, she was well aware of every one of those changes, those losses. It wasn't like she was suffering from some deep dark secret issues. She was just having trouble sleeping.

John stood up and cleared the dishes. He unloaded and loaded the dishwasher and wiped the counter. The kitchen looked better after he'd cooked dinner than it had before. Her big brother had driven all the way here and cooked her dinner and cleaned up afterward. Maybe she wasn't managing as well as she thought.

"Thanks." Abbie stood up from her perch at the counter. It was the time in the evening when a non-Mormon host would offer coffee or tea and dessert and retire to the living room. "Do you want some milk and a little something sweet before you leave?"

Abbie opened the drawer in her kitchen that she lovingly referred to as her "snack drawer." Sometimes it was full of chips, popcorn, cookies, chocolates, and the occasional nut mix. Sometimes it was empty. Luck was on her side. A friend had sent her a box from Neuhaus a few weeks ago. She arranged the chocolate gems on a small silver dish. John popped a truffle in his mouth while Abbie poured each of them a glass of milk.

"Ooh. These are good." He ate two more truffles and finished his milk.

He stood and Abbie did, too. She walked with him to the door, his arm draped across her shoulders.

"Will you at least think about it? No pressure." He opened the door. "Well, maybe a little bit of pressure." He gave Abbie a solid squeeze and then headed out.

"Drive safely," she said. "I love you."

"I love you, too, Abs."

John walked down the steps to his car. He didn't turn around. If he had, he would have seen a single tear roll down his sister's cheek. She wiped it away.

SEVEN

Abbie put on the kettle and removed a tiny white bag from a box claiming that the mix of passionflower, chamomile, and lavender would induce calm. The kettle dinged when the water came to a boil. She dropped the bag into a cup and poured hot water over it. She was skeptical, but John's visit had reinforced what she already knew: she needed to sleep.

Abbie took her cup of herbal tea into the living room. She stretched out on the couch and tried to think of nothing but the tea. Instead, a glimmer of a memory slipped into her mind. Something that related to her dad's students. She had read an article somewhere about demographics. No, not exactly that. What was it? Marriage, marriage in religions that discouraged interfaith unions.

Abbie leaned toward the coffee table so she could reach her laptop. She typed in every search term she could think of. Finally, the article popped up. It was about a group of Orthodox Jews in New York and Mormons in Utah. Both groups encouraged early marriage and large families. Both groups discouraged marriage outside the faith. And both groups were facing a gender imbalance: men were leaving their faiths at rates much higher than women. The writer claimed that for every 150 LDS women of childbearing age, there were only 100 LDS men of the same age. A lot of young Mormon women weren't having children because they couldn't find young Mormon husbands.

Abbie put down her not-so-sleep-inducing tea. She walked upstairs, pulled the ladder down from the attic, and climbed up into the space beneath the steep pitched roof. She'd spent so much time with her dad's notes on blood atonement during the Smith murder that she now had a pretty good sense of how he organized his research.

She moved the box filled with first- and second-edition books from the early days of the Church and opened the box behind it. She pulled out a Redweld with a yellowing label in the upper right corner and the words NEW AND EVERLASTING COVENANT written on it.

Was she crazy? The New and Everlasting Covenant was how polygamy had initially been introduced back in the early to mid-1800s. The revelation had officially been recorded in 1843, but Joseph Smith and a few of his close friends had been practicing it for years by that point. Abbie sat cross-legged on the floor among the boxes. She pulled her dad's notes out of the rust-colored folder and started reading.

Non-Mormons joked about polygamy, but what most outsiders didn't know was how much most LDS wished polygamy had never been part of their history. After the practice was expunged from the main Church in the early 1900s, suggesting the practice might not have been so bad is akin to saying there might be something to Marxism during the height of the Cold War. Abbie's own maternal grandmother had denied there was polygamy on her side of the family until the day she died. It wasn't until Abbie was an adult and saw an old photo of a headstone with the names of two wives that she knew her grandmother had lied. It wasn't just the Taylor side of her family who had practiced the Principle.

Abbie held a single sheet of paper in her hand. Her father's neat script on top said 1886 REVELATION. John Taylor, Abbie's great-great-great-something-grandfather, had been the third President of the LDS Church. Lore had it that he had claimed Heavenly Father had revealed to him that polygamy "cannot be abrogated" and "will stand forever." But the revelation had been hotly contested ever since the Supreme Court had ruled the practice was not constitutionally protected. Even so, many saw the 1886 Revelation as a call to members to continue the practice, even if they had to do so in secret and even if it was illegal.

Abbie shook her head. Over the years, she'd heard a lot of explanations for why Joseph Smith had taken spiritual wives years before he announced the Revelation. Most didn't mention that many of those young wives were already married to other men.

Abbie placed the copy of the 1886 Revelation back in the Redweld. She stood up, the large folder in hand, and made her way down the ladder, closing the drop-down door to the attic behind her. She went downstairs to lock the door, set the alarm, and turn off the lights. Tonight would be the night she would get some rest. *Please.*

Sleep came, but only in spurts between disturbing dreams. In the early-morning light Abbie could remember only fragments, like pieces of broken glass. She'd seen images of stoic women pushing handcarts through mud and snow. There was a sepia-toned photo of bearded men in black-and-white-striped uniforms imprisoned for having more than one wife. There was a glimpse of a crowd listening to her great-great-great-grandfather talk about the polygamous colonies in Mexico and Canada. And there were the babies, babies waiting in heaven with Heavenly Mother and Father, waiting to be born.

Was she losing her mind?

Abbie lay under the covers, listening to the robins call to each other, thinking about the Principle, polygamy, plural wifery . . . whatever you wanted to call it. It would make for an elegant solution to the current gender imbalance.

If it weren't insane.

Abbie reached for her phone, charging on her nightstand. She scrolled through the photos she'd taken of her dad's notebook. Who were these young women? They were all devout. Even without her father's comments about the strength of their testimonies, it was obvious that if you were getting your master's in religious studies from the Y, you were dedicated to your faith. Most of them had served missions. All of them were unmarried.

Where were they now? Where had they gone?

Abbie should have listened more carefully to that part of her brain that knew something was off when her dad had mentioned his lunch with Heber and the notebook. She should have trusted Heber. Something had already started when he and her dad had their lunch. Abbie didn't want to think what she was thinking, but pieces of her dad's story fit together a little too well with a uniquely Mormon logic.

If she could track down the young women, she could know. What she was contemplating wasn't reasonable. It wasn't normal. A conversation with one of these dropouts might be able to put her mind to rest—on that one front, at least.

Abbie tossed the covers aside and dashed downstairs to where she'd left her computer. She opened it and started an email to Clarke. She typed in the names from the notebook.

PLS RUN CHECKS. WANT TO KNOW WHERE THEY ARE. THX!

She hit send.

Then she Googled the current Utah anti-bigamy law: "A person is guilty of bigamy when, knowing the person has a husband or wife or knowing the other person has a husband or wife, the person purports to marry and cohabitates with the other person."

Abbie ran back upstairs, showered as quickly as she could manage, pulled her wet hair into a ponytail, dashed past her coffee machine, and darted out the door.

If she was right, and she hoped she wasn't, she'd need her passport.

EIGHT

Clarke had managed to track down five of the seven young women by the time Abbie walked into the station. She stood next to his desk as he tracked down the final two. At different times, each woman had crossed the Texas–Mexican border in El Paso. None of them had returned.

"Are you going to clue me in?" he asked.

The entire drive from her cabin, Abbie had rehearsed a plausible explanation for looking into the whereabouts of the young women. By the time she had parked, she was confident she had an answer that was as close to the truth as possible without sounding utterly mad.

"They were students of my dad's," she told Clarke now. "Heber had asked about them the week before he was killed."

Chief Henderson came out of his office and stood next to Abbie while she was talking. "Well, what are you waiting for? Go talk to them. Maybe they know something. These girls were students at the Y?"

"Graduate students in religious studies," Abbie said. That was true.

"There are only a few days until the funeral and, as far as I can tell, no progress. Not on the 911 call, not on the phantom white car, and not on this Caleb Monson, whose fingerprints are on President Bentsen's car. Not that I put any stock in your young climber's story, but we don't have a sketch based on his"—Henderson cleared his throat—"recollection either."

Henderson was right. He had every right to be frustrated. They were nowhere.

The chief turned to Clarke, "I want you to find this Caleb Monson. Then go back and get Bryce Strong in here with a sketch artist. The tech guys are still working on the burner phone. As far the white car, the only camera around the area is at the gas station near the mouth of the canyon, and it's broken."

Then Henderson looked at Abbie. "You find these women. It's a stretch, but right now that's all we have."

"They're someplace in Mexico."

"I don't care. You get yourself to El Paso. See if anyone remembers them. You're a detective. Figure it out."

Henderson had no idea what he was asking Abbie to look into. She doubted he would have been quite so supportive if he had. As it was, she couldn't have hoped for better orders if she'd written the script herself. She knew exactly where she needed to go once she passed through the border at El Paso.

The trip wasn't pleasant. A cramped flight to Texas, no help from anyone at the border, and then a drive through one of the most dangerous parts of northern Mexico to Colonia Juárez, home to one of the smallest LDS temples in the world.

If you weren't a serious student of early Church history, there would be no reason to know that in the latter part of the nineteenth century, when it was becoming clear that Mormons were going to have to give up polygamy in the United States, the Church had established a number of colonies beyond the jurisdiction of the U.S. government, in Canada and Mexico. Of the nearly half a dozen colonies established by early polygamous settlers in Mexico, two remained: Juárez and Dublán. Dublán had the distinction of being the birthplace of George Romney, the Michigan governor who ran for president in 1968, as did his son a few decades later. Juárez, unlike Dublán, did not have any famous sons, but, importantly, it did have a temple.

It was the temple that had convinced Abbie that Juárez was the most logical place to find the young women. If Heber's death was somehow connected to the young women and to children being born in the covenant, then it was critical that each man be sealed to the women who would bear his children. That eternal covenant could be performed only in the temple.

Abbie knew it was sort of crazy, but she also knew the legalistic tendencies of the religion she'd been born into. Mormon history was full of examples where the letter of the law was followed while its substance was flouted. Joseph Smith had helped found the Kirtland Safety Society Anti-Banking Company after Church leaders were denied a bank charter. The Anti-Banking Company functioned as a bank, but was not, as its title announced, actually a bank. In the same way, Brigham Young and John Taylor had established polygamous colonies so that if the Supreme Court ruled against the Church on polygamy, they could continue the practice while technically not performing plural marriages within the borders of the United States of America.

These thoughts swirled through her mind as Abbie drove through the scruffy desert. Her back never relaxed and her grip never loosened as she drove her rented black SUV to her final destination. When she saw the skyline of the tiny town of Colonia Juárez, she had never been so happy to see the angel Moroni gleaming atop a temple spire.

Juárez looked like what many small towns in Utah would have looked like a hundred years ago—a few official, stately, red-brick buildings surrounded by well-tended green fields in a small valley between dry foothills. Juárez was not a big town; just over a thousand people. At over 5,000 feet, its elevation was a little higher than Salt Lake City's. Despite the distance from Utah, the early polygamous settlers had probably felt familiar in the topography of desert and mountains.

As soon as she parked the SUV, Abbie sensed she was being watched. The street was deserted, but Abbie felt eyes follow her. She walked down a side street to a new four-story, red-brick building reminiscent of the Academia Juárez, still an elite high school in the LDS educational system. For a building of its size, it was odd that there was no sign identifying its purpose. She walked up the steps and tried the door, but it was locked. She knocked. An older woman with carefully coiffed white hair opened the door. Abbie looked past her and saw three young women holding babies.

"May I help you, dear?"

Abbie had practiced her cover story on the flight to Texas. A little research had uncovered the names of some of the founding families of the polygamous colonies. Abbie had decided she would be related to the McClellans.

"I hope so. My name's Jennifer Sweeten. I'm a descendant of William C. McClellan. I'm doing some genealogical research." Every member of the Church was supposed to do genealogical research—the Second Coming of Christ couldn't happen until every soul born had the chance to hear the true restored Gospel of Jesus Christ, whether in this life or in the afterlife. That's what baptisms for the dead were for. Abbie herself had probably been baptized and confirmed for hundreds of strangers when she was a teenager. Members of the Church performed important temple rituals, including baptisms, confirmations, and marriages, for dead people.

The woman's face brightened. "A McClellan! Oh, dear, it's so nice to meet you. I'm Donna Charlesworth. Please." She stepped aside and motioned for Abbie to come in. "I'm sure I can find someone to help you. In the meantime, where are you staying? There aren't many options here." Abbie hadn't given much thought to accommodations. She could sleep in the enormous SUV if she needed to.

"Uh, I don't know." Abbie shook her head.

"Wonderful!" Sister Charlesworth clapped her hands together. "Why don't you stay with me? I have a big empty house and would love the company."

"I don't know what to say. Thank you." Abbie meant it.

Of all the stereotypes about Mormons, the one about them helping each other out was accurate. No matter where you went, you could rest assured that you'd be welcomed by fellow Saints. If you moved across the globe, a contingent of local elders would help carry boxes into your new home and local sisters would deliver enough prepared food to feed a small army.

"First things first," Sister Charlesworth said, "it's hot out there. Would you like some water?"

"Yes, please." Abbie sat down on a navy upholstered chair in a comfortable sitting room that looked a lot like a doctor's office. On the coffee table, fanned out like a deck of cards, were Church magazines in both English and Spanish along with a vase of silk flowers. The three young women with infants Abbie had seen through the window earlier were gone, but Abbie heard crying down the hallway.

Sister Charlesworth returned with a glass of water for Abbie, accompanied by another smiling woman.

"This is Sister Robbins. She has some time right now and knows the history of Juárez better than anyone I know."

Abbie stood up to shake Sister Robbins's hand. The lines around her eyes pointed to her being in her midforties or maybe early fifties, but her energy and smile gave the impression of someone at least a decade younger.

"Sister Charlesworth tells me you're a descendent of William McClellan. Do I have some stories for you! Are you up for walking in this heat?"

"I live in St. George," Abbie lied. St. George, in

southwestern Utah, had climate more like Las Vegas than Salt Lake. Summers could be brutal.

The woman smiled. "Okay. You can handle the heat, then."

Abbie finished her water, then followed her energetic guide outside into the sauna-like temperatures beneath the cloudless sky.

"I'm sure you'll want to see the temple first. It's one of the smallest in the world in terms of square footage, but I believe it's true what was said when it was dedicated: Heavenly Father still has plans for the Saints here in the Mormon colonies."

"I agree." Abbie smiled at her kind tour guide.

"Several of our more prosperous families donated the land for it," Sister Robbins went on. "We all gave what we could, contributed our labor and talents to bring this temple into being." Even to Abbie's apostate eye, the temple was beautiful, white stone glowing in the sun.

"I saw the Academy when I arrived, but haven't seen the Old Tithing office. Do you mind?" Abbie asked. She had memorized everything she could from the Colonia Juárez, Chihuahua, Wikipedia entry.

"Of course not. It's a fun building. So charming."

They crossed the street in front of a single-story, square, red-brick structure with a high-pitched roof and a white-trimmed triangular portico above arched double doors.

"This building reminds me of when working together was part of everyone's day-to-day life. Without cooperation, there's no way we could've made it here." The woman waved her hand at the place that used to be the tithing office. "It's being used as a Family History Center now. You'll probably want to check it out again on your own."

"Definitely," Abbie agreed. Her cover story was that she was here doing genealogical work, after all. Then Abbie tried to broach the real reason for her visit with as much discretion as possible. "Not that I know anything at all about architecture, but the style of the Old Tithing office looks a lot like the building we just came from."

"Good observation. When we built the orphanage, we wanted it to look like it had always been part of the community. I know it doesn't—well, not quite. Goodness gracious, it's bigger than the Temple in terms of square footage, but at least it's partly obscured by trees. I think they did a pretty good job."

Orphanage?

"They certainly did," Abbie said. "It must be nice working with kids."

"I don't do much of that. I'm a little more comfortable with computers than most of us who volunteer, so I spend the majority of my time maintaining records."

Records. The Church of Jesus Christ of Latter-day Saints was a church of records. Whatsoever ye shall bind on earth shall be bound in heaven.

"I love kids," Abbie said. "Do you think I could help out while I'm here? I'm sure I'll need a break from genealogy from time to time."

"We can always use an extra pair of hands in the nursery. One of our regulars is up in Alberta visiting grandchildren, and the moms need as much rest as they can get. If you're up for it now, I think we could use you."

"I'd love that."

Like most Mormons, Abbie had been brought up to be helpful. If there was work to be done, it was bad form not to help doing it. The genuine friendliness of the two women she'd met so far was beginning to make Abbie doubt her instincts. Maybe nothing was going on at the temple. Maybe this new large building was just a place to take care of children without parents.

Sister Robbins brought Abbie to the back entrance of the orphanage. She swiped a key card and opened the door. Abbie followed her new friend up a flight of stairs into a large, bright playroom. A child-friendly mural of the Salt Lake Valley in the 1860s, complete with the temple and horse-drawn wagons, covered the walls. Somebody had taken the time to attach actual tree trunks in places where there would have been trees. Silk leaves fluttered from the air-conditioned breeze. Toddlers sat in a circle listening to a woman read. In another corner, three silver-haired women sitting in brightly painted chairs rocked dozing infants. A few older kids, four- and five-year-olds, were at short round tables. A little blonde girl was coloring, and a tawny-haired boy was building a tower of wooden blocks.

The woman reading to the circled toddlers looked at Abbie. The woman tried, unsuccessfully, to stifle a yawn.

Sister Robbins announced, "We have a new volunteer, Sister . . . uh . . ."

"Sweeten. Jennifer Sweeten," Abbie said. "Would you like me to take over?"

"Yes, please, I'm getting too old for this." The older woman used her arms to push herself up from her chair.

The children sat in silence while Abbie pulled a book from a shelf: *Girls Who Choose God: Stories of Strong Women From the Book of Mormon.* Abbie flipped through the short children's book. It was relatively new, published well after Abbie would have been its target demographic, but she did find something she wanted to read: "Abish, the Daring Missionary."

Abbie had almost finished the story when another woman came to retrieve the children. In a few efficient moments, the entire room was emptied of its young charges. Abbie stayed behind to straighten up. She retrieved a bottle of lemon-scented cleaning spray from a high shelf in an open cabinet. She spritzed the table and chairs where the kids had been just moments before. As she wiped the surfaces, two other women neatening the room looked over at her and smiled. Smiles that played across the surface of their mouths but not in their eyes.

Abbie wiped away tiny handprints from every surface she could find. She was slow and methodical.

"That little girl has such a sweet spirit," one woman said. "I'm going to miss her when she leaves."

The woman's friend nodded. "I wish Sister Bentsen would listen to us. I think it's better to keep the brothers and sisters together. The children will have no memory anyway. A few extra months can't possibly make any difference."

Sister Bentsen? That couldn't possibly be *her* Sister Bentsen, could it?

The woman not speaking shot her companion a death stare. Silence was immediate. Both women's eyes glanced toward Abbie, trying to determine if the stranger in their midst had been listening. Abbie kept her head down and stared at the tabletop she was wiping for the fifth time.

"It's not our place to make those decisions. I, for one, am glad not to have that responsibility." Now, the older woman's voice was quiet; her anger, though, was loud. "I choose to follow the direction of our leaders. Of course," she added in the tone you use when you mean the exact opposite of what you're saying, "I'm not judging you for having your own opinion."

The two women looked over toward Abbie again. The stern one said, loudly this time, "Thank you, Sister." The chastened woman, the one with her own opinion, kept her eyes on the floor.

"You're very welcome!" Abbie smiled broadly and waved as the women left. She put the cleaning supplies back one the high shelf.

What had she just overheard?

NINE

Sister Charlesworth was as generous with her food as she was with her hospitality. After a heavy dinner and a home-made pie with crust that would have been the envy of any pastry chef in the world, Abbie collapsed into bed. The flight from Salt Lake, the drive from El Paso, the tour of the town, and volunteering at the orphanage had well and truly worn her out. She was, in Sister Charlesworth's words, "bone tired." For the first time in months, the whirring in Abbie's head couldn't prevent sheer exhaustion from forcing her body to sleep.

Until a phone rang.

It took Abbie a moment to orient herself. She was in a ruffled canopy bed upstairs in one of Sister Charlesworth's bedrooms on a well-maintained street in Colonia Juárez. It was a tidy room, decorated with pale-peach and lavender flowers. In the darkness, the floral pattern was played out in shades of dark and darker gray.

Sister Charlesworth's voice was soft, but Abbie could tell the older woman wasn't far down the hallway.

Abbie set her right foot and then her left on the floor. The floorboards creaked. She shifted her weight and moved toward the door in slow motion, which allowed her to walk through the space in almost complete silence. She leaned her ear against the door.

"Sister Robbins, please calm down. I can't understand what you're saying."

Before Sister Charlesworth said anything else, men's voices rumbled outside the window. A loud knocking echoed through the house. Abbie tiptoed back to the window and peeked through the lace curtains without moving them. Early sunlight was beginning to streak across the sky. There were five men standing at the white picket gate in front of Sister Charlesworth's house, all of them carrying guns of one kind or another.

"I'm coming, I'm coming." Sister Charlesworth's voice was loud enough for the men outside to hear. Abbie heard her hostess set down the phone and answer the door. "Brother Johnson, what's the matter?"

"Brittany ran away last night."

"With the children?" Sister Charlesworth asked.

"Yes. We think she left around four in the morning."

"Oh my," she said. "What can I do to help?"

"Do you have any idea where she would hide? We don't think she could have gone far, particularly carrying the kids. I don't need to tell you that we need to find her before something happens. She's due any day now."

"She kept to herself," Sister Charlesworth said. "She

didn't chat much with the other young ladies. She liked to go on walks by herself in the orchards, I think—"

The man interrupted Sister Charlesworth with a "Thank you" before she could finish her sentence. He waved his arm at the men standing at the white picket gate. "The orchards!" They started walking west.

Abbie climbed back into bed as quietly as she had climbed out of it. She curled on her side, facing away from the door. Abbie heard the knob turn and the door creak open just enough from someone to peek through. Abbie didn't move. The door closed.

Abbie waited until six thirty to get up and shower. Sister Charlesworth was already in the kitchen making breakfast when Abbie came down.

"Orange juice?" Sister Charlesworth asked.

"That would be great." Abbie could've used a cup of coffee.

"I usually just eat toast in the mornings. When you get to be my age, your appetite sort of disappears." Sister Charlesworth patted her round stomach and chuckled. "Even if it doesn't look like it."

"I'm not big on breakfast, but that toast looks delicious."

Sister Charlesworth stood up and went to the counter. She cut a thick piece of bread from a homemade loaf and slid the slice into a toaster. A few minutes later, she presented Abbie with perfectly golden toast, melted butter glistening on top.

"I had so much fun with the kids yesterday. I can do genealogy later. Could you use an extra pair of hands this morning?" As much as Abbie wanted to, the mention of Sister Bentsen was impossible to dismiss entirely. It was a common last name. Abbie had gone to high school with at least three different Bentsens.

"We can always use extra hands, and it's nice to have someone new around. We don't get many visitors." Sister Charlesworth paused for a moment, the way people do who have a lot of stories to tell but don't assume others necessarily want to hear them. "What inspired you to make the trek?"

When you lie, especially when it doesn't come naturally, it's best to stay as close to the truth as possible. Abbie already felt bad about not being honest with this kind woman who had opened up her home and heart to her.

"My mom died a few years ago. We were really close. There are still times when I pick up the phone to call her." Abbie took another bite from the toast. It wasn't warm anymore, but the chewy bread was good enough to stand on its own.

"Then my husband died. It was a lot. I was pretty overwhelmed. The only person in the world who could've comforted me was already gone. I don't think I've ever felt more alone. I spent a lot of time praying and thinking about life, about family. A few weeks ago, I was prompted to visit where my mom's family came from. I had vacation time, so here I am."

"It sounds to me like you're following what our Heavenly Father wants you to do." Sister Charlesworth reached her hand across the kitchen table and squeezed Abbie's. "It's hard when someone passes through the veil, especially when they're young. Take comfort that it's all part of His plan. You were right to listen to the voice that prompted you to come here."

Abbie used to laugh at the thought of a still, small voice—the Holy Ghost—guiding a prayerful person through life. Now, she thought listening for those divine promptings wasn't all that different from sitting in silent meditation to find clarity. Both were ways of quieting the noise.

"Dear, you'll find what you're looking for. I knew the moment I saw you there was a reason Heavenly Father sent you to us now."

After Abbie cleared the kitchen table, she and Sister Charlesworth walked to the orphanage together. The streets were quiet, but people were out and about, standing in small groups and talking too quietly to be overheard. No one looked Sister Charlesworth in the eye.

Once they walked through the doors of the orphanage, the anxiety floating through the streets of this tiny town took on a darker tone.

"It's awful, just awful," a woman said. Her eyes were red and swollen; her cheeks were splotched with pink. Abbie recognized her but didn't know her by name. She burst into tears when she saw Sister Charlesworth.

"Brittany Thompson?" Sister Charlesworth asked.

"Yes," the crying woman confirmed.

"Sister Charlesworth." Abbie heard a familiar male

voice. She turned around to see the man who had been on the porch earlier that morning. He was tall, at least six foot three, and heavyset. He had thick gray hair, his skin permanently tanned from years spent in the sun.

"Where's Brittany?" Sister Charlesworth asked him.

"The mother and children are gone."

"Gone? How?"

"It looks like she managed to get the Jacksons' old truck working again. It's missing, along with some rifles Brother Jackson kept in the barn."

Brittany Thompson. The name rang a bell, but Abbie couldn't place it. She needed some quiet to think, but the lobby and front steps of the orphanage had become Grand Central. Everyone in town was stopping by to offer help and, more importantly, to gossip. While Sister Charlesworth explained what she knew to one more concerned neighbor, Abbie slipped outside.

It was still early, but the air promised a hot day. There was a bench facing the street, but Abbie wanted a more privacy. She walked around the corner of the orphanage and found a bench shaded by a tall tree and nearly hidden by bushes. She sat down. Henderson had sent her here because Heber Bentsen had been interested in the list of young women who'd dropped out of the Y. Her boss was grasping at straws. He wanted Heber's murder tied up in a nice little bow before the funeral. But Abbie didn't think the line between Heber's murder and young women dropping out of the Y was going to be quite so direct.

She started scrolling through the pictures from her

dad's notebook. It was hard to read his tiny script on the phone's screen, but she kept at it. Brittany Thompson wasn't an unusual name, but it was too familiar for Abbie's taste. She had to confirm that her dad's notebook was not the place where she'd seen it. She cupped her hand over the screen of her phone to shield it from the sun and squinted at her dad's handwriting. There it was: Brittany Thompson, the first student to leave. Her dad had written that she had an exceptionally strong testimony of the Church, had served a mission in France, and showed extraordinary academic promise. YALE and EARLY MISSIONARY WORK IN GB were jotted in the margin on the second page of notes.

Abbie's thoughts were interrupted by the sound of women's voices coming from around the corner. Apparently, Abbie was not the only one seeking escape from the chaos of the orphanage. The conversation was too hushed for Abbie to make out what the women were saying, but one of them was sniffling loudly.

Then Abbie heard a deep man's voice. Her stomach clenched. She knew that voice.

"Good morning, sisters."

"Good morning, Elder Bowen."

Abbie felt her blood run cold. When was the last time she'd actually seen Bowen? When he and his goon in the flannel shirt had searched her house? Or was it when he'd lied to her during her investigation about his involvement with Celestial Time Shares? Either way, their shared history was not a friendly one, and she had no desire to see him here in this Mormon colony. He would never believe she was doing genealogical research. He also knew her name was not Jennifer Sweeten.

"I know everyone is upset. There's no reason to worry. I'm sure we'll find the mother—Brittany?—and the children, but it's dangerous out there. It's important to follow the rules the Brethren have laid out for you while you're here. Your Heavenly Father will protect you if you follow the path He has shown you."

"Yes, Elder Bowen." The voices of the young women were docile, eager to please.

"I would also like to take this moment to remind you that your special missions here, like all sacred things, must not be discussed with those who are not part of our Heavenly Father's plan. He will reveal the fullness of what we are doing when that time is right." Bowen paused for a moment. Abbie could almost sense his glare, like a high school principal scowling across the desk at a wayward student. "This is an orphanage, you understand?"

"Yes, Elder Bowen." Two female voices, in unison.

Something was off. The youngest member of the Quorum of the Seventy and the de facto spokesman of the Church of Jesus Christ of Latter-day Saints was nothing if not the consummate salesman. But right now Bowen didn't sound like himself. What exactly was she hearing in his voice? The tone was wrong. He didn't sound calm and controlled; he sounded worried and angry.

An unpleasant wave of anxiety spread from Abbie's stomach, tightening her chest and constricting her throat. The theory forming in her mind was outlandish, and yet some pieces were falling into place. Abbie couldn't escape the fact that Brittany had been the first student to disappear from her graduate studies at BYU, and she apparently had borne two children here in Juárez. It was hard to imagine a scenario where a chaste LDS returned missionary would have had premarital sex at all, let alone managed to get pregnant two times, outside of temple marriage.

Abbie couldn't quite bring herself to admit the idea that this could be a small-scale plan to increase the number of children being born into the Church. But it made more and more sense as she thought about it. Technically, it didn't run afoul of Utah's antibigamy law: no purporting marriage, no cohabitation. And it might not even be marriage for time on this earth—maybe the young women were being sealed for eternity, like when women were sealed to Joseph Smith or Brigham Young well after those two men had died. If you were sealed for eternity, but not for time on this earth, were you married in this life at all in terms of the law of the United States?

And Bowen was here.

The LDS Church was known for its missionary work, for all those clean-cut teenagers sent around the globe to share the restored Gospel of Jesus Christ, but Abbie had long suspected the real secret to the Church's staggering growth was that most Mormon families had at least four children, with five and six being not at all uncommon. It didn't take too many generations for a church of six people in the early 1800s to grow to a church of fifteen million when every family had that many kids.

Abbie's mind jumped to conversations she'd had with her dad about the "preexistence." If you didn't grow up with a cosmogony that included a war in heaven between supporters of Jesus Christ and those on Satan's team, the idea that there was a finite number of spirit brothers and sisters in heaven waiting to receive earthly bodies might have seemed strange. Abbie, however, had grown up with this creation myth. Before being born into earthly bodies, all human beings lived as spirit children with a Heavenly Father and a Heavenly Mother. In the last days before the Second Coming, it was especially important to have as many of those remaining spirits as possible born into solid LDS families. There would be the final battle before the Millennium. The more Mormons, the better.

"Jennifer! There you are." Sister Charlesworth exhaled loudly when she saw Abbie sitting on the bench. "Can you help with the little ones again? You had them enthralled yesterday. We're a bit short-staffed, and, well, we can use you."

With Bowen at the orphanage, Abbie knew the smart thing to do would be to tell the kind Sister Charlesworth she had a family emergency and had to get back to St. George as soon as possible. The smart thing to do would be to avoid Bowen. The smart thing to do would be to get as far away from Juárez as quickly as she could.

Abbie did exactly the opposite of the smart thing.

"Of course, I can stay as long as you need me." She did, of course, have to check in with Henderson. He wanted to have everything buttoned up before Heber's funeral. She'd try to leave him a message later that morning. Abbie had found a few spots around town with reliable cell phone coverage.

"Thank you." Her gracious hostess took Abbie's right hand in both of hers and squeezed gently. "That's wonderful. I'll get you a key card so you can get in and out of the building without me. Security is going to be tighter now, since what's happened."

Sister Charlesworth accompanied Abbie to reception. They both had to weave between small clutches of people, deep in conversation about the news of the morning. A woman in her early eighties asked Abbie to stand in front of a white photo backdrop and took her picture. A few minutes later, Abbie was holding a card with her picture on it and the words SISTER JENNIFER SWEETEN, VOLUNTEER, JUÁREZ LDS CHILD CENTER.

Abbie would have thought that someone working with children, even voluntarily, would be subject to rigorous background checks, but it seemed as far as this orphanage was concerned, one only had to pass the Sister Charlesworth test. Apparently, Abbie had.

"We're going to take the older ones over to the church for some crafts and singing as soon as we finish with story time. Do you remember the way to the playroom?"

Abbie did. She walked up the back stairs and opened the door to a loud sigh. A harried-looking woman glared at her, then pasted a smile on her sour face. Evidently, Abbie was late.

"Good morning!" the woman said in a falsetto that did not mask her irritation. She turned to the circle of children.

"Sister Jennifer is here to finish this story." She handed Abbie *The Holy Ghost Is Like a Blanket*, opened to the page she had been reading, and was gone before Abbie could say anything.

Abbie read, "The Holy Ghost is like the wind. You can feel the power of the wind, but you cannot see it. You can feel Him in your heart as He helps you choose the right."

The kids sat quietly. Then, as if out of thin air, another sister appeared. She instructed the children to line up. They did so in silence, then filed through the door. After the kids left the room, the same woman turned to Abbie and said, "Sister Sweeten, it's so kind of you to help out. Let me apologize for Sister Jamison's rush out of here. She's been very emotional since what happened."

"Of course. It's fine," Abbie said.

The woman looked at her watch. "We need to get down to the lobby."

The children were already waiting when Abbie and her fellow sister arrived in the entrance hall. The kids' faces were freshly clean, their hair combed. A few of them looked to be about four or five years old, and the rest were younger. Abbie was assigned to walk with two of the older girls. They followed the neat line of kids and sisters out the front door, down the steps, and onto the street.

"My name is Sister Sweeten," Abbie said in her talking-to-young-children-and-dogs voice. "I'm visiting Juárez for the first time. What should I see while I'm here?"

"The temple," the first little girl said. "Mommy said that's where I came from." Abbie looked around to see if either of the other chaperones was listening to her conversation. They weren't.

The other little girl chimed in, "Yes, that's where we all came from. It's a secret." Her voice dropped to a whisper. "The sisters don't even know."

"What do you mean"—Abbie imitated her young friend's hushed tone—"that you came from the temple?"

The girls sized up Abbie. One stopped walking and put her hand to her chin, looking intently into Abbie's eyes. The other put her small hands on her narrow hips. The first asked, "Can you keep a secret?"

"Yes." Abbie nodded. "I can."

"We're very special children of our Heavenly Father. We come from the temple because our mommies were chosen."

"I understand," Abbie said, but she didn't understand. She didn't understand at all. "Have you met your daddy?"

"I don't know my daddy's name, but my mommy does. When I leave here, I'll have a family in Utah who wants to take care of me and—" Before the first girl could finish, the other interrupted. Both wanted to impress the outsider.

"There aren't enough worthy daddies in this 'spensation." Abbie assumed the girl was trying to say "this dispensation." Mormons defined the term as a period of time when there was at least one divinely authorized servant on the earth. Now was the final dispensation—the Restoration—which had begun when the fullness of the Gospel was revealed to Joseph Smith.

The girl continued her explanation. "Some mommies

have been chosen to marry special daddies so our brothers and sisters can come down from heaven."

Abbie wanted to ask about the special daddies, but they were already at the front door of the church. They had no choice but to follow the other sisters and kids in front of them.

Holding the girls' hands, Abbie entered the lobby. She was not prepared for what was waiting for her. Before Abbie could duck into a side hallway or a bathroom, Bowen looked over the shoulder of the man he was talking to and directly into Abbie's eyes.

"Sister Taylor," he said loudly, "it's so nice to see you. What brings you to this neck of the woods?" Abbie looked around to see if any of the sisters from the orphanage had heard Bowen call her by her real name. Luckily for Abbie, they were busily giving the children instructions.

"Elder Bowen," Abbie said. "I could ask you the same."

"As the Prophet told us all when the temple here was dedicated," Bowen responded, "the Mormon colonies in Mexico are as important as ever."

Indeed.

"Sister Sweeten!" Sister Charlesworth's voice pierced through the chatter in the church lobby. Abbie's generous hostess approached the General Authority with a wide smile. "President Bowen, it is such an honor to have you join us here."

Bowen shook her hand and flashed his perfect smile. "It's entirely my pleasure to be here among the Saints whose hard work and dedication to the Gospel have created this haven."

Sister Charlesworth basked in Bowen's flattery, but then remembered herself and shared the praise. "Sister Sweeten has been such a blessing since she arrived."

Bowen didn't miss a beat in playing off Sister Charlesworth's honest compliment. "I'm sure she has. Sister Sweeten is nothing if not diligent." Bowen's lips smiled. His eyes didn't.

Sister Charlesworth was not ready to let her General Authority slip away from her anytime soon. "So, President Bowen, how long will you be with us this time?"

Bowen had no choice but to be polite. "Well, I wish I could stay—"

It was now or never.

"Please excuse me." Abbie walked toward the bathroom. She might have five minutes, if that, before Bowen would be able to extricate himself from Sister Charlesworth's attention. Then he would make a phone call to alert someone in Salt Lake that she was here.

Abbie passed the door to the women's restroom and walked out of the church as quickly as she could without drawing attention to herself. Then she sprinted to the orphanage, up the stairs to where the young mothers slept. The doors were all open. It was like a college dorm. The rooms were the same: two twin beds, two desks, and two dressers, but the young women had personalized their spaces with photographs, homemade quilts, and stuffed animals. Abbie looked through open doors on either side of the hallway, reading the temporary name tags inserted into slots at each door. Where was Brittany Thompson's room?

Abbie made it to the end of the hall, where she found what she was looking for. Brittany's roommate jumped when Abbie came in. She was crying. Abbie closed the door behind her.

"Are you okay?" Abbie asked.

The whimpering girl attempted a smile.

"I need to look through Brittany's things. Where are they?"

Brittany's roommate seemed surprisingly nonplussed by the question. She pointed at a dresser. "She . . . she kept her special things here." The young woman stood up and opened the top drawer. She handed Abbie a pale-teal box of tampons. "The older ladies here are really squeamish with feminine hygiene products of all kinds; tampons make them especially squirrely. They have never looked in here."

"Have you seen Sister Sweeten? The new volunteer?" The words floated through the window open to the street below.

Brittany's roommate stared at Abbie, not blinking. "Brittany didn't want them to take her babies. She changed after she found out she was pregnant again."

"Pregnant?"

"Yeah. She's due any day now. I wouldn't want to be driving back to Utah with two kids and worrying about my water breaking."

"Utah?" Abbie asked.

"Where else would she go?" Brittany's roommate couldn't hide her surprise at Abbie's question. It was as though Utah were the only place in the world.

Abbie heard the sound of men's voices. They were nearer this time, inside the building.

"Thank you," Abbie whispered. With the pale-teal box in her hand, she left the room. She ran to the back stairs. The voices were behind her, but she didn't look back to see who was there. If she was lucky, by the time they searched the orphanage and Sister Charlesworth's home, she'd be well on her way to the Texas border.

TEN

Abbie's heart rate returned to normal somewhere on I-40 in Arizona. She pulled over at a rest stop. The contents of Brittany's special box had been calling to her since the orphanage. Underneath a layer of tampons were a small diary, three ultrasounds, and a Polaroid of Brittany wearing a long white dress holding the hand of a septuagenarian, also dressed entirely in white: Elder Bragg, one of Port's closest friends in the Quorum of the Twelve.

"Jesus," Abbie muttered to herself. Brittany was beaming. She certainly didn't look like a reluctant bride.

Then Abbie opened the diary.

This morning, after I prayed, SB called. She said she was the secretary to TSC. At first I thought it was a prank, but it wasn't. She told me TSC would like to see me and she asked if I could meet him. She told me he was going to be in Provo for business and gave me an address and a time. I told her I would be there. She said thank you and reminded me that this was not a social visit. I should treat it as a sacred meeting and could not tell anyone about it. I assured her I wouldn't say a word to anyone. I thought my heart was going to jump out of my chest. I couldn't believe TSC wanted to meet with me.

When I met him, I felt the spirit of the Holy Ghost everywhere! I think TSC almost glowed, like Joseph Smith described when Heavenly Father and Jesus first visited him in the sacred grove. TSC asked that we kneel and pray. It was the most beautiful prayer I have ever heard! I must have started crying, because he handed me a tissue. Then we sat. He took my hand and told me he knew of my devotion to the gospel. I couldn't speak, but I nodded. He smiled. He said that we were in the last days, and that it was important that we press forward with bringing down our brothers and sisters from the pre-existence.

We talked a little about the new and everlasting covenant. Then he kissed me on the forehead and asked me to wait for a moment. TSC left. Then PB came in. I had seen him in person one time before when he spoke at the Y. I was so overwhelmed by the spirit that I couldn't speak. I could only smile when he introduced himself. He asked me to stand up and he put his arms around me. His hands caressed me. He leaned toward me and kissed me, touched me. When he stopped kissing me, he asked me if I would help with Heavenly Father's work. I said yes!

I was shaking. I had never felt so close to my Heavenly Father!!! I don't know how long I stood there before TSC returned. It could have been minutes; it could have been hours. I was basking in the light of the spirit. He told me

I had been chosen to be PB's fourth wife. He asked if I could keep this a secret. I told him of course! He told me I would receive an official letter from his office calling me to a special mission. It was a letter I could show my parents. It would say that I was being called to do important work for the Church and I may be gone for several years. I would be able to send my parents a letter at Christmas and on the 24th of July, but not on Tuesday, like regular missions, and I couldn't send pictures. He promised great rewards awaited me in the Celestial Kingdom.

Jesus.

ELEVEN

Abbie loved the desert southwest: the red-then-pink-then-white earth that formed into mesas, small round mounds, and otherworldly spires. She loved the smell of sagebrush and the sky that made you feel like you were the size of a speck of dust with about as much importance. The open space gave Abbie's mind room to roam.

Hours after she turned on her headlights, she finally made it to Utah 39. As far as she could tell, no one had followed her. Abbie turned on the blinker as she rounded the curve just before the entrance to her driveway. The promise of crawling into her own bed crowded out almost every other thought in her head. She exhaled and felt the knotted muscles in her neck relax. She was home.

Then she saw the car. It was parked on the side of the narrow road. Barely noticeable. If the passenger hadn't been reading something on his phone, Abbie wouldn't have seen the glow reflected on his white face. Without slowing down, she drove past her own driveway. She was one coincidence past worrying if she was being paranoid.

She drove up the canyon and then took a back road toward Riverdale. She found the long private driveway she was looking for and turned off the road, pulling up in front of the three-car garage. For a moment, she wondered if she should find a motel instead. It was the middle of the night and she wasn't even sure if Flynn was here. In her keyed-up, sleep-deprived state, Flynn's was the only place she could think to go. She simply didn't have the strength to drive anywhere else or think of anywhere else to drive.

When Flynn had texted her after Heber's death—when they'd thought it was a tragic accident—he hadn't mentioned anything about where he was. For all she knew, he could be in Oslo or Tokyo or Montana. If he was here, though, he would take her in and wouldn't ask questions. The other flurry of feelings about him—them—could wait until later.

Abbie climbed out of her SUV and knocked on the front door.

The house was dark and silent.

She knocked again, this time with more force. She heard the sound of movement upstairs. Then faint light seeped out from one of the windows on the second floor; a few moments later there were footsteps.

The door opened.

"Abs? What are you doing here . . . now?"

"Do you have room for me to park my car in the garage?" Yes, she was now feeling fully paranoid. If the guys in the car by her driveway had any sense, they'd seen her big black SUV driving up Utah 39 in the middle of the night. Even if they hadn't followed her (and she was pretty sure they hadn't), they would have informed someone.

"Okay, weird question, but I'll play," Flynn said. "The answer is yes, but I need to move a car out so there's room."

Even in his rumpled pajama bottoms and T-shirt, Flynn was easy on the eyes. The shirt looked comfy, but it didn't hide his defined shoulders and arms. Not that Abbie was paying attention to Flynn's shoulders.

"Thank you." Abbie walked to her dusty rental and waited while Flynn backed out his mint-condition, navy Karmann Ghia. Abbie pulled into the empty space. She remembered that it was a tight fit for her Rover, let alone this gargantuan SUV from the airport in El Paso, but she managed to pull in without scraping anything. When she walked out of the garage, Flynn was leaning against his beautiful car, his arms crossed. He had a lopsided grin on his face. There was no denying he was handsome: short-cropped hair, a little silver at the temples, eyes an impossible shade of blue between topaz and tanzanite, and a little scruff on his jaw.

"Do you want to wait outside and watch the sunrise or would you like to go in?" Flynn's eyes crinkled at the corners. "It looks to me like you could use something to eat."

Abbie knew she was a mess. She had driven straight from Mexico.

"Inside is preferable." Her voice sounded shakier than she thought she felt.

"*Après toi.*" Flynn bowed slightly and motioned toward the door.

They walked into the entry hall and then down the hallway to the kitchen. He turned on the lights in the classic kitchen, all white cabinets and Carrara marble. Abbie sat down at the island counter.

"I have to admit that my knowledge of what meal exists between dinner and breakfast eludes me. Dinfast? Breakner? We could just go British and call it extraordinarily high tea."

Abbie loved that Flynn knew that high tea was a simple supper and not, as many misguided hotels seemed to think, a particularly fancy snack of tiny scones and pretty finger sandwiches.

"If I recall," Flynn went on, "you're not really a breakfast person."

"No, I'm not, but I am a coffee person."

"You'll have to wait for that. By the looks of you, I'm making an executive decision to ban caffeine for now. As soon as you've eaten a proper meal, you need to sleep."

"Thanks," Abbie said in her deadpan voice. "I look that good?"

Flynn raised that rakish eyebrow of his and walked around the kitchen island. He leaned over and kissed her gently on the forehead.

"I have some leftovers." He turned to the fridge and pulled out what looked like seared fish (probably Utah trout), haricots verts tossed in olive oil with shallots, and a quinoa pilaf. "I think it's all edible cold, but I'm happy to heat it up if you'd like."

"Cold is good."

Flynn set the plate in front of Abbie. She stifled a yawn and ate. After a few bites, exhaustion beat out hunger. She couldn't keep her eyes open.

"Let's get you upstairs."

Abbie didn't argue. She followed Flynn up the back staircase that led from the kitchen to the second floor of the house. He opened a door on the right side of the hallway. Sunlight was beginning to hit the large field in front of the house that had once been home to horses.

Flynn opened the door to a different bedroom than the one Abbie had stayed in before. This one was painted a very pale yellow. There was a cherry-wood four-poster bed against the left wall flanked by two matching nightstands. Two windows overlooked the field. The trees obscured the road beyond. In front of the window on the right was a comfortable cream chair with a matching ottoman. A large dresser stood across the room from the bed.

"I'm not sure what we have in here." He opened a drawer and pulled out a women's white T-shirt and red sweat pants with UTAH emblazoned down the side. "My oldest daughter likes this room. She keeps some things here. These will probably work as pajamas." Abbie took the sweats.

"The bathroom is through that door. I'm fairly sure there are fresh toiletries, but if not, let me know. I have more clean toothbrushes than a dentist."

"Thanks."

Flynn was standing close enough for Abbie to smell a hint of whatever cologne he was wearing. Despite her utter physical exhaustion, part of her hoped he would wrap his arms around her. Instead, he said, "Good night, Abs. I'll be here when you wake up. Then you can tell me what the hell you've gotten yourself into."

When Abbie first opened her eyes, she thought she hadn't slept more than a few minutes. The light outside the window looked almost exactly like it had when she'd nestled under the covers. The bed looked like it was still perfectly made except for the spot where Abbie was lying. Then she realized it wasn't dawn; it was dusk.

She went into the bathroom. As promised, there was a neatly organized drawer of travel-sized soaps, shampoos, lotions, and dental hygiene products. She showered and brushed her teeth. She hadn't done either before she climbed into bed. To be honest, it hadn't even occurred to her. Abbie thought about trying to find something to put on other than the sweats she'd slept in, but the growl from her stomach convinced her to head to the kitchen before searching for clean clothes.

"Good morning." Flynn was sitting at the counter with a cup of tea and his computer open in front of him.

"Good morning."

"I was thinking of grilling some steaks. Baked potatoes, roasted Brussels sprouts, tossed salad, and a nice California Cab."

"That sounds like a perfect breakfast," Abbie replied.

"In the meantime, you can nibble on this." Flynn placed a platter of cheeses, Marcona almonds, red grapes, and an assortment of crackers in front of Abbie. He already had a small plate with some crumbs and a few grapes on it.

"I was about to pour myself some Schramsberg. May I interest you in a glass?"

"Yes, you may."

"My housekeeper came today. I asked her to wash what you were wearing. I hope you don't mind. I think she left everything in the laundry room."

"Thank you."

He popped the sparkling wine, handed Abbie a glass, then snapped his computer shut.

He raised the narrow goblet. "To the story that brought you here."

Abbie raised her glass and took a sip of golden bubbles. Then she started talking.

TWELVE

After Abbie had verbalized the jumble of facts jostling around in her brain, Flynn repeated them back to her, straightening out the tangle.

"What you know to be fact is: One, Heber was murdered. Two, Heber was interested in the female students who'd dropped out of their graduate studies at the Y. Three, Heber had lunch with your dad the week before he died and they talked about those female students. Four, Brittany Thompson, one of your dad's students, left Colonia Juárez with her two children and a third on the way. Five, Bowen was in Juárez. Six, Brittany's diary states she was happily going to become a fourth wife."

"Yes," Abbie said. "What falls under the 'not demonstrable fact but need to check out' category: Who called in Heber's accident and why? Did Bryce Strong really see a man get out of a white car and check on Heber? Was what the little girls in Juárez told me true? Was Bowen's presence in Juárez related to Brittany's disappearance, to me being there, or was he there coincidentally on Church business?"

Abbie took another sip from her glass. "Whatever's going on with my dad's students shouldn't be any of my business. But if it's connected to Heber's murder . . ." Abbie trailed off. She didn't want there to be a connection.

She looked at the clock on the kitchen wall. She had slept away an entire work day. Hours when she should have been investigating. An entire day when Chief Henderson was probably calling for her head on a silver platter because she hadn't checked in.

"I have to check my phone," she said. It was charging upstairs on the nightstand. There had been almost no reception in Mexico, and the drive from El Paso hadn't been all that much better, although checking in with her boss had been the last thing on her mind as she drove across the desert. Now she did have to respond to messages.

Henderson had sent her a text, but just to see whether she'd found anything. She sent a noninformative but accurate response. She didn't want to get into a conversation about President Bragg being sealed to four women. Standard parlance dictated that all Apostles were referred to as "President." A confusing practice for outsiders, but an indication of the Church's long-standing admiration for hierarchy.

Clarke had texted a few times. He had made progress on a white car. Caleb Monson, the man whose prints were on Heber's car door, owned a white Mercedes. Clarke was suspicious about how the former soldier had enough money for such an expensive car.

Abbie walked back downstairs to the kitchen. Flynn had reopened his computer, his brow furrowed.

"I need to get rid of the rental. If the guys waiting outside my house saw it, and they had to, they'll be looking for it. Plus, I don't want to end up with the license plate making it into some database for a stolen car."

"Unlikely," Flynn said. He was probably right, but then added, "You can drop it off in Roy. I checked." He pointed to his screen, open to a page for the car rental company. "I'll follow you and give you a ride back."

"Okay." She did want to drop off the SUV as soon as possible. She didn't like the feeling of not having returned it in Texas like she was supposed to. "Can we go now?"

Flynn scrolled down to the bottom of his screen. "Yep. Open twenty-four hours."

Abbie's phone vibrated. A photo of her dad appeared on the screen. She answered before the second buzz.

"Dad? Are you okay?" Fear gripped her heart. If someone had been waiting for her, then it was not at all unlikely that someone was keeping an eye on him, too.

"Oh, yes, Abish. I'm fine, but I could use your help. I know it's late, but this really can't wait." Abbie's eyes widened as she listened to her dad. She put the phone on speaker so Flynn could hear, too.

When her dad finished with his too-lengthy explanation, Flynn said, "We'd better get going."

Abbie backed out of the garage and started for the car

rental place. The drive to Roy didn't take long. In a few minutes, she walked up to the counter with a lengthy apology prepared for why she hadn't returned the car at the airport in Texas. She needn't have worried. The young man managing the desk was polite and helpful. If he didn't believe her story about having missed her flight and needing to visit a sick aunt in St. George, he didn't let on. He gave her a friendly smile and offered to reduce the extra fees because of her extenuating circumstances. Abbie insisted on paying everything she owed, including the fines. Taking financial advantage of her lie would have made her feel awful.

She climbed into the passenger side of Flynn's car, and they drove south on I-15 toward her dad's. It took only about an hour and ten minutes before they were turning onto her old street in Provo. The light from the kitchen window spilled out onto the yard. The rest of the house was dark. They parked in the driveway and walked up the steps. She turned the doorknob. It was locked.

Abbie knocked and waited as the sound of footsteps approached.

"Abish." Her dad exhaled her name. He was wearing flannel pajamas underneath a robe that was older than Abbie. "Flynn," he said. "I didn't know you'd be here."

"It's a long story," Flynn said. Flynn was John's best friend. They'd been inseparable since elementary school. That was enough of an explanation for the professor.

They followed Abbie's dad to the kitchen. A very pregnant young woman with hair the color of pale caramel sat at the table sipping a glass of chocolate milk. A long-sleeved T-shirt stretched across her round belly and almost covered the black fabric panel insert of her maternity jeans. On her feet were white sneakers that had seen better days.

"Hi, I'm Abbie."

"I'm Brittany. Brittany Thompson. I used to be one of your dad's graduate students."

It was Brittany. *The* Brittany. Before Abbie could say anything, her dad interjected. "One of my best students. Yale offered her a five-year scholarship in religious studies to complete her dissertation. Her area of research is the experience of early Mormon converts from the United Kingdom."

"My area of research *was* early converts from England and Scotland." Brittany Thompson stifled a yawn. "I'm so sorry you drove all the way down here so late. The kids are already asleep, but Professor Taylor insisted."

Abbie glanced at her dad. He looked all of his seventy-eight years and then some. He needed to get to bed. He couldn't handle a houseguest, let alone a pregnant one with toddlers in tow.

"No offense, Dad, but you're not really set up for hosting. Flynn has more than enough room at his place."

"It's not a problem at all," Flynn said without missing a beat. "I've even got a playroom downstairs. My kids live with their mom most of the time, but I'm fully set up."

Her dad looked relieved, Brittany less so.

"Flynn is a family friend," Abbie's dad said to Brittany. "You'll be in good hands until you decide what you want to do. As much as I hate to admit that I'm getting old, I am. If there were an emergency, I'm not sure I'd be of much use."

"Okay." Brittany slurped the last of her chocolate milk. Grains of the cocoa mix stuck to the bottom of the glass.

She pushed herself up from her chair. "Thank you so much, Professor Taylor. I'm sorry. I just didn't know where else to go."

"You are always welcome here. All of my students are."

Brittany hugged Abbie's dad as closely as her swollen belly would allow. Once she released him, it was Abbie's turn.

"Let me help get the kids into the car," Flynn said.

"They're in Abbie's old room," the professor said. Flynn and Abbie tiptoed upstairs. Abbie took Jacob, the smaller of the two. Mary, the older daughter, stirred for a moment, but then snuggled her head into Flynn's neck and fell back asleep.

Brittany didn't have anything beyond her oversized handbag. A well-loved bear was peeking out the top, along with the white folded tops of a few clean diapers, a package of wipes, and spines of three navy passports.

"I don't have car seats," Brittany apologized. "I know that's terrible."

"It'll be okay," Flynn reassured the pregnant mom. Abbie felt an inordinate sense of guilt that they would be driving without the kids safely strapped into car seats, but Flynn's words were all the security they had at the moment. Flynn did his best to buckle in the kids, making sure that neither one had a neck against a strap. Then they started the drive north.

Abbie had expected the exhausted mother to fall asleep in the back seat between her two children. Instead, Brittany got a second wind.

"I don't know where to start. It's going to sound crazy." Apparently the mom wanted to talk. Abbie made an encouraging sound and Brittany Thompson started her tale.

"I was your dad's student years ago, at least ten months before Mary was born." She leaned over and kissed the top of the sleeping girl's head. "I got this phone call. I was convinced it was a joke at first, but when you're asked to meet an Apostle, well, you go. We prayed and he started talking about the Second Coming and how concerned he was that so many active LDS women, like me, aren't getting an opportunity to become mothers."

Abbie couldn't think of the proper response to this statement. She made a noncommittal *hmmm* sound.

"Then he told me the 1890 Manifesto was never intended to be permanent. Anyone who reads it carefully and understands the doctrine and the history of the era knows that. Plus, there's President Taylor's 1886 Revelation. Now is the time."

"The time for what?" Abbie asked.

"To continue the practice of the New and Everlasting Covenant, just as Joseph Smith intended."

Those words hung in the air for a moment. Flynn was

doing his best to pretend he wasn't there. He kept his eyes on the road.

"You mean plural marriage?"

"Yes." Brittany did not hesitate. "I know it's a lot to take in for some, but for me, it was easy. I've always had a strong testimony that this is the one true restored Church of Jesus Christ. Our Apostles are guided by revelations from our Heavenly Father. I have no doubt that we're living in the last days. There are challenges in this dispensation. When President Bragg first met with me, it was, uh, sort of a physical interview. We prayed first, but then, well . . . it doesn't matter. A few days later, we met again. He asked if I wanted a blessing. I did."

"Did he give you the blessing by himself?" Abbie asked. "Without another priesthood holder?" In most circumstances, two priesthood holders gave a blessing. They usually anointed the head of the person to be blessed with sacred oil, then laid their hands on top of that person's head.

Brittany didn't answer at first. Then, rather unconvincingly, she said, "Uh-huh."

"Who else was there, Brittany?" Abbie asked.

"Does it matter?" There was an edge in Brittany's voice.

It did to Abbie. She had known Elder Bragg from family dinners her parents hosted when she was a kid. He was a follower, not a leader. He was not the kind of man to instigate a major shift in Church practice, certainly nothing like reintroducing plural marriage. Elder Bragg was not a man to be out in front on something like that. He very well might believe in plural marriage and might even have been happy to practice it, but only if he were follow-ing instructions from someone higher up on the food chain. There were only three men in the Church who fit that description, and one of those men was now lying on a slab in the Utah Office of the Medical Examiner.

"It does matter," Abbie said. Much as she tried, she couldn't escape the thought that whoever was guiding this polygamy experiment was connected to Heber's murder.

Brittany took a deep breath. "The covenants I made are sacred. What I'm doing is part of the Lord's plan."

The tone in Brittany's voice made it clear that she was not going to say anything more on the matter.

This faith-inspired silence was strange to people who hadn't grown up in the Church. Abbie had never been able to fully explain it to her late husband Phillip, who simply couldn't wrap his mind around a religion that demanded members keep secrets not only from outsiders, but some-times also from each other. Abbie had grown up believing silence could be a manifestation of obedience to God. It had been a few years now, but she remembered feeling the devotion she heard in Brittany's voice.

There was silence for the rest of the drive, until they turned down the long tree-lined driveway to Flynn's house. Brittany spoke again. "I would've stayed in Juárez, but they were going to take my babies."

THIRTEEN

Brittany insisted she sleep in the same room with her kids, so Flynn put together a travel crib for the little boy. The little girl slept in the queen bed with Brittany. They managed to find pajamas for everyone, all a little bit too big, but clean and soft. Once her children were settled, Brittany collapsed into the bed without brushing her teeth.

Abbie and Flynn went downstairs to the formal sitting room. The light of the almost-full moon cast long shadows across the lawn outside.

"A nightcap?" Flynn asked.

"Tea."

"That can be arranged." Flynn disappeared to the kitchen. Abbie heard him fill the kettle and then heard the sound of bubbling water. A few minutes later he returned with a mug of milky tea. He handed her the cup and helped himself to a generous pour of Scotch.

They sipped their drinks in silence.

"Polygamy? The 1886 Revelation?" Flynn shook his head. "I've heard the same stories everyone else has about the five copies John Taylor made. You ever heard of the Prophet John Taylor?" He winked at Abbie.

"Yeah, I think so." She was grateful for Flynn's good-natured teasing about her great-great-great-grandfather. She could use a smile right about now. Yes, Abbie was the direct great-something-granddaughter of the Prophet John Taylor, who had allegedly claimed polygamy must always be practiced regardless of U.S. law.

"I got to tell you, Abs, I always figured that 1886 Revelation was a hoax to sustain the break-off polygamist sects."

"I did, too. Not sure Brittany's word is sufficient for me to believe in a document that purportedly no longer exists, if it ever did."

"True," Flynn said, "but she told a fascinating story."

"And left the most interesting part out."

"What part was that?"

"Who else was in the room when Bragg gave her the blessing." Abbie couldn't help but wonder if Brittany understood how important that bit of information was.

"Abs, a lot has changed since we were kids. The Church isn't a persecuted sect. Americans don't hate Mormons like they used to. They don't even think Mormons are weird. In fact, most people vaguely like Mormons. They think we're friendly, hardworking, and"—he cleared his throat—"honest and trustworthy."

That was just it. Abbie's drive back from her little jaunt to Mexico had given her plenty of time to think about just how carefully crafted the Mormon brand was.

Flynn continued. "You know as well as I do that the

main source of embarrassment for the Church, at least when it comes to plural marriage, stems from the fact that Joseph Smith began practicing polygamy well before he officially claimed, and with some women already married to other men. You know what I think about polygamy?"

"What do you think?" Abbie asked.

"I think the reason we don't seriously talk about the New and Everlasting Covenant is that members of the Church have become *comfortable*. Your dad, and mine, would use the word 'complacent.' Fact is, most members like their politically conservative image today. They like being liked. It's no longer a church made up of people willing to face extraordinary hardship to practice a persecuted faith. It would be hard to follow a principle that made you weird again. Not just I-don't-drink-tea weird, but really, truly weird. Polygamy would do that."

Flynn wasn't wrong. Plural marriage was anathema to most members. Selling it to the larger world would probably be easier than selling it to Mormons. Practicing polygamy would force active members of the restored Church to ask themselves how far they would be willing to go to practice their faith. How many would be willing to risk what their pioneer ancestors had?

FOURTEEN

"Abs. Abs." There was knocking at the door. Abbie had gratefully accepted Flynn's offer of a guest room instead of taking a car and driving home. After she'd crawled into the unfamiliar bed, she had expected her mind to race over the events of the day, but exhaustion had won out. Now Abbie opened her eyes to a room full of sunshine.

"Come in," she said.

Flynn opened the door. "Abs, someone's been trying to reach you. Your cell phone buzzing is driving the rest of us crazy."

"I didn't even hear it." Abbie pulled the sheets over the camisole she had slept in. She reached across the bed for her phone. "Sorry."

"No worries." Flynn winked at her. "I'm making breakfast downstairs. The kids were up with the sun. Brittany's still asleep." He was awfully chipper for a man who'd been up for who knows how long with two young children he didn't know. Abbie had only seen Flynn with his own young family years before, before his divorce. The kids had been small then. Her memory involved them rolling down a hill at a picnic. Flynn had ended up as dirty and grass stained as his kids.

A delighted shriek echoed from the kitchen.

"Gotta go." Flynn shut the door.

Abbie sat up in bed. Clarke had been calling, six times in the last hour. She pressed his name and the phone dialed.

"Good morning," she said.

"Good morning." Clarke made no mention of how long he'd been trying to reach her, for which Abbie was grateful. "There's been an accident. A climber up Ogden Canyon. We're making our way out there now, but it's going to take some serious hiking to get there. I've already called the ME."

"It's not . . . ?" Abbie asked, dreading the answer.

"I think it is. At least, that's what the 911 caller said."

Damn.

Clarke texted Abbie where the trailhead was. A shower helped wash off the day before. Day-old clothes would be fine for a hike. Peals of laughter guided her to the kitchen, where she was greeted with Flynn in an apron dropping oversized dollops of whipped cream onto homemade pancakes. There was bacon, too, and sliced bananas and Nutella. Brittany was sitting at the kitchen table, drinking a glass of milk. Her plate was empty until Flynn placed another pancake on top of the pool of golden syrup. The kids had opted for Nutella.

"Two more pancakes are just about ready." Flynn flipped the golden spheres. "Bacon?"

Abbie took a slice from the plate lined with paper towels. It had perfectly crisp edges, nice chewy bits of meat, and just a hint of soft fat. Exactly the way she liked it.

"I wish I could stay for breakfast, but there's been an accident. A climber."

Flynn pretended to be severely wounded after Brittany's son stabbed him with an invisible sword. The boy clapped his hands in delight as Flynn slumped to the floor in front of the stove.

"I'll see you later," Abbie said.

★ ★ ★

Clarke hadn't been kidding about the hike. It wasn't impossible, but it certainly was challenging. By the time Abbie arrived at the site, her T-shirt was sticking to her back.

"You don't get it. He's done this climb a hundred times!" Bryce's roommate said to the young officer who was trying to take a statement. Sir Robin, at his side, was alert, but not the happy puppy Abbie had seen the other day.

Her heart broke for both the man and the dog. Bryce Strong's roommate, barely in his twenties, was dressed like the kid he was, in khaki cargo pants and a well-worn Star Wars T-shirt. His light brown hair was pulled into a ponytail. His scruffy beard looked more like the result of forgetting to shave than a purposeful fashion statement.

"Why don't we go sit down over there?" Abbie said in the most soothing voice she could muster. "Would you like some coffee?"

The roommate looked at her like she was speaking a

foreign language, but then the words sank in. He'd been alone with his friend's body for a few hours now. He was a little crazed. Perfectly rational people could get a little unhinged when they were with a body, especially a body of someone they cared about.

"Yeah," the young man said. "Coffee."

Sir Robin followed them to a clearing where they could sit with their backs to the body. Abbie pulled two indestructible mugs out of her backpack, along with a thermos of black coffee she'd stolen from Flynn's. She balanced the mugs on a tree stump and poured. She handed the first mug to the young man. He stared into it and then took a sip. Abbie poured another for herself. Then she pulled out another thermos and a tin bowl. She poured water into the bowl. "Here you go, Sir Robin." It was early in the morning, but summer in Utah was hot and dry. Not the ideal environment for Sir Robin.

She overheard a clean-cut officer tell Clarke it was "obviously" an accident.

"It's too soon to tell," Clarke admonished the junior officer. Abbie heard the same dread in Clarke's voice that she felt in her stomach. This was no accident.

"He's wrong," the roommate said, pointing to the young officer. "Bryce could do this climb blindfolded with an arm tied behind his back. He made it to semis at Psicobloc last year. People were talking about him taking it this year. This"—the young man said, waving toward the cliff behind their backs—"was nothing to Bryce. He did it just because it was one of his first climbs when he was a kid. It was sentimental, like eating your mom's cookies. You may have had better since, but they would always be good because they were first."

"Tell me what happened," Abbie said.

"I have absolutely no idea. We were going to head up to Bear Lake for the weekend. Bryce liked to climb before he had to get in a car for a long drive." Sir Robin sat up from his spot at the roommate's feet. He set his chin on the young man's knee and gazed up at his friend. They were both grieving.

Abbie turned to survey the rock face. She wasn't a climber. It didn't look at all easy to her. "Do you climb?"

"Yeah, but I wasn't in Bryce's league."

"Is there any way he might have slipped on his own? Could he have just misjudged something?"

Sir Robin whimpered.

"No way." The roommate pulled the bottom of his T-shirt up to his face and wiped his eyes. "No freakin' way."

Abbie believed him.

FIFTEEN

It was well into the early afternoon by the time Abbie and Clarke could leave the scene. It took an eternity for the local ME to hike in and even longer for him, and the junior officers, to move the body. Abbie gave instructions for every inch of both the top and bottom of the cliff to be searched. There was some grumbling, but Clarke gave his fellow male officers a stern look and they fell in line.

Clarke's stomach alerted them to the fact that it was past time to eat. They stopped by their favorite barbacoa for lunch. The restaurant, with brightly colored plastic flowers and trees peeking from every corner and crevice, managed to be cheerful despite a complete lack of natural sunlight. Clarke inhaled his first carnitas burrito before Abbie was a third of the way through her shredded-chicken taco.

"They're connected, aren't they." Clarke said the words, between gulps of his Diet Coke, as a statement, not a question.

"It's unlikely they're not," Abbie replied. "We'll have to wait for the report from the ME. But falls are tough. It's difficult to distinguish between someone falling or jumping and someone being pushed."

"Do you think the person who did this is the same person who killed Heber?" Clarke asked.

"I think we need to follow the evidence," Abbie said. "I want you to follow up everything related to Bryce Strong. Everyone he talked to between Heber's accident and today, every message he sent, everything he did. We need to find out if anyone knew he'd seen Heber's accident."

"What about you?" Clarke asked.

"I've got to follow up on something else."

★ ★ ★

Abbie knew Flynn would be livid if he knew she'd gone back to her place on her own, but she didn't see any other convenient option. Even if someone was watching her house, she was a professional. She was trained to take care of herself. Plus, no one would think her plan was a good idea. She needed to do this alone.

Abbie stopped at the local drugstore on the way home to pick up everything she needed. According to the box, she would be sporting long honey-colored tresses within thirty-five minutes. While her hair was slathered in lotion-y chemicals, she painted her fingernails a bright shade of coral. She watched the clock. Another twenty minutes to go.

Wrapped in a bath towel, she walked from her bathroom to her closet. She didn't want to risk the hair dye touching anything, but she also didn't want to waste a single minute. She surveyed her closet. When her timer alerted her that she could rinse out her hair, her nails were already dry, and she had picked out the perfect outfit.

Within half an hour, Detective Abbie Taylor was dressed in a knee-length khaki skirt and a simple white blouse. She had sensible loafers on her feet. Her hair was a mass of tousled blonde curls. She applied her makeup with a heavier hand than was her norm.

She grabbed her scriptures, set the alarm on the fancy security system Clarke had installed, and climbed back into Flynn's SUV. It was a Jeep. Better to be driving American. As she made her way toward Salt Lake, she rehearsed her plan.

Turnabout is fair play. You go rifling through my home turf, I'll go rifling through yours.

★ ★ ★

Heber's funeral was in two days. The viewing would be held tomorrow, in the Conference Center instead of the smaller Tabernacle. The Church leaders evidently expected a lot of people to pay their final respects.

She parked, scriptures in hand, and crossed Main Street into the labyrinth of buildings that made up the city-within-a-city around the Salt Lake Temple. The main administrative buildings for the Church were here. So were Bowen's and Port's offices.

Pasting a friendly smile on her sparkly peach lips, Abbie looked younger than her age. Her modest blouse and skirt, along with her long thick blonde hair, made her look like any one of the sister missionaries cheerfully answering tourist questions on Temple Square—well, except for the fact that Abbie wasn't wearing a black badge announcing that she was SISTER ABISH TAYLOR of THE CHURCH OF JESUS CHRIST OF LATTER-DAY SAINTS. Abbie moseyed her way toward CAB, the Grecian-inspired Church Administration Building on South Temple. Smiling at everyone who smiled at her, Abbie stopped to chat with an elderly woman who asked her a question about the *Handcart Pioneer Monument*. Then Abbie stopped to read her scriptures near the Reflecting Pool. Well, that's what anyone watching the young blonde would have thought.

In reality, Abbie was waiting. It wasn't a complicated plan, but it did require her to be patient and quick. Finally, the moment came. An older man walked into a side entrance. Abbie slipped in the door right behind him. The man, a General Authority, stopped to chat with the security guard. The guard glanced at Abbie's well-thumbed scriptures and continued his conversation with the important Church leader.

One lucky break. Abbie didn't expect another one.

An advantage of growing up the daughter of one of the most prominent Church historians was that you got to play in hallways everywhere while your dad had important meetings with important people. Abbie and her siblings had played many a game of hide-and-seek in this 1917 granite structure that housed the offices for the Church VIPs.

Led by childhood muscle memory and a fair amount of reconnaissance training, Abbie slipped into a staircase off the main hall. The offices of the member of the First Presidency were generally on the first floor. The rest of the

Quorum of the Twelve were scattered on the next few floors, along with certain General Authorities, including Bowen.

Abbie emerged onto the second floor and strode purposefully down the hall. Just as she came to the main stairs, she heard male voices. She kept her eyes down as two older men walked past. She didn't recognize either of them, and they didn't seem to even register that she was there. She kept walking. Bowen's office was not on this floor. When the hallway was empty, Abbie opened the door to the unofficial staircase. If she met anyone here, it would be a janitor, a personal assistant, or someone delivering lunch. No one likely to ask her any questions.

She heard a door up the flight of stairs open. A woman's heels clicked on the steps. Abbie crumpled a Kleenex, opened her Book of Mormon, leaned against the wall, and sniffled. The woman passed her. She averted her eyes so as not to embarrass the crying blonde woman. Abbie waited until she heard the door to the first floor close before she stopped her faux crying and walked to the next floor.

Abbie opened the door from the stairwell slowly. She peeked around the corner of the hallway. She saw Port's profile as he opened a door and disappeared behind it. Port's office was on the first floor, along with the Prophet's and whoever would be taking Heber's place. Abbie felt fresh pain as she thought about Heber, but instead of tears, she felt resolve. She walked directly to the office where she just seen Port. The name on the door was KEVIN BOWEN.

SIXTEEN

For now, the coast was clear, and Abbie strained to hear the voice on the other side of the door.

"She called herself Sister Sweeten," Bowen was saying. "Nobody suspected anything until she disappeared. A very sweet, older sister had taken her in. She left all her things when she took off. I went through it. Nothing interesting."

"She rented her SUV in El Paso?" Port asked.

"Yes."

"Has she returned it?"

"Yes. In Roy." Bowen's voice sounded like a straight-A student who had just handed his homework in late. "We found out after the fact."

"I knew she'd come back here. She can't help herself." Was she that predictable? Port had known her since birth.

"Why do you say that?" Bowen asked.

"She feels compelled to not be idle, 'put her shoulder to the wheel,' as it were. She thinks she's left her religious roots behind, but she hasn't. Not entirely. She's driven by a desire to have a purpose. She took this job, one she clearly doesn't need, because she wanted to be in Utah, with the family who has rejected her because she rejected the Church. She's a stubborn one."

There was a moment of silence. Neither man spoke. Abbie could feel her heart beating so loudly she was convinced Bowen was about to open the door and yell, "Gotcha!"

Instead, Port asked, "Were there any signs Sister Thompson was planning to leave?"

"No. We had no idea," Bowen said. Again he sounded like a Boy Scout who was getting in trouble for the first time.

"Sometimes that maternal instinct sparks an independent streak. Children can turn an obedient woman into a difficult creature." Port laughed at his own humor; Bowen didn't. Then Port instructed, "Keep an eye on Professor Taylor."

Abbie heard someone turn a doorknob. A sliver of sunshine from an office three doors down became an entire semicircle of natural light. Abbie turned her back to whoever was emerging from the office and made a quick, though not too quick, escape onto the back stairs.

She kept walking, and smiling, past the Tabernacle, past the monument to the seagulls, past the very pretty Salt Lake Assembly Hall. Her heart was, as they say, in her throat. She didn't even try to breathe deeply until she was sitting inside Flynn's SUV, doors locked, in the darkness of an underground parking garage.

★ ★ ★

John and Libbie's place was in the Avenues, not that far from where she was parked. Abbie needed a friendly face and a place to sit for a minute, a safe place where no one would ask her questions about what Port had said. His observations about her, her motivations, hit a little too close for comfort.

Sunlight hit her face as soon as she emerged from the darkness of the subterranean garage. She drove toward the mountain with the white *U* painted on its side. A few turns and she was in the shaded streets of gracious homes from another era, a time before houses were supersized.

Abbie pulled into John and Libbie's driveway. Her sister-in-law, her face mostly hidden beneath a wide floppy brim, was kneeling in front of a flat of flowers bursting with pinks, blues, and purples. John teased his wife mercilessly about her gardening hat. She had been wearing it, or some version of it, practically ever since John married her.

Libbie stood up when she heard Abbie pull in. She arched her back as if she had been stooped down for too long, then turned toward Abbie. Abbie saw a polite smile beneath the straw brim. It took another moment for Libbie to put her hand in front of her mouth in a not-too-subtle effort to stifle a laugh.

"Sorry to stop by unannounced. I was in Salt Lake. Hope you don't mind!" Abbie said. Libbie pulled off her hat and gave Abbie a hug.

"I need a break. Let's go inside. I'm thirsty."

Abbie followed Libbie inside. They walked into the kitchen. Libbie giggled.

"That's quite a . . ." She choked on the words before she could finish. "Look."

Abbie walked in front of the microwave door. She gazed at her reflection and slowly shook her long blonde hair, like she was the star of a shampoo commercial. Abbie caught Libbie's eye, and they both collapsed into uncontrollable laughter.

Between belly laughs, Libbie touched the pale tips of Abbie's hair. "It's so you."

Abbie tried to take a deep breath so she could talk, but every time she saw Libbie's face, she started laughing again. Finally, the deep laughs subsided into a few chortles.

"I was trying not to stand out."

"Well, I hate to be the one to break it to you, Abs, but with all that"—Libbie waved a hand from Abbie's neck to her toes—"going on, and Barbie hair, well, ya sorta stand out."

"Okay, okay." Abbie couldn't deny that the change in hair color gave her a very different look. "It's not so much 'not standing out' as not looking like myself I was going for."

"In that case, you certainly succeeded." Libbie's eyes twinkled. She took another look at her husband's baby sister and her eyes stopped smiling.

"What's going on? It's not like you to stop by without letting us know—not that I'm complaining—but, you know."

"I'm okay. Don't worry, the dye job is not the manifestation of sleep-deprived mania. I'm working on a case and I wanted to be able to move around Temple Square without anyone knowing I was there."

Libbie made duck lips, then shrugged. "If you wanted to blend in, I could've gotten you a little black name tag with Sister Taylor and The Church of Jesus Christ of Latter-day Saints written on it."

Abbie rolled her eyes, "You're wicked."

Libbie handed Abbie a glass of water with a slice of lemon floating on top of two square cubes of ice. "So I've been told."

SEVENTEEN

Abbie drove home on autopilot. She was glad Libbie had given her the buffer she needed after listening to Port's psychoanalysis. Those few moments of laughing so hard she cried were the only moments she'd had without low-level dread since Heber's death.

It wasn't until she climbed out of her car to open the old gate at the bottom of her drive that she remembered she wasn't supposed to be here.

Abbie looked around. No one was watching. She opened the gate. Then she went to grab the mail from her rusty mailbox. She paid almost all her bills online, so she rarely checked the actual post. It generally consisted of coupons for local businesses, the odd postcard from a real estate agent who had sold property in the area, and an occasional request for donations. This time there was only one pristine white envelope. The return address printed in a proprietary font indicated the letter was from the Church of Jesus Christ of Latter-day Saints.

She slipped her index finger under the corner of the

flap and pulled across the envelope, leaving a jagged edge along the top. There was a neatly folded letter inside:

> *Dear Sister Abish Violet Taylor:*
>
> *The Stake Presidency is considering formal disciplinary action in your behalf, including the possibility of disfellowshipment or excommunication, because you are reported to have participated in conduct unbecoming a member of the church.*
>
> *You are invited the join this disciplinary council to give your response, and, if you wish, to provide witness or other evidence in your behalf.*

Abbie didn't recognize the Stake President's signature because she didn't know her Stake President. She hadn't been to her own church since she'd moved back to Utah. She didn't intend to.

When she'd lived in New York and heard about an LDS scholar or podcaster being excommunicated, she'd dismissed the possibility that the same could happen to her. It seemed unlikely anyone would go through the trouble of reporting her to the Strengthening Church Members Committee. She wasn't prominent enough in her own right to cause the Church any discomfort. It didn't, however, take much imagination to figure out why she was being scrutinized now, or how her disciplinary hearing would end. She would be excommunicated for apostasy because she was, after all, an apostate.

Excommunication was mostly an academic matter for

her. She wouldn't necessarily lose her job, although it certainly would make it harder. The few new friends she had managed to make since she'd moved back to Utah wouldn't care about her status as a member of the Church; they might even find the entire situation amusing. Her family, though, would not.

Being excommunicated would force them to make a decision about interacting with her. Abbie wasn't sure if she could compete with the promise of eternal exaltation.

Abbie got back in Flynn's SUV, letter in hand, and drove up her driveway. She tried to convince herself she didn't care about the disciplinary hearing, but if she was being honest with herself, she didn't really want it to come to this. She didn't believe Joseph Smith had been visited by God, Jesus Christ, and an angel in upstate New York. She didn't believe the history he'd translated from the gold plates about people coming from Israel to the Americas. She certainly had no faith that the current President of the Church was a prophet who received revelations from a god of any sort. She didn't pay tithing. She didn't follow the Word of Wisdom. Her laundry list of Mormon sins was a long one. Still, excommunication was so final.

She got out of her car, but didn't go inside. She walked around the side of her house and sat down on a chair with a view of the mountains. She felt the sun of a cloudless sky.

This letter was inevitable. Those quiet personal choices she'd made after prayer, after fasting, after years of trying to stay in the Church would be judged by two men she had never met. The familiar weight of hopelessness pressed on her. She'd experienced it too many times before not to recognize it, the heaviness of truth that comes with a diagnosis but no cure.

Port had known her since birth, but she also knew him. The dread she was feeling wasn't all about her. That she knew. She wasn't the only Taylor to have gotten a letter like this today. If she still believed in the power of prayer, she would have dropped to her knees. Instead, she called her dad.

He sounded like the wind had been knocked out of him. Even disfellowshipment would mean he couldn't maintain his position as a professor. Being excommunicated would end his career at BYU, and probably everywhere else. There simply were not that many religion departments around the country, not ones in need of professors well past their publishing prime. This letter was a threat not only to her dad's spiritual life, but to his worldly life as well.

The despair in his voice and in the silence between words was so deep, Abbie felt like they would both drown in it. Her rail-thin, widowed father was sitting all alone in his study, surrounded by stacks of books that covered every horizontal surface, with a letter that was more terrible to him than a death sentence.

Tears welled in her eyes. She closed them and listened to her father's silence.

He was not going to say the words, but they both knew that he would bear the loss of his profession, he would bear the loss of his Church, but he could not bear the threat that he would not be worthy to be united with her mom in the Celestial Kingdom.

"Dad?" Abbie had let him sit in silence as long as she could stand. "I'm so sorry. Don't worry. I don't think they'll really do anything to you. Someone just wants to scare us."

"Well, they've succeeded, with me at least."

"It'll be okay," Abbie said, "I know it will."

"You don't know that." He was right. She didn't.

"When's your date? Do you want me to come?" Abbie asked.

"Your presence," he said softly, "would undoubtedly make things worse."

If only. If only he and Heber hadn't had their lunches; if only they had never talked about his students dropping out; if he hadn't mentioned those lunches to Abbie; if Bowen hadn't seen her in Colonia Juárez. If Heber hadn't been killed. A wave of remorse washed over her.

"Dad?" Silence. "Dad? Are you still there?"

Abbie heard her dad exhale.

"Blame it on me," she instructed.

"What?"

"We both know I've been in the crosshairs before and will again, if I don't get excommunicated this time. Tell them you don't know anything. Nothing about Mexico, nothing about the students, nothing about Brittany Thompson. Tell them you don't believe my crazy ideas. Tell them—"

"Abish, that would be a lie."

"Think about what really matters. You're as worthy a member of the Church as this world will ever know. You keep your covenants, you walk the path, you believe."

"I will take responsibility for what I've done. I'll do whatever I need to do to repent." Nothing Abbie could say or do would comfort or help him. There was silence on the line again as they both processed what their neatly folded letters meant.

Then he said, "Abish, I love you. I will always love you."

Abbie didn't respond immediately. She wasn't used to such raw emotion from her dad. "I love you, too, Dad."

Silence again. Abbie wasn't sure if he'd already hung up the phone.

EIGHTEEN

Abbie closed her eyes and leaned her head back, facing the sun. She breathed in the dry air. It smelled of dirt and pine. Port wouldn't really have her dad excommunicated, would he? Her dad had done everything Port had ever asked of him, including leaving his dying wife's bedside to authenticate early Church documents found in upstate New York. Port owed her dad.

Her phone vibrated. It was Flynn.

"Brittany's in labor," he said. "The OB/GYN is on her way. Everything's fine, but if you'd like to be here for the delivery, I'd suggest you get here now. The contractions are two and a half minutes apart and it's progressing pretty quickly." Flynn had been through five deliveries himself, so he knew what he was talking about.

"On my way."

From the moment Abbie set eyes on Brittany Thompson in her dad's kitchen, it had been clear the young mother was going to give birth any moment. Still, Abbie had hoped for more time. Abbie was grateful the baby could be born in relative peace at Flynn's place, but they wouldn't be able to keep the new baby a secret for long. Under Utah law, they had ten days to register the birth. The people looking for Brittany Thompson would soon have a leg up in their search.

★ ★ ★

When Abbie opened the front door to Flynn's, she heard the supportive voice of the obstetrician. "You're almost there, Brittany. You're doing an amazing job. Just another few pushes."

Abbie walked upstairs and into the makeshift L&D room. Flynn was holding Brittany's hand.

"Okay, push."

Brittany bore down. Tiny red spots sprouted all over her face, like new freckles. Her hair was stuck to her head with sweat.

"One more time!"

Barely a minute later, the doctor held a squirming red baby covered in whatever it is babies were covered in. In the next few busy moments, the placenta was delivered. Flynn cut the cord. The obstetrician wiped the baby and set him on Brittany's chest. The young mother looked beautiful, broken blood vessels and all. The word *radiant* was overused in describing both brides and new mothers, but in this case it was an apt description. Abbie thought there was nothing like watching a new baby being handed to his mom for the first time to restore your faith in humanity.

"Congratulations on the birth of Baby Boy Thompson!" Flynn said.

Brittany grinned. "Moroni. I'm going to call him Moroni Hyrum."

Flynn shot Abbie a look from the other side of the room then turned back to the doctor. Brittany was naming her son after the last Nephite prophet, the one who visited Joseph as an angel, and Joseph Smith's brother.

"Dr. Roberts is on his way. He's the pediatrician in the group," the obstetrician said. "My expertise ends once the baby comes out. But, in my inexpert opinion, this is one healthy little boy."

On cue, the doorbell rang.

"I'll get it." Abbie returned with the pediatrician. He was on the young side, but carried himself with an authority one hoped was an accurate reflection of skill and judgment.

The doctor walked straight to the baby without wasting time on pleasantries. Abbie sat down on one of the upholstered chairs in the reading nook with a view of the field in front of Flynn's house. The birth certificate was on the side table. In the space for NAME OF FATHER, Brittany had written DALLIN BRAGG.

The same Bragg whose fireside chat at BYU had gone viral after he advised young women who wanted to get married to put on lipstick and make an effort to look pretty. Usually, the Church posted fireside chats on an official website for months, but this one had disappeared within twenty-four hours. Bowen had made an official statement about President Bragg's lighthearted joke being misconstrued.

Bragg's name alone could cause a scandal if anyone thought the Dallin Bragg on this birth certificate was *the* Dallin Bragg, President of the Quorum of the Twelve Apostles. An individual tryst between an Apostle and a pretty, young returned missionary was unthinkable. The reality, of course, was worse.

NINETEEN

For a few moments, Abbie let herself relish the new baby. Moroni's brother and sister piled onto the bed with their mom as soon as everything was cleaned up. Flynn had managed to rustle up two new stuffed animals for baby Moroni to "give" his older siblings. They became bored with the baby pretty quickly and happily took their new toys down to the basement playroom.

Once Brittany was settled, nursing the newest addition to her brood, Abbie and Flynn left her in the hands of the baby nurse Flynn had hired, which was probably entirely unnecessary. A woman who could hotwire a truck with two children under the age of five and drive across the desert while nine months pregnant could certainly handle breastfeeding a baby on her own.

Flynn and Abbie settled in the library. It was one of her favorite rooms in this house. Flynn made a beeline for the butler's tray. He poured himself a good three fingers of deep-amber liquid.

"Mud with a little whiskey?" Abbie teased. Flynn liked

his Scotch on the peaty side. Her description wasn't that far off.

"I need this. It has been one hell of a morning." He took a long swallow, then glanced at his watch. "And, yes, in case you're wondering, I am very well aware that this constitutes day drinking." Another swallow. "Care to join me?"

Before Abbie could answer, her phone buzzed. It was Clarke.

TAYLOR? WHERE ARE YOU? THE CHIEF IS MAD. LOOKING ALL OVER FOR YOU.

"I wish I could, but my day's not over yet."

"You're going to head in to the station? What are you planning to tell Chief Henderson?"

Abbie hadn't though that far ahead, but she'd have time on the drive over. "I'll tell him most of the relevant facts."

"What exactly would those be? You and I are helping to hide the fourth wife of one of the Apostles, a young woman who escaped from an orphanage in Colonia Juárez? Oh, and by the way, she just gave birth to his third child, a boy."

Abbie raised her eyebrow. "I think perhaps I'll phrase things differently."

"You'll be back for dinner tonight, right? You can't stay at your place."

Abbie chose not to disclose that she'd already been there. Twice. She also chose to wait for another occasion to mention her disciplinary council letter.

"I'll text you later." The thought of leaving Flynn alone to take care of Brittany Thompson and her three children seemed selfish. Flynn's life had been turned upside down because of her. "I'll be back to help with the kids."

Flynn kicked his feet up onto an eighteenth-century chest he used as a coffee table. "See you tonight, blondie."

Abbie turned around before he could see her blush.

TWENTY

Hair color was the least of her worries. She was certainly going to get some ribbing for it at the station. Henderson's door was closed, so Abbie walked to her own office. There was no attempt to hide the sniggering.

Abbie stopped, turned to her fellow officers, and said, "It's good to mix things up every now and then."

Someone in the back of the room said, "Yeah. It is."

Abbie wasn't sure who'd agreed with her, but she was sure she'd just stopped being the butt of a blonde joke.

She'd barely stepped into her office when Hazel knocked at her open door. "The chief would like to see you."

Abbie stood up from her desk. Hazel patted Abbie's shoulder as she passed and said, "It'll be okay," in a voice soft enough no one but Abbie could hear.

Henderson's door was open now. Abbie walked through.

"Come in and shut the door behind you."

She did as she was told.

"Detective Taylor, I've looked the other way with you more often than I care to count. Every time I think I can trust you, you demonstrate unprofessional behavior. This must stop. You were hired to work for the good people of Pleasant View, and that is what you're going to do."

"Sir. What behavior of mine was unprofessional?" Abbie didn't want to sound combative but needed to know exactly what he was talking about.

"I don't want to get bogged down in a debate with you right now. The fact is, I asked you to close the investigation before the funeral of one of the most beloved men in this state. From what I gather, you've made absolutely no progress in the matter. On top of that, you delegated all your responsibilities for the investigation into that pot-smoking climber's death. And apparently, instead of working, you went to the beauty salon."

Ouch. He was right. Well, about everything but the beauty salon. Abbie had mixed the hair dye herself.

"I can't, in good conscience, let this situation persist."

Abbie wasn't sure where Henderson was headed next. Was she about to be fired?

"I'm reassigning you. We've had a rash of thefts at Weber High. Someone is breaking into lockers and stealing valuable items. I want you to find the culprit. Until you do, you'll be reporting to the campus of Weber High every morning at six thirty AM and staying until the school closes up for the night. I'd like a detailed report of the day's events emailed to me by midnight, every night. Check in with the principal and the school security officer to find out how you can best assist them in their efforts."

Was he serious? Henderson was asking Abbie to spend

twelve hours a day as a hall monitor? She would rather be fired. The thought flashed before her eyes. She didn't need this job. She could move back to New York.

But it disappeared almost as quickly as it came. Port was right about her. She needed to put her shoulder to the wheel. The reason she had moved back to Utah in the first place was because she knew, deep down, she couldn't spend her mornings with a private trainer, meet friends for lunch and shopping, and go out to glittery events in the evenings. There was travel, too, but she could only distract herself with amusements for so long. All of those activities—yoga retreats and visiting the wonders of the world—were fine when they added to a life that already had meaning. Without a purpose in life, though, they were only shiny objects to distract from a hollow existence.

Abbie wanted this job. She loved her crazy Swedish summerhouse in the canyon. She loved the powdery snow in the winter. She loved the warm springs in the valley when everything sprouted flowers. She loved the hot, dry summers that baked the grasses on the foothills to a pale shade of gold. She loved the splashes of bright yellow and red on the Wasatch Mountains against the deep blue skies in the fall. And, most of all, she loved her family. Even if they didn't love her back. Yet.

"Yes, sir." Abbie said the words with determined clarity and complete acceptance.

Henderson stared at her with wide eyes. He looked like he had picked up a battering ram—ready to use it—when someone just opened the door from the other side and invited him to walk through.

"Uh, well, uh, drive over there right now and get things set up. I'll expect a report tonight."

"Yes, sir," Abbie said. "Sir?"

"Yes, Detective Taylor."

"Who will be overseeing the investigation into President Bentsen and Bryce Strong's deaths?"

"I will."

Abbie opened the door and walked out of the office. The showdown everyone was expecting hadn't happened. It would be humiliating to spend her days at Weber High, but Abbie was not going to let anyone get even a whiff of the professional embarrassment she was feeling. She went into her office, closed the door, and sat down behind her desk. She could probably sit for five minutes before Henderson would expect her to be on her way to the school. She needed each of those minutes. The schedule Henderson had laid out was going to mean she would have no time and no resources for anything else.

Abbie could guess how this story would end. As soon as sufficient time passed, Henderson would let the two investigations wither on the vine. No one wanted to think about an Apostle being murdered, and no one cared about the death of a marijuana-smoking climber.

Four minutes to go. Abbie turned on her computer, inserted a thumb drive, and downloaded everything from the Bentsen and Strong investigations. She ejected it, slipped it into her wallet, and turned off her computer. Without saying a word, she walked through the front office of the police station. She felt everyone's eyes watch her as she left the station.

TWENTY-ONE

Abbie met the earnest and well-past-his-prime security officer at Weber High. He took an inordinate amount of time giving her a rundown of the locker thefts, and then he insisted on giving her a tour of every inch of the high school. He offered to do a "stakeout" that evening. Abbie was happy to oblige. She gave him her number so he could reach her if "things got ugly." Abbie headed straight back to Flynn's. The kids were getting out of their bath and into pajamas when she arrived.

"I've got to write a quick report for Henderson. I'll be right there to help."

"No rush. Your timing is perfect," Flynn teased. "We've already fed and bathed them. By the time you finish your report, they'll be asleep."

Abbie set herself up at the kitchen counter and started typing. She finished, hit send, and snapped her computer closed. She walked back upstairs to help. Flynn greeted her with his index finger pressed against his closed lips. She turned around and tiptoed back down the stairs to the kitchen. Flynn followed.

The sky had turned lavender with pink clouds.

Flynn opened the wine fridge and took out a bottle of Grüner Veltliner.

"Join me now?"

"Yes, please."

As the pleasantly acidic wine began to do its job, Abbie's defenses softened and she let herself feel the full weight of the day.

"You look like your puppy died," Flynn said. His T-shirt was still damp from bathing duty, his hair was mussed, and there were circles under his eyes Abbie hadn't noticed before. Still, there was some of his regular sparkle, even if it was a more tired version. He gave her one of his lopsided grins.

Sitting next to her at the kitchen table, he took another sip of wine. She handed him her disciplinary council letter without looking at him.

He read it. "Does it matter?"

"My dad got one, too."

"Oh." The grin disappeared. "Sorry about the puppy joke. Is he okay?" Before Abbie could say anything, Flynn said, "Dumb question. Of course not. Do you think he'll get through this?"

"It all depends on the outcome. Mom, his job, his world." Abbie couldn't string together words in a coherent sentence.

"I wish I had connections that mattered, that could help. Do you think John does?"

"He might. My sisters might, too, but I'll never hear the end of it from them. They'll blame me."

"Yep, they will." Flynn understood the state of Taylor family relations. He was also not one to pretend things were prettier than they were.

"You think the disciplinary hearings are related to your trip to Mexico?"

"Kind of hard not to."

Flynn took a long swallow of his wine, then another. "Abs, if you were beginning to doubt yourself, to doubt that Heber's murder and Brittany Thompson are unrelated, this letter should put those doubts to rest. This can't all be coincidental."

Then Abbie told him about Henderson assigning her to hall monitor duty. Flynn was right: there were too many coincidences.

TWENTY-TWO

Growing up in a world where people saw miracles everywhere, Abbie had taught herself to question coincidence and conspiracy. She knew how easy it was to believe. If she was being completely honest with herself, she also knew how comforting it was to believe.

When you were taught to see miracles, you could see them all over. As a girl, she remembered reading the missives from missionaries out in the field. They described miracles wherever they went. If they met an investigator while it was raining and then, while discussing the Book of Mormon, the sun came out, it was a miracle. If they missed a bus but then someone on the next bus asked them a question about the Church, it was a miracle.

Abbie hated the idea she might be seeing connections that weren't there. She put down her mostly full glass of wine. "I'm going to head home. I'll need a dress for Heber's funeral tomorrow. John is going to pick me up. Even Henderson couldn't bring himself to say anything about me going."

"No." There was anger in Flynn's voice. Abbie was surprised, and looking at Flynn, she saw he was surprised by the edge in his voice, too. He was not a man who often felt angry, and even when he did, he rarely showed it. The next words he spoke, he spoke quietly, but the tone was the same. "You showed up on my doorstep for a reason. As crazy as this all is, it is happening. You can't just go home and think everything will be normal because you don't want to believe in conspiracies. Two people are dead, there's weird stuff going on in Colonia Juárez, and both you and your dad are being called in for disciplinary councils. Not to mention your demotion meant to keep you as far away from the investigation into Heber's murder as possible."

"Listen," Abbie said, "even if everything is connected in a way neither one of us has figured out, there's no reason to think I'm in danger. Clarke put in a state-of-the art security system at my place. I'm safe."

"Two people are dead," Flynn repeated.

"And?"

Flynn exhaled. "There's no talking you out of this?"

Abbie shook her head.

He put his glass down. He looked skeptical, but calmer than a few moments before. "I'll stay there with you. At least until we're sure there is no connection between what you know about Mexico and the deaths here in Utah."

"I don't need a babysitter." Abbie heard her own voice. She sounded like a petulant teenager.

"Hey! I excel at childcare." A hint of a smile crinkled

around his eyes, despite his mock indignation. "But it's not my only skill. I know you can handle yourself, but so can I." Abbie knew he was talking about his skill as a marksman.

Abbie was conflicted.

"Okay." As she said the word, she realized there were butterflies in her stomach that had nothing to do with murder.

Flynn made sure everything was settled with his housekeeper and the baby nurse. Brittany was, for the moment, consumed with feeding baby Moroni and sleeping as much as she could. Her kids were well behaved and seemed enthralled by the variety of diversions in the basement playroom. Flynn, Abbie had to admit, ran a tight ship.

★ ★ ★

Abbie drove Flynn's SUV. He'd had a little too much Scotch to drive himself. She turned up the driveway to her cabin when Flynn saw the gate. "Do you ever close that?"

"I don't. The wind occasionally does."

"Mind stopping?" Abbie did, and Flynn hopped out. He swung the gate closed and looped the chain around the post. "I'll deal with that tomorrow."

"It would be a pain in the neck to stop and open it every day."

"Maybe." He shrugged. "But I want it to be a pain in the neck for anyone who visits you."

Abbie pulled up next to her ancient forest-green Range Rover.

Flynn said, "Here we are. Your little *sommarstuga*."

Abbie rolled her eyes. She called it a cabin, but to most eyes, it looked a bit grander than that.

Flynn followed Abbie into the house. She took him upstairs and showed him to his room. In contrast to the elegance of Flynn's place in Riverdale, the style at Abbie's was casual. The entire inside of the house looked like a watercolor of slate blues, pale grays, and white. Nothing fussy, nothing fancy.

"May I offer you something to drink?" she asked once they were both back downstairs. Abbie walked over to a narrow liquor cabinet and took out a bottle of Laphroaig. She poured two fingers into a heavy crystal tumbler. She handed him the glass and poured another for herself. Flynn didn't move. She felt him watching her. Her stomach fluttered.

When she turned around, he took the glass from her and set it down next to his own. He lifted her chin toward his face and kissed her.

"I've wanted to do that for a long time."

Me, too.

TWENTY-THREE

Flynn was still asleep when Abbie headed to Weber High. As she walked past his closed bedroom door, her heart skipped a beat.

Abbie was patrolling the halls by six thirty when the first high school students started their days. Before third period, she changed into something appropriate for a funeral and made the drive to Salt Lake. Abbie didn't expect to feel emotional at the funeral. LDS funerals were such dry affairs: a lot of talk about how blessed everyone was to know the principles of the restored Gospel. Someone of Heber's social station warranted talks by members of the Twelve, which were essentially long recitations of Heber's service to the Church.

Abbie sat with her dad and John. Her sisters and other brothers sat together with Heber's extended family. They pretended not to see Abbie. Behind the podium, Port sat between the Prophet and Eliza Bentsen. Looking at the Prophet, Abbie wondered how much he understood about what was happening. Rumors of his dementia didn't seem to be far off. He had a half smile on his face and the glazed eyes of a person who was in the later stages of Alzheimer's.

As hymns were sung and prayers given, Abbie found herself falling into a dark hole. Heber was about to buried, and she had no idea who'd killed him. With Henderson taking over the case, she might never find out.

Abbie looked at the hymnbook open on her lap. She sang the last verse and then quietly closed the book. She folded her arms, bowed her head, and closed her eyes for the last invocation. As Heber's oldest daughter prayed, Abbie opened her eyes and glanced around the gathering. There were supposedly twenty thousand people in attendance. As many as usually come for a Prophet.

When Heber's daughter finally said "Amen," Abbie looked up toward the dais and saw Port watching her. It was unnerving. He smiled when their eyes met. Abbie didn't want to be the first to look away, so she waited. A young man in an ill-fitting suit tapped the Second Counselor on his shoulder. Port turned toward the man. Abbie watched. She recognized the face. How did she know him?

Her dad wanted to talk to Eliza, so Abbie and John followed him past the very discreet security detail assigned to keeping the assembled Church leaders safe. Being a respected LDS apologist had its advantages. The small Taylor group was allowed onto the podium.

"It's so good to see you." The widow held her dad's hand for a moment, then let it go.

"We know you have to leave for the cemetery with

family. I just wanted to tell you that I'm here for whatever you need. I understand."

"I know." Eliza bowed her head. "You like few others know the sacrifice the Church can ask of us."

That seemed like an odd thing to say, even at a Mormon funeral. Abbie glanced at her brother to see if he had any response. If he did, it hadn't registered in his expression. Her dad hugged Eliza. Then it was their turn. Abbie hugged her; then John did. Eliza turned back to Abbie and squeezed her hand.

"Don't worry, my dear. Heavenly Father knows everything and is just."

One of Eliza's adult grandchildren, who clearly had been tasked with keeping Grandma on schedule, announced that the car was waiting. It was time to leave.

★ ★ ★

The rest of the day at the high school was nearly unbearable, hours opening lockers and patrolling the parking lot. Henderson would have wanted her to bust the kids smoking behind the bleachers on the football field, but Abbie pretended not to see them. It had been a long time since she had felt such a sense of relief to have the workday behind her rather than in front of her.

She wrote her report for Henderson's pleasure and emailed it from her car. Then she started toward Flynn's place in Riverdale. From the flurry of texts he'd sent, it had been a busy day. He'd walked her property with a security expert and arranged for the gate to be upgraded along with tall fences and motion-detecting cameras. Then he'd driven back to his own place to make sure all was well with Brittany and the kids.

She knocked on the front door of Flynn's place.

"Come in!" She heard his voice from down the hall. "We're in the kitchen."

Abbie did as instructed. The scent of searing beef and onion met her as soon as she walked through the door. Flynn was dicing tomatillos and jalapeños. There were limes, lemons, avocados, thinly sliced red onions, and cabbage marinating in lime juice. Brittany was sitting at the island wearing a nightgown and robe. The newborn was swaddled and fast asleep in a Moses basket at her feet. The older kids were spread out on the floor with paper, crayons, and a variety of coloring books.

Flynn glanced up from mixing salsa verde.

"Detective Taylor, so nice to see you. Our guests were in the mood for tacos. There's plenty to go around; can I entice you to join us?"

Damn, he was good-looking.

"Yes, yes you can."

A timer beeped, and Flynn turned down the heat under the cast-iron skillet where strips of beef were sizzling.

"Mind making the guac?"

Abbie washed her hands, finely chopped some red onion and cilantro, and then scooped the soft innards of three avocados into the *molcajete* on the counter. She squeezed lemon and lime on top, added a little salt and white pepper, and then engaged in the distinctly satisfying process of smushing everything together. When the soft green mixture was just the right amount of mixed, she sprinkled a few of the prettier cilantro leaves on top.

Flynn arranged the taco ingredients on the center island along with a bottle of Marie Sharp's habanero sauce from Belize. Tabasco might have its place in a Bloody Mary, but if you could find it, Marie Sharp's was the way to go for tacos. Everyone grabbed a plate and began assembling their toppings of choice inside the warm flour tortillas.

The satisfaction of sharing good home-cooked food silenced the room as everyone chewed their first few bites. Abbie contemplated the ingredients wrapped in the tortilla Flynn had warmed over a flame. The paper-thin slices of crisp cabbage and red onion marinated in lime played off the umami of the seared meat; the fattiness of the guacamole was the perfect foil to the fresh citrus of the tomatillos. This taco was pretty close to perfect.

They drank Mexican cokes; even Brittany did. Abbie felt certain she could tell the difference between the soda made south of the border from real sugar and its American counterpart sweetened with corn syrup, but she knew she might just like the Mexican cokes because they came in little glass bottles reminiscent of another era.

Abbie finished half her taco and about as much of her coke, then broke the silence. "How was your day?" she asked Brittany.

"Oh, Flynn's been so nice." Brittany tucked her tangle of loose curls behind her ears. For a brief moment, she looked more like an innocent teenager with a crush than a woman who'd just given birth to her third child and anything but an ingenue. "I napped for almost four hours this afternoon. Flynn's housekeeper made me a lovely lunch and then I had shower. The kids played outside most of the day, so they're happy and tired out."

Brittany yawned. "I think it's time for bed." Moroni stirred in his basket, and his big brother rubbed his eyes with both fists.

Abbie helped Flynn get the kids bathed and into pajamas while Brittany nursed the baby. It had been a long time since Abbie had read *Goodnight Moon*.

When the two older kids were at last quiet in their beds, Abbie and Flynn went back downstairs.

"You're a bit of a nomad," he said, gathering the dishes. "I know you want to go back to your own place tonight, but would you humor me and wait until my security guy gets everything done? He's promised me it will be within the week. He's pulled his guys off of other jobs to get this done. Oh, and you can tell your partner—Clarke?—my expert was properly impressed with your home security system. Your colleague knows his stuff."

Abbie had begun picking up the crayons scattered across the floor and crawled under the table for an orange one. She didn't realize Flynn was waiting for her to say something, to answer his question about staying with him.

"So?" Flynn took the box of crayons from Abbie as she emerged from underneath the kitchen table.

"I don't really have a choice, do I?"

Flynn smiled wryly. "No, you don't."

"Okay." Abbie's voice sounded neutral, but if the butterflies in her stomach were any indication, she was feeling anything but.

"I have a nice Montepulciano, if you'd like."

"That sounds perfect." It did, actually.

Flynn opened a bottle and poured two generous glasses. They sipped while they finished cleaning up.

"Let's go outside. It's a nice night."

Abbie followed Flynn through the formal dining room and the sitting room to French doors that led to a flagstone terrace overlooking the lawn and a peach orchard beyond. The sky turned a deep purple streaked with rose as the sun slid down behind the mountains.

"How was the funeral?" Flynn asked.

"About how you would expect."

The wine, the sky, and Flynn's blue eyes were distracting her. She set down her glass of wine. Flynn did, too.

With his hand on the small of her back, Flynn pulled her toward him. He kissed her, this time with more certainty than he had last night. His fingers caressed her neck and then grazed the hollow above her breastbone. He leaned down to kiss the soft skin. Then, with agonizing slowness, he toyed with the top button of her shirt. She took his hand in hers.

"I've got work. Not to mention that there are two little kids, a baby nurse, a baby, and a new mom right inside."

"We have to stop?" Flynn said, kissing her forehead.

"Yes, it's the grown-up thing to do."

He groaned. "Being a grown-up is highly overrated."

TWENTY-FOUR

In the morning, when Abbie left Flynn's house for her job as hall monitor, she heard baby Moroni stirring, but the rest of the house was still in deep slumber. She had managed to get some rest between some really weird dreams. In the way that happened in dreams, she remembered being in places and seeing people that were impossible. Yes, there had even been some flying involved. Abbie had glided over the small temple in Colonia Juárez and then landed outside her house in Utah. She had watched Bowen and his cohort in the flannel shirt rifle through her office, looking through her dad's old research.

Was that why Bowen and his friend had broken into her place last year? Had they been looking for something of her dad's? Some research he'd done long ago? They had looked through her study and everyplace else where books and papers would logically be kept, every place except the attic. They hadn't looked in the attic.

She turned into the parking lot at the high school for another fun-filled day on the trail of the Weber High locker thief. Before she walked through the doors of the institution of teenage learning, she texted Clarke to see if any progress had been made on Caleb Monson or the ME report on Bryce Strong. Henderson had taken over her cases, but he hadn't specifically prohibited her from asking about them.

Clarke didn't respond. It was early, even for him.

Abbie checked in with the principal and the security guard. There hadn't been any robberies overnight. The dance team arrived just when Abbie did and began practicing a routine in the gym. Abbie watched the dancers practice their jump splits while their coach clapped the beat. In a wave, the girls flew into the air, touched their toes, and then landed in splits on the ground, jazz hands stretched to the sky in victory. It looked painful, despite the girls' toothy smiles.

Her phone rang. She'd forgotten to turn it to vibrate. The dance coach shot her a dirty look. Abbie quickly stepped into the hallway.

"Good morning, Clarke!" She was happy he'd called. She wasn't sure if Henderson was making his life difficult. She hoped not.

"Taylor, we do know more about Caleb. I'm sending you the most recent picture we have of him. Looks like he's the driver of our white mystery car."

"Thanks!" Abbie said.

"The other guys have all been reassigned. I'm pretty much the only person following anything up." There was a loud crash in the background. "Gotta run."

Abbie glanced at her phone. She tapped the image Clarke had sent.

She recognized Caleb Monson. He was Bowen's brawny partner from the break-in last year: the man in the flannel shirt. He'd also been the man in the ill-fitting suit at Heber's funeral. And Clarke had said he was the mystery driver who talked to Bryce Strong at the scene of Heber's fatal crash.

Caleb Monson might just be the person who connected everything.

★ ★ ★

Time passed so slowly at Weber High that Abbie was convinced all the clocks were broken. Nothing like uninterrupted boredom to make time stop. Another day, another wordy report sent to Henderson about the Weber High caper.

She put the car in drive and backed out of the high school's parking lot. Her phone vibrated. She ignored it. Abbie was vehemently opposed to using the phone while driving, so she let the phone go to voicemail. It immediately started ringing again. She ignored it a second time. It started ringing again. She pulled back into her parking spot and looked at her phone. It was her dad.

IF YOU COULD DRIVE ME TO THE DISCIPLINARY COUNCIL I WOULD VERY MUCH APPRECIATE IT.

Abbie's dad had just learned how to text. Her brother John had finally convinced him to use a smartphone. His texts were as formal as Professor Taylor was.

OF COURSE, DAD. HAPPY TO.

Abbie would barely make it to Provo in time to drive her dad to the church if she left right then. Nothing like an absent-minded professor to wait until the last minute. She headed south on I-15.

Her dad was standing in the window waiting for her when she pulled into the driveway. He was dressed like he would for church: a well-pressed gray suit, white shirt, and subdued navy tie. The color of his face matched his suit and hair.

It took only five minutes to drive to the meetinghouse where the council was to be held. Abbie watched her dad walk inside with all the enthusiasm of a convicted criminal going to a sentencing hearing. The Church called disciplinary councils "Courts of Love." It didn't feel that way.

Abbie sat outside in the parking lot and waited. Her presence, even if only in the lobby of the church, would not be helpful. Her dad hadn't told anyone about the council, not even John. He didn't like to drive after dark. That's why he needed her help.

Abbie tried to distract herself from the sick feeling in her stomach by scrolling through news articles on her phone. Her efforts were unsuccessful. The minutes ticked by with excruciating slowness, and she felt increasingly nauseated. She couldn't concentrate on anything she read. When her dad emerged from the church, he was pressing a carefully ironed handkerchief under his eyes. After he pulled the seat belt across his chest, he said, "I've been disfellowshipped."

There wasn't anything to say. Being disfellowshipped meant you couldn't offer public prayers or give talks in church. For her dad, it meant more than that. Abbie had already checked BYU's honor code, which confirmed her fear that by accepting a position on the Y's faculty, her father had agreed to observe the honor code standards. Excommunication, disfellowshipment, or disaffiliation from the Church automatically resulted in the loss of good honor code standing at the school. Her dad could lose his job.

Disciplinary councils were supposed to be confidential. Lately, though, disciplinary councils for high-profile people were being leaked on social media. Then one of the papers would pick up the story. Professor Taylor was a popular teacher and noted historian. If he were fired, it would make the front page of the *Trib*. The *Deseret News* would print the official Church position.

"Abish, I've been asked to take a leave of absence from the Y until this is 'sorted.' That was the word they used."

"I don't know what to say." Abbie couldn't ignore the dull ache in her chest and the sick feeling in her stomach. She felt heat behind her eyes. She blinked.

"There isn't anything to say." Abbie started the car and pulled out of the church parking lot. They were back in the driveway in front of her dad's house, her family house, in minutes. Her dad just stared at it, but he didn't make any move to open the car door.

"Do you want to talk about it?"

"Not really." He opened the door and got out.

"I love you." The words were from her heart, but she

knew they were cold comfort to a man who had given his entire life—personal and professional—to the Church. A Church that had just told him he was no longer worthy to participate fully in his faith.

Until this council, her dad had always found a way to navigate the shifting winds of Church ideology, which was no easy feat. Modern religions faced challenges older religions hadn't. History didn't allow new religions to blur the darkness, the violence, the all-too-human greed, pride, and hatred endemic to so many religious communities.

There wasn't anything Abbie could do but drive home and stew in her sadness and growing anger at a world that had let this happen to her dad. It wasn't fair.

She was nearly to Riverdale when she saw the shiny blue pickup truck make a quick turn behind her. It had been following her since Provo, but in her emotional state she hadn't really registered it. Abbie took a detour through Roy to check if she was being paranoid. A few late turns without putting on her blinker and a stop at a convenience store confirmed her instincts. The pickup truck was following her.

Abbie was more comfortable on the back roads around Ogden than she had been when she first moved here, but if the person in the truck had grown up in the area, she would be at a disadvantage. She stayed in the parking lot of the convenience store while she planned the next move.

Her phone buzzed. It was Flynn.

You almost here? Brittany wants to see Bragg.

Brittany wanted to see Bragg? Talk about taking a bad day and making it worse. The last thing in the world Abbie wanted to do was lead whoever was driving that slick pickup truck directly to Brittany and her kids. That was problem number one. Problem number two was that Brittany wanted to see Bragg.

SOMEONE'S FOLLOWING ME. LET ME LOSE HIM. STALL.

She watched as the light at the three-way stop turned red. It was long past rush hour. Traffic was light. She backed out of her parking space and drove out of the lot, turning into the lane to make a left-hand turn. Nobody was behind her. Then the truck slipped back onto the road. No other car pulled up behind the truck. She glanced at the light in front of her—still red—then back in the rearview mirror. The blue truck loomed high just a few feet from her bumper.

The light turned green. Abbie waited. The truck didn't honk, but someone who had just pulled up behind him did. Abbie waited. The light turned yellow. Now there were two cars honking and at least six cars waiting behind the blue truck. The light in front of Abbie turned red. She gunned it. She turned straight in front of the oncoming traffic. There was nothing the truck could do but wait. By the time Abbie turned off onto a side road that would eventually lead her to Flynn's, she'd lost her tail.

The third garage was open and empty. She pulled in. If anyone was looking, no one would spot her old Rover. She exhaled and climbed out of her SUV. Then she remembered problem number two: Brittany wanted to see Bragg.

It shouldn't have come as a surprise. Brittany had made no secret of the fact that she wanted to stay in Colonia Juárez, presumably to have more of Bragg's children. Maybe, with the new baby in her arms, Brittany thought she could convince the father she should keep her children with her and not have them raised by a good Mormon family here in Utah. Brittany had chosen her life as a plural wife, but she might not have expected to become so attached to her children. In many ways, Brittany wasn't so different from many of the early polygamist wives who'd defended the practice even though it was difficult, maybe especially because it was difficult. Early plural wives had, as Laurel Thatcher Ulrich wrote in *A House Full of Females*, an "intense religiosity." Brittany was nothing if not intensely religious.

Abbie walked inside Flynn's without knocking. She tripped over a heavy suitcase. Three car seats stood in a line next to two very full diaper bags. Abbie heard voices upstairs. Flynn's was calm. Brittany's wasn't.

"I've been praying since yesterday for guidance. Today, it's clear what I must do. It's the only way for me to join the Anointed Quorum. It was the pregnancy hormones that made me crazy. I wasn't thinking straight when I left," Brittany said. "I want to bring the children to their father."

"Do you think his wife knows . . ." Flynn took a moment to find the words to finish the question. "About this arrangement?"

"I don't know," Brittany responded. "It may be like the early days before Joseph could tell Emma. My duty is to follow what is revealed to me, not to question it."

Abbie followed the voices up the stairs.

"All right," Flynn said. He sounded supportive, but Abbie knew he was trying to mollify the young mother without giving in to her wishes. "It's getting late. Why don't we figure out the details in the morning?"

Flynn's eyes smiled when Abbie arrived in the doorway. Moroni was fussing. Brittany pulled up her shirt to start nursing.

"We'll just be downstairs," Flynn said, stepping outside before softly closing the door behind him. Once out of earshot, Flynn said to Abbie, "I guess that's that. Maybe it's all for the best."

Abbie gave him a hard stare.

"Okay," he admitted, "helping Brittany visit Bragg feels a lot like we're sending Daniel into the lions' den."

"That would bode well for Brittany, but not so hot for us," Abbie pointed out.

Flynn sighed. "I keep forgetting how well you know your scriptures." He kissed Abbie's forehead. "Okay, I'll quote a source I know better than the Bible: 'I've got a bad feeling about this.'"

"'I *have* a bad feeling about this,'" Abbie said, then winked.

"Star Wars, too? I can't win," he said. "Yeah, I have a bad feeling about this."

"I do, too."

TWENTY-FIVE

Flynn convinced Brittany that the kids needed to be well rested for such an important meeting. Waiting until tomorrow to reach out to Bragg was the best course of action. The kids would get a good night's rest and a healthy breakfast before meeting their father for the first time.

Abbie and Flynn sat at the kitchen table.

While Abbie had been waiting in the church parking during her dad's disciplinary council, everyone here had eaten dinner. Flynn reheated lentil soup and crumbled goat cheese on top.

"Bread?" He held up the last quarter of a crusty baguette.

"No thanks." Abbie took the soup and a glass of un-oaked Chardonnay Flynn offered her.

As she ate, she brought him up to speed: Caleb Monson's white Mercedes, Clarke being the only person working on the investigations, her dad being disfellowshipped and forced to take a leave of absence until things were "sorted."

"Sorted?" Flynn asked.

"That's the word he used."

"It's sounds to me like it's a message to you: if you leave well enough alone, your dad can come back to the Church."

This wasn't the first time the thought that her father was being used as a pawn had crossed Abbie's mind, but she'd dismissed it as paranoid. If Flynn was thinking the same thing, though, maybe it wasn't so paranoid. "Do you mind if I eat and work?" She placed her laptop on the table next to her soup.

"Not at all. What are you thinking?" Flynn scooted his chair next to Abbie's so they could view the screen together.

"I have an idea to narrow down our suspects."

With a few taps on her keyboard, Abbie logged in to her Family Search account. Non-Mormons had Ancestry .com. But if you had a Church ID number, you could access all the information on that website for free, plus a lot of information not available to nonmembers.

Abbie typed in Brittany's full name and clicked on the temple icon to see the list of effective ordinances: Baptism and confirmation, both when she turned eight. That was standard. Initiatory and endowments had been done about ten months before her daughter was born. Brittany herself had been "born into the covenant," which meant her parents had already been sealed in the temple when Brittany was born. Brittany's own SEALED TO SPOUSE icon, which would indicate whether she was sealed for time and all eternity to her spouse, was encircled in a dotted line followed by the words NOT AVAILABLE.

Abbie checked Brittany's children. Mary and Jacob were recorded, both were said to be BORN INTO THE

Covenant, and neither had a father listed. This was not standard. There was no record of Moroni yet.

Abbie tried a few more things but came up against an online brick wall: This sealing-to-parents ordinance is valid, but the parents are not listed because of privacy or they may not match those in Family Tree.

The information icon suggested that if she had further questions about the sealing ordinances, she should please see your ecclesiastical leader.

Well, she wasn't about to do that.

Flynn let out a low whistle.

Everything was in order for Brittany and her children in the afterlife. It also meant that someone with access to that website knew what was happening in Colonia Juárez.

TWENTY-SIX

Long after the house was quiet, Abbie stayed at the kitchen table, at her computer, tracking down information on Caleb Monson. He had a low-level job working in the Church IT department. Abbie had trouble seeing Caleb as a mastermind. Sure, he was the one link that touched everything, but he seemed more like a piece in someone else's chess game than the player himself. Still, he was involved.

Abbie slept for a few hours before getting up for her shift at the high school. She was tiptoeing downstairs, trying not to disturb the rest of the house, when Brittany emerged from her room. She was dressed in one of the outfits Flynn, or rather Flynn's housekeeper, had bought for her. Little Moroni was dressed, as were Mary and Jacob.

"President Bragg is expecting us this morning," Brittany announced when she saw Abbie.

"I thought we were going to wait until after breakfast to decide what to do," Abbie said, hoping she didn't sound as unhappy as she felt about Brittany's decision. "I don't think Flynn's up yet."

"I heard his shower running an hour ago," Brittany countered.

"Well, let's get the kids something to eat. You haven't had breakfast yet, have you?" Abbie was stalling.

"Mommy!" Mary announced, "I wants Uncle Flynn's pancakes."

Thank goodness for small blessings.

Abbie took the kids' hands and walked them down the stairs to the kitchen. The clock on the wall informed her that she was already fifteen minutes late for her shift at Weber High.

Once Mary and Jacob were settled at the table with milk, Abbie searched the house for Flynn. She found him outside on the patio with a cup of coffee. Butterflies fluttered in her stomach when she saw the spot where they had stood the other night.

Abbie updated him on the events of the morning.

"Pancakes and polygamy." Flynn's alliterative attempt to introduce some levity to the situation only highlighted the fact that he and Abbie felt the same dread.

There was an upside, though. Abbie delivering Brittany Thompson and her children to Bragg would invariably be viewed favorably by the powers that be, the powers that could decide if her dad was worthy to "return to fellowship." The sooner that happened, the better. Whatever misgivings Abbie had about plural marriage, Brittany Thompson was an adult woman who had made her choice deliberately and voluntarily.

While Flynn prepared breakfast, Abbie stepped into the

front hallway to call Henderson. She exhaled when his cell went to voicemail. Happy to avoid an actual conversation, she said something about a family emergency and that she'd be to Weber High as soon as things were sorted, which was exactly what she hoped a morning drive to Elder Bragg's house would do: "sort" her family emergency.

Abbie stepped back into the kitchen. Brittany said to Flynn, "Elder Bragg asked me to meet him at his house in Midway. I have the address. He told me to come as soon as I can. He's up there now. He forgave me and promised I can return to Mexico with all my babies, and we can even have more children if I want!"

Brittany grinned from ear to ear. She was a smart young woman. No one had tricked her. No one had taken advantage of her. Brittany had not only agreed to be sealed to a man old enough to be her grandfather, but she'd agreed with enthusiasm. Still, Abbie felt protective of the young mother, even though Brittany was only a few years younger than Abbie was herself.

Flynn had dragged out the pancake making as long as he could. Even with a syrup mishap that meant a complete change of clothes for Mary, breakfast did indeed come to an end.

"Okay. Let's go," Brittany said with the happy anticipation of a kid on Christmas morning.

Flynn loaded suitcases and baby accoutrements into the back of his SUV while Abbie attached the car seats. Brittany held her sleeping baby until she fastened him into his safety seat. She sat next to him in the back. Mary and Jacob were fastened in their seats in the SUV's third row.

The drive from Riverdale to Midway took about an hour and fifteen minutes. Flynn opted for the I-84 route, which is what Abbie would have done as well. It took a little longer, giving Brittany more time to change her mind, plus it was a prettier drive.

The kids, thankfully, fell asleep not too long after the car started moving. Even baby Moroni snored quietly.

"Thank you, guys," Brittany said. "I mean, I show up on Professor Taylor's doorstep all crazy from pregnancy hormones and you two just help me out."

"Of course," Flynn said. "We are happy to help."

"I mean it. I don't know what I would've done if you hadn't been there. I knew I could go to Professor Taylor, but he's old. I know he has tons of grandkids, but my pregnancy sort of freaked him out."

Abbie smiled. Brittany was right: pregnancy and child-bearing were not something her dad was well equipped to handle. He got light-headed at the sight of blood. Once, when Abbie was about twelve or thirteen, she'd cut her thumb while slicing cucumbers. It wasn't a trivial cut, but nothing that required stitches. Her dad was in the kitchen, and the moment he saw the blood dripping from her hand, he sat down, pale as a ghost. Her mom came in from the dining room, efficiently wrapped the injured hand in a clean tea towel, and took Abbie to the bathroom, where she dowsed the cut with antiseptic and applied a bandage. Professor Taylor would not have been able to help with a scraped knee, let along help out when a woman went into labor.

As they drove into Heber Valley, Abbie's mind was

whirring with all the things she didn't understand about Brittany. Abbie and Brittany were similar in so many ways: both had been good students in school, both had been born into the same conservative religion, and both had married at a relatively young age. And yet, Abbie didn't understand the path Brittany had chosen.

"Why did you leave Colonia Juárez? I know you've said it was pregnancy hormones, but I've done that drive to the border. It's not easy. I can't imagine doing it with two kids."

"I guess I owe you an honest answer," Brittany said. "From the first time I learned about Joseph Smith's revelation about the New and Everlasting Covenant, I knew it was true. I had a strong testimony that plural marriage was part of our Heavenly Father's plan in the past and that it would be again. I know it will be part of our lives in the Celestial Kingdom. That day when I was sealed to Elder Bragg in the temple was the happiest day of my life."

Brittany looked directly at Abbie. "I know you don't think that's possible, Abbie, but it really was a very happy day for me." Brittany's cheerful tone wavered, and she added, "I'd given up hope of ever becoming a wife, a mother."

If only for that brief moment in time, Abbie understood Brittany Thompson. The two women shared knowing what it was like to lose hope of ever becoming a mother. That was not a pain Abbie would wish on anyone.

"When I found out I was pregnant, we were both overjoyed. I knew it was Heavenly Father's way of telling me I was on the right path holding fast to the iron rod."

Mormons joked that there were two kinds of members

of the Church: Iron Rods and Liahonas. The second group, so the joke went, were future former Mormons. The description came from a dream recounted in the Book of Mormon. The prophet Lehi saw a treacherous path to the tree of life. The only way to get there safely was to hold fast to an iron rod. Brittany was the epitome of an Iron Rod. She wanted to believe and she did. She treated doubt not as a reason to question her faith, but rather as a challenge to be overcome in order to maintain her faith.

"Why did you leave, then?" Abbe asked.

"Like I said, it was just out-of-control pregnancy hormones. After Mary was born, it was hard that Elder Bragg was away almost all the time, but I came to appreciate the sisters at the orphanage. They think we're single mothers, which was a little hard on us there because the sisters were all a little judgy. You know, they thought they were living their faith and we, well, that we had made some serious mistakes. Sometimes I just wanted to shake those smug grins off their faces as they 'served the Lord.' None of us ever said anything, though. We know we're sealed for eternity to an Apostle and are blessed to bear his children."

Abbie wondered if it were true: the sisters believing they were helping single mothers. If so, the sisters must have thought it strange that these young women managed to get pregnant over and over even though they all lived in dorm rooms at the orphanage.

Moroni stirred. They had turned onto the road that would lead them to Elder Bragg's Midway home.

"In some ways, living down there is probably more fun

than having kids here in Utah with just one husband. We were kind of like a sorority, all of us living together in this big house, going through the same pregnancy stuff at the same time. There were lots of kids and lots of women helping each other."

Brittany went on, "I'm not ashamed of what we're doing." Her voice dropped almost a full octave. She sounded serious. "I haven't told my family and friends about what I'm doing because it is not my revelation to share. If you read the 1890 Manifesto, or even the Second Manifesto in 1904, it's clear the Church abandoned polygamy because the earth was not ready for the practice. The U.S. government was against us. The Supreme Court was against us. Americans were against us. Now things are different."

Brittany wasn't entirely incorrect. When the practice of polygamy had gone from being a poorly disguised rumor in the 1840s to being openly practiced, early members of the Church faced animosity from both fellow citizens and government officials. The Church learned its lesson in 1890 when the Supreme Court of the United States directed all Church assets to be turned over to the federal government in the case *Late Corporation of the Church of Jesus Christ of Latter-Day Saints v. United States*. Within a few months of the decision that promised to leave the Church without money, Prophet Wilford Woodruff received the revelation that Latter-day Saints should "refrain from contracting any marriage forbidden by the law of the land." By disavowing polygamy, the Church managed to keep its material goods.

Since then, the LDS Church had become a model citizen of conservative respectability.

Abbie didn't have anything else to ask. Brittany Thompson believed. Abbie watched as Flynn drove toward Bragg's house. Midway was in a wide valley. There had been a time when almost all the land between the mountain peaks was farmland with a few lazy streams winding between the pastures and fields. Now there were huge houses, luxury resorts, and at least three solidly nice restaurants.

Flynn turned off a road that probably hadn't existed twenty years ago. A lot of the houses here were built as second homes. Elder Bragg's place was at the end of the cul-de-sac.

Brittany must have sensed they were just about there. She said, "I shouldn't have left," almost like she was asking for forgiveness.

As Flynn drove into the driveway, dread gripped Abbie. She took some deep breaths to calm herself, but they didn't help. A sick feeling of foreboding spread through her body, a heaviness completely at odds with Brittany's happy anticipation. As soon as Flynn parked the car, Brittany bounced out and unstrapped Moroni. He was still asleep. Flynn carried the bags up the front walkway while Abbie helped the older kids out of their car seats. Brittany rang the doorbell before Abbie, Mary, and Jacob made it up the front steps.

The door opened. It was Elder Bragg, grinning.

TWENTY-SEVEN

"Do come in." He stepped aside to open the door wide. Mary held on to the back of Brittany's legs. Jacob hid his face in his mom's hip. Flynn waited for Brittany to struggle into the house. Abbie followed the whole crew.

Bragg glanced outside the door before closing it. Then he put his arms around Brittany, holding the newest addition to their family. He kissed her with a fervor Abbie wouldn't have thought possible for a man his age.

"I thought I'd lost you," he said softly in Brittany's ear.

Flynn shot Abbie a look. This display of affection seemed strange to him, too.

After the couple finished their amorous greeting, Bragg turned to Abbie. "Detective Abish Taylor? I'm glad you helped reunite us. I'm sure I don't need to stress the importance that everything you think you understand about Brittany and Juárez is not yours to share." Then he added, "I know how much you love your father."

Any thought Abbie might have entertained that Bragg possessed a single molecule of compassion in his being was eliminated with that last sentence. He had no real authority to keep Abbie from talking to anyone about anything, but he knew didn't need authority. He had all the power he needed. He held the keys to the priesthood and, Abbie knew, the keys to her father gaining full fellowship.

"Of course. I understand," Abbie said, kicking herself for the flimsy response. She wanted to say something sharp and hurtful, but that wouldn't help her dad.

"Under the circumstances, Mr. Bragg, I expect we'll hear from Professor Taylor this evening that he has been restored to full fellowship." Bragg, Brittany, and Abbie all looked over at the source of the deep voice. Flynn commanded the room.

Bragg stared at the man, nearly four decades his junior, who exuded his independence unapologetically. The Apostle was clearly not used to such a confident lack of deference. He looked both startled and defensive, although he must have sensed that Flynn was the wrong person to mess with.

"I expect you'll hear before you get back to your house in Riverdale." Bragg was looking straight at Abbie. He had chosen his words carefully, and she heard the threat he wanted her to hear: *I know where he lives.*

"We'll leave you with your family." Flynn opened the front door.

Brittany turned away from Bragg, who was holding Moroni with such awkwardness you would have thought it was the first baby he had seen. She flung her arms around Flynn. "Thank you! Thank you! I don't know what would have happened to all of us if you hadn't helped." She hugged him and then she hugged Abbie. "Thank you!"

"You're welcome." Abbie had never meant the phrase less in her life.

Abbie and Flynn left Bragg's house and climbed into the SUV. As Flynn backed out of the driveway, a white Mercedes pulled in. Abbie held her breath while she waited to see who was in the car.

Caleb Monson, wearing jeans and a red flannel shirt, got out of the car, walked to the front door, rang the doorbell, and waited. The door opened, and Caleb Monson disappeared inside.

★ ★ ★

Her days at Weber were blurring into one mass of lockers and students. As soon as it was six thirty in the evening, Abbie bolted from the high school. She'd spent the last hour of the day writing her detailed report for Henderson. She wanted to keep her boss happy, or at least not unhappy, with her.

She climbed into the Rover and drove directly to the station. It was empty except for Clarke and the nighttime officer. Abbie made a beeline for her office and closed the door. She sent her report to Henderson, then got to work on Caleb Monson.

She must have fallen down the rabbit hole. She hadn't looked away from her research until Clarke knocked on her office door to say good night. He handed her a copy of the ME's report on Bryce Strong.

"Just got this. Homicide."

"Really?"

"You can read the report for yourself, but the gist is that

there was too little external damage to the body. If Bryce Strong had fallen naturally, his body would have bounced against rocks and trees on the way down. ME's pretty sure he was pushed pretty hard at the top of the cliff. There were a few defensive wounds, too."

"No DNA matches?" Clarke certainly would have led with that bit of information if it were there.

"Nope. What are you looking at?"

"Caleb Monson."

Clarke didn't know about her seeing Caleb at Heber's funeral or at Bragg's house. She hadn't told her partner about Bragg at all. Abbie didn't want to admit it to herself, but she hadn't been forthcoming with her partner because she was afraid of what would happen to her dad. If she told Clarke, it would be impossible to keep from Henderson. If Abbie had learned anything from her last case, it was that Henderson reported everything to Bowen, who reported to Port.

"Something is off about him," Clarke said.

Abbie couldn't have agreed more.

"What have you got?" he asked.

"When he returned from his mission, he joined the military. He excelled at taking control of places where other soldiers failed. The reports I found were redacted, but it's clear that in the military he had no trouble using violence. He was discharged. When he got back to Utah, he lived at home, did odd construction jobs, got into a few fights that got him on the wrong side of the police but nothing major. Then he enrolled at LDS Business College in the six-week 'Discovery Experience.'"

"What's that?" Clarke asked.

"It's a program designed to help students discover next steps in their lives. The course focuses on what the school calls 'principles and practical applications to help young single adults tap into the powers of heaven.'"

Even her earnest partner couldn't resist smiling at the marketing language. "I've got to see this myself." Abbie opened up the website. Clarke came around to her side of the desk and read from the screen. "The goal of the program is for the student to have 'individual, revelatory moments to empower and inspire.'"

Abbie bit her tongue that wanted to say, "And so it was revealed unto him that he, Caleb Monson, should go forth into Information Technology."

Instead she said, "After he finished the program, he enrolled in coding and video production classes. Now he works in the back office of the Church IT department."

"Soldier to videographer?" Clarke asked.

"Looks like it."

Clarke's stomach growled. He stifled a yawn. "It's late. I've got to get home," Clarke said. "We can visit this Caleb Monson tomorrow. We don't need to pull an all-nighter. Henderson isn't breathing down my neck on this."

"Okay. I'll see you in the morning." Abbie watched her partner leave.

She had just seen Caleb at Bragg's. She was not about to wait until tomorrow.

TWENTY-EIGHT

Abbie signed out the Pleasant View City Police Department's only "surveillance" car, a nondescript sedan. It was mostly used when an officer brought an opioid addict to a treatment center, the idea being that a squad car was intimidating. Sadly, that sedan was getting more use than it should.

Her Range Rover, no matter how old and beaten up, would stick out. It was better to drive something made in America.

Caleb Monson had been married in the temple early that year. He and his wife lived in Herriman, a place that had grown in the past two decades from a population of barely over fifteen hundred to over fifty thousand. A single land developer was responsible for the rows of identical houses lined with newly paved roads. Trees with trunks narrower than Abbie's arms sprouted from neatly trimmed lawns the size of postage stamps. She wondered if in the morning, all the kids would bounce identical balls in sync.

She pulled her sedan to the curb across the street from Caleb Monson's house. Lights were on inside, but Abbie couldn't see any activity. She waited. Lights went on upstairs. Through the window, Abbie watched as a pregnant woman leaned forward and carefully lined her lips with a deep pink pencil, then dabbed lipstick with her fingers on top. She spritzed her wrists and neck with perfume, fluffed her hair, and then disappeared from view. Abbie waited.

The garage door rolled open. A white Mercedes backed out and stopped. The pregnant woman emerged from the house. Caleb Monson popped out of the car and opened the door to the passenger side. He closed it after his wife lowered herself into the car. They drove away.

Abbie had one moment to decide what to do. Follow or not? If she followed, she could get a better sense of the kind of guy Caleb Monson was. If she didn't, she could check out the house. Not that she was thinking of breaking in.

Not really.

Abbie watched until the Mercedes disappeared from sight. Caleb had left the garage door open. *Be grateful for small blessings.* She walked with purpose toward the garage. In the corner of the garage was a tripod leaning against a single metal filing cabinet. She crouched down to open the bottom drawer. It was full of manuals; the next two drawers were filled with camera equipment; the top drawer housed batteries of all kinds. On top of the cabinet sat three plastic CD cases. Two were new and unopened. The third was labeled QUORUM MEETINGS, 2016–. Abbie peered through the semiopaque plastic. The CD on top was dated the day of Heber's murder.

Abbie slipped that CD into her bag, then turned around and walked back to her car. No one paid any attention to the blonde getting into the dark sedan parked across the street.

Abbie started driving to Flynn's.

TWENTY-NINE

Flynn answered the door as soon as Abbie knocked.

"Don't do that to me again!" he said, ushering her inside. "Where have you been?"

"Work." Abbie reached into her bag. She pulled out her phone, which had run out of juice, and then she pulled out the CD. "Well, I paid Caleb Monson a visit."

Flynn looked at Abbie's phone. "You wanna charge that so you can call people who might want to know that you're okay?"

Abbie handed him the phone. They walked down the hall to the kitchen. Flynn set the phone on a charging station.

"Going back to the 1990s? What's with the CD?" Flynn asked.

"I'm not sure. This was just lying around at Caleb's. But do you see the date? It's the day Heber died. Do you have anything that would show us what's on this?"

"As a matter of fact, my old laptop has a slot for discs." Flynn left the room and returned a few minutes later with a computer. He opened it and slid the disc in. Abbie sat next to him at the kitchen table in front of the screen.

The video camera was pointing at a wall. The recording started midsentence.

". . . comments President Bragg made about how young women should make an effort to look pretty and put on some lipstick is just one such an example." It was Elder Bowen.

"Brother Monson, is that camera working?" a disembodied voice asked.

"Uh, yeah, just a sec." The camera jostled. Caleb Monson stood in front of the camera, adjusting something. Then the lens focused on the faces of two older white men in suits. A third man in the background, slightly out of focus, was dozing.

Bowen continued. "It's important to remember that even innocuous comments can be portrayed as sexist or racist or both when they fall into the wrong hands. A single offhand remark can spread across the globe in a matter of minutes. This is the new world, Brethren."

A man's voice asked, "We took that video down?"

"Yes," Elder Bowen replied, "but you can still find versions on YouTube if you know how to look. Legal has taken steps, but once something like this gets out, the First Amendment makes things tricky. We need to be careful, particularly when it comes to meetings like this one."

The Quorum of the Twelve Apostles were accustomed to a certain degree of respect. Abbie imagined it was difficult adjusting to a world in which the very characteristics that had once been the source of their power had become a source of doubt and, in some quarters, derision.

Someone coughed; there was the sound of a few chairs scraping against the floor and papers being shuffled. The camera angle changed. Abbie and Flynn saw Elder Bowen standing at a lectern.

"Good evening, Brethren; thank you all for being here. There's a lot to discuss, so I will not waste any of our precious time together. We all are aware of the dismal numbers: for every hundred and fifty LDS women of child-bearing age, there are only one hundred LDS men of the same age. This is a crisis the Church hasn't faced since the early days of the Restoration. We have changed the missionary ages, we have spoken about the importance of marriage, and we have highlighted the importance of starting families. Still, we have not managed to restore what we once had. As you all know, we have engaged some fresh eyes to address the problem of marriage and demographic imbalance in the Church." Bowen said. "May I introduce our first guest, Dr. Humphrey Steiner, chairman of the Harris Poll."

A balding man with expensive heavy-rimmed glasses came to the lectern. He was wearing a dark-gray suit and pale-lavender shirt with a tie in a shade of dark purple. Abbie was fairly sure Dr. Steiner was a man who wore amusing socks. He said, "Thank you, Elder Bowen. It has been a pleasure working on this project."

Dr. Steiner pressed his finger on the computer, and a colorful graph appeared behind him. "Our polling data suggests that plural marriage is not objectionable to fifty-two percent of Americans between the ages of eighteen and thirty-five, as long as all parties are at least eighteen and enter into the arrangement of their own free will. That percentage drops to thirty-one percent for those between the ages of thirty-six and forty-five, and to eleven percent for those between the ages of forty-six and fifty-five. Eighty-three percent of Americans over the age of fifty-five overwhelmingly find plural marriage objectionable. For those over seventy, the number rises to ninety-seven percent."

The polling expert went on to dissect different questions that were posed, how there were regional variations around the country, and how education and religious affiliation affected tolerance for polygamy. The takeaway was that younger, more urban people who didn't know a Mormon personally and didn't attend a religious service regularly were more open to the practice. The older, the less urban, and the more religious the person, the more likely the person was to object to plural marriage.

The camera stayed on Dr. Steiner. "The details are elucidated in the report. I'm more than happy to personally discuss the findings of the project with any one of you."

"Thank you" could be heard well off-camera. It was Heber Bentsen. Abbie wished she could see him.

"I know you're also interested in the results of my polling within the LDS community," Dr. Steiner continued. Abbie wondered how much the Church had paid this high-priced polling guru to conduct the survey without any news outlet in the country picking up the story.

There was no sound from off-camera. Absolute silence. Nobody shifted in his seat or moved his chair. No one even coughed. Abbie couldn't move her eyes from the screen, and neither could Flynn.

"I can't emphasize enough that given the restrictions I was working under, in terms of keeping this research discreet, the margin for error is rather larger than I would like." The suspense in the room radiated through the computer.

Dr. Steiner cleared his throat. "There was a positive correlation between members with temple recommends and a willingness to follow the Prophet, even on publicly unpopular issues. However, that correlation breaks down when those members believe a directive does not align with their conservative Christian values."

"Are you saying there are Saints who would fall in line behind whatever Fox News is saying rather than follow the Prophet?"

"That's not exactly how I would phrase it," Dr. Steiner said.

There was some murmuring among the male voices. Someone cleared his throat; another voice came from beyond what could be seen on the video. "So, bottom line: we could have more trouble convincing a fellow middle-aged Latter-day Saint that the practice of plural marriage is okay than we would convincing a graduate student in San Francisco?"

"Yes," Dr. Steiner replied.

Silence again.

"Thank you so much for your presentation, Dr. Steiner," Bowen said. Offscreen, a door opened and then closed.

Bowen then said, "I'm happy to introduce Brother McConkie, who has generously donated his time to provide us with his legal opinion concerning a number of cases we all know well." A well-coiffed man in a three-piece suit complete with cuff links, burgundy bow tie, and coordinating pocket square appeared behind the lectern.

"Brethren, it has been my great honor to assist the Church in this way. The details of my opinion are contained in the binders that are being passed around to each of you. While there were a dozen or so cases relevant to my analysis, only three—*Reynolds v. United States, Davis v. Beason,* and *The Late Corporation of the Church of Jesus Christ of Latter-day Saints v. United States*—were my focus.

"Before getting into the details of my legal analysis, it is important to understand that these cases were decided after the enumerated powers doctrine had lost much of its force, but before the constitutional guarantees of individual liberty had begun their modern expansion under the 'heightened scrutiny' approach. In other words—"

Bowen interrupted Brother McConkie. "Brother, we so appreciate your detailed analysis of the case law concerning those early religious freedom cases. I look forward to reading the entirety of your opinion. Unfortunately, we are short on time. Would you be able to give us your bottom-line answer concerning the likelihood of success if there were a case to challenge the current precedent concerning the practice of polygamy in the United States?"

The lawyer looked a little deflated. Abbie was fairly sure he wanted to explain enumerated powers. She was grateful Bowen had interrupted him.

"It's my considered opinion that given the current climate concerning certain Middle Eastern religious groups in the United States—not to mention the current slate of justices on the Supreme Court—this would not be an opportune time for the Church to draw attention to the aspects of our belief system that do not fall in line with traditional Christianity."

"Thank you so much, Brother McConkie." Bowen got up and opened the door for the lawyer, who could not hide his displeasure at being dismissed.

The door closed. For a moment, no one said anything; the camera shifted. Heber came into focus and began speaking. His tone was calm, quiet, and strong.

"Brothers, I know we're all struggling with the imbalance in the number of young women and young men in the Church right now. No one is more aware than I am of the challenges we face. However, I feel moved by the spirit to warn you that we are embarking on a dangerous path. There is another way. We can seek to understand the reasons so many of our young men are becoming inactive or abandoning the Church entirely. How are we failing them? If we address those issues and concerns, our problem with our young women not being able to enter the sacred covenant of marriage will end. We will not have to be concerned with our brothers and sisters in the preexistence. Measured discussion and prayer will bring us all to a place where we can address the issue of gender imbalance."

Then another voice, from well off-camera, started speaking. The camera shifted to the source of the words. It was Port. Even through the small screen of the old laptop, Abbie sensed the energy shift in that wood-paneled board-room where the Quorum of the Twelve were meeting.

"My dear brothers, this is the time to gird our loins for the final days. If we are truly guided by the spirit of our Holy Ghost, each one of us knows we are in the last days. You all know we have Brethren in the Senate, in the House, in high positions of power in the White House. It is vital that this Church remain strong. We cannot let anything harm the image of the Church at this important juncture. Those who do not know the fullness of the Gospel will not understand what we do. We cannot let the views of the uninitiated keep us from doing what we must do. The path is clear, and yes, it is narrow. We must move forward, but we cannot do so in a way that could damage our public image. If our Heavenly Father wishes us to keep that which he has revealed secret, we must do so."

Port paused, a long moment of absolute silence. No one in that room seemed to even breathe. Damn, Port was a sharp orator. Abbie felt her neck muscles tighten.

"There has been a shift in popular opinion on this matter. Some of us probably never thought we would live to see the day when the New and Everlasting Covenant could once again be practiced. I'm told there are several television shows that portray plural marriage as a normal lifestyle choice. However, we here are not talking about temporal issues that concern gentiles. We are dealing with eternal matters with eternal consequences. We cannot wait to bring souls from the preexistence. Each one of us in this room has seen Prophet Taylor's Revelation."

Was Port admitting the polygamy revelation actually existed? The 1886 Revelation commanding members of the Church to continue practicing plural marriage regardless of earthly laws? The revelation the Church had officially denied? Abbie pushed her fingers into the space just beneath her eyebrows. She closed her eyes and felt the intense pain. It was a welcome break from listening to Port.

Port kept talking. "That revelation was for us, that revelation was for now. My dear Brethren, I bear my testimony to you that I know we must follow a path of growth for the Church, just as surely as I know Joseph Smith restored the fullness of the Gospel. However, we cannot risk the success of the Church because we have been tempted by the popularity of liberal ideas like transparency and openness. Some matters are sacred and must remain secret."

So, Port was telling everyone to lie?

Whatever support for open discussion Heber might have sparked among his Brethren was gone. Port wielded the power of hard conviction. There was no room for any other point of view, no dissent, no debate.

The seconds counted by on the bottom of the screen. Then the voice of the man off-camera said, "Brothers, let us pray."

The men bowed their heads.

It was over. Whatever Heber's goal had been, he had not achieved it. Port controlled his apostolic audience.

The Brethren shuffled out of the room. Abbie looked for Heber, but the camera never rested on his face. The video kept going, with no one in the eye of the camera. Abbie was about to snap Flynn's old laptop shut when Port spoke off-camera.

"Brother Bowen, this went well. I'd like to discuss with you a small experiment I've started. Only a very select few are aware of the details in Colonia Juárez."

The screen went black.

THIRTY

Abbie was experiencing sensory overload. First, there was the content of the video. Second, there was the fact that this meeting had happened hours before Heber died. Finally, there was the realization that Caleb Monson knew about all of it because he recorded it.

"Did we just watch the Apostles have a due-diligence meeting about the possibility of reintroducing plural marriage?" Flynn spoke at a speed so slow Abbie could hear the silent space between each word he articulated, just like white blanks between words on a page.

"Yes. I think we did."

"Do you want some wine?" Flynn asked.

"Yes. I think I do."

Flynn got up from the table. He returned a few minutes later with two very full goblets.

"It was a long time ago when I went on my mission," Flynn said.

"I know," Abbie said. "I was there for your homecoming."

Flynn took a drink from his glass before setting it down.

"Most people think the Church has grown to its current fifteen million members because of the missionaries, all those clean-cut young men and women knocking on doors and teaching the Gospel."

Flynn's usually playful tone was absent. He sounded sad.

"When I got to the MTC, I started to see things differently. I think the missionary program was being used as a way to keep young people from leaving the Church. We were kids. At an age when we should have been heading off to college or work, an age when we should have been asking questions, staying up late at night with friends talking about the meaning of life, we were shipped off to spend two years without friends or family. We're told what to think, what to say, what to write in our letters home. We get back, hormone crazed, and we get married as soon as we can. Before you know it, you've got three kids and another on the way, plus a mortgage. You never had your chance to think, to question or doubt. By the time you look up from the responsibilities of marriage, parenthood, and work, the Church is too big a part of your life to leave."

"Is that what happened to you?" Abbie asked.

Flynn looked into his glass. "The Church becomes your life; it gives you meaning. You stay because you can't imagine not staying."

"What changed?" Abbie asked, "Do you understand what Bowen was talking about when he brought up the missionary program?"

"The world has changed. When our dads served their missions, they met people who had never heard of the

Church. Back then, missionaries could stick to their rehearsed lesson plans. Now, all you have to do is Google JOSEPH SMITH POLYGAMY to find out about Fannie Alger and Lucinda Harris. The same is true for the very premise of the Book of Mormon. You'll be hard-pressed to find many reputable scholarly sources supporting the notion that people from Israel came to the Americas and inscribed their history on golden plates, which eventually fell into the hands of Joseph Smith via an angel."

"Okay. I get it. It's rough being a missionary now."

"No, that's not really my point. It used to be that the worst that could happen to those young missionaries was to have doors slammed in their faces. Now, missionaries have to face facts about the Church and the scriptures they may have never known before because we as a Church don't talk about history in any way that isn't faith affirming, which means we don't really talk about it. Learning those facts when you're on a mission can be the basis for disillusionment. It's a tough on a good LDS kid when everything he believed was true isn't."

Abbie felt that pain of disillusionment, the ache of wanting to put things back to the way they were before she knew more. "I know," she said.

Flynn took Abbie's hand and pressed it to his lips. "I know you do."

Abbie didn't know what to say.

Flynn continued. "I was in the Stake Presidency before the divorce. I talked to these young people when they got home. They struggle. Most want to stay in the Church, but it's hard, because once you've seen good and kind people who don't live anything like the way the Church teaches, you may start to think that there is more than one way to live your life. Still, a lot of them stay because they really believe the Church is the one and only true church; some stay because they want to believe, even when they don't; some stay because it's where all of the friends and family are. For a reason I can't explain, young men are more willing to leave than young women. That's a problem. The real source of the Church's growth had always been good, old-fashioned procreation. Fewer young men, fewer potential fathers."

Abbie felt a sense of relief to hear someone else say out loud what she had long thought. Traditionally, young LDS women married in their early twenties and had children from then until their late thirties or early forties. It wasn't at all unusual to have one child in college and another in kindergarten with three or four in between. Membership growth had been slowing for a while, but the numbers in the past few years had been lower than any in recent memory, maybe as low as 1.7% in the last year. With young men abandoning the Church, their faithful and fertile female counterparts were being left without husbands. A lot of Mormon babies weren't being born.

THIRTY-ONE

Abbie was still processing what she'd seen on the CD from the night before when she arrived at the parking lot at Weber High. She was a little early. She entered through one of the back entrances near the gym and walked through the hallway where the cheerleader and varsity athletes had their lockers. She heard rustling around the corner. Abbie stopped and walked quietly to the corner. She looked around to see the janitor placing an iPad in a large duffel bag.

"Stop!" Abbie yelled.

In a flash, the janitor bolted. Abbie dashed after him. He was no match for either her speed or her strength. As she was handcuffing him, the security guard walked in through the front entrance. His eyes lit up when he saw them.

"I think if you check that duffel," Abbie said, "you'll find that we've found our thief."

The security guard rifled through the bag, then set it down and puffed up his chest. "As I suspected."

The security guard escorted the janitor to his own closetlike office. The janitor sat down on a plastic chair with his hands cuffed behind him. They waited for one of Abbie's fellow Pleasant View police officers to arrive.

When one finally did, Abbie was happy to hand over responsibility.

"I'll give you my statement at the station," she promised her fellow cop. "Mr. Johnson here, the senior security officer of Weber High, has been invaluable to this investigation. He should be able to answer any questions you have."

The security guard beamed. Abbie's fellow officer shot her a look of despair. She smiled back and walked out into the sunshine, grateful for small blessings.

Abbie would now be able to devote herself full-time to the investigation into the murders of Heber Bentsen and Bryce Strong.

It was time to tell Clarke everything.

★ ★ ★

The foothills were still covered in early-morning shadow when Abbie pulled into the police station. Henderson's parking spot was empty. Clarke's was not. Abbie took in the familiar quiet at her place of employment. Within the hour, Hazel would bustle through the door. The other full-time officers would follow. At some point, there would be a call, but it wouldn't be anything serious. Abbie poured herself some very bad coffee from the break room. She smiled. It was good to be back.

With her coffee in hand, Abbie stopped by Clarke's desk and asked him to meet her in her office as soon as he could, which turned out to be right then. They walked together. Abbie shut the door behind them. This was going to be a long conversation and not an easy one.

Clarke listened as Abbie told him about Colonia Juárez, Brittany Thompson, and Elder Bragg. Then she slipped the CD into the computer. They watched until the screen faded to black.

Clarke sat stone-faced. His chest rose and fell several times before he spoke. "There's no evidence directly implicating anyone in Heber's murder."

"No, there isn't," Abbie agreed. She'd been on her own with all these weird related-yet-unrelated facts for too long. Had she made connections that weren't there? It would be good to have Clarke's perspective.

"We can't ignore the strong motive, though," Clarke said. "There are people who didn't want to risk President Bentsen going public."

Abbie exhaled. She felt just a little bit lighter than she had moments before. She wasn't crazy.

"How did you get this CD?" Clarke asked.

Abbie explained.

"You know, our DA is not going to like that." That was true, but then Clarke added, "It was an open garage, though." That was true, too. Right then, though, Abbie cared more about figuring out who had killed Heber and Bryce than worrying about the intricacies of the rules of evidence.

"There's no way Henderson is going to let us question the Apostles about their whereabouts," she said.

Clarke shook his head. "No, he's not going to admit how damning that meeting is. I think, though, we can make some discreet inquiries. I can probably rule out most of the Apostles pretty quickly without raising any eyebrows."

"That would be great," Abbie said.

"You know," Clarke added, "I don't like this Caleb Monson."

Even though Abbie felt the same way, she reminded herself and Clarke, "We need to keep an open mind."

"Of course," Clarke agreed. "Oh, by the way, Henderson won't be in today because of some medical issues. Technically I'm in charge of this investigation. I'm going to suggest moving forward without bothering the chief during his convalescence."

"Agreed." Abbie felt the muscles in her shoulders relax.

Clarke pushed his shirtsleeves up past his elbows. "Let's get to work."

He set about checking calendars and calling personal assistants to determine alibis for as many of the Apostles as he could without alerting anyone to what he was doing. Clarke was charming and knew exactly what to say to get information without giving any in return.

Abbie left him to it. She went to talk to the one person who knew every single one of the Brethren at that meeting.

THIRTY-TWO

Abbie walked through the unlocked front door to the sound of fingers madly clicking away at a keyboard. She walked down the hall to her dad's study.

"Hi Dad!"

"Abish. So nice to see you." He stood up, walked around his desk, and hugged her. An uncommon gesture for him, but nice.

"Everything back to normal in terms of the disciplinary council?"

"Yes, I was fully reinstated yesterday evening. The whole thing happened so quickly that I didn't even miss any classes." He paused for a moment, then added, "Thank you."

Abbie felt relief. The Church meant everything to her dad. She couldn't imagine what his life would be without it.

"I can't take any credit," she half-lied. "Brittany was adamant that she wanted to go back. I still have my reservations, but she's an adult woman capable of making her own decisions."

"Do you know if she's returning to Mexico?" he asked.

210 I D. A. Bartley

"I don't. I know she wants to, but I have a feeling it isn't entirely her decision to make."

Her dad was quiet for a moment; then, in a voice just louder than a whisper, he said, "You're going to keep this Mexico information to yourself, aren't you?"

"We're staying focused on the facts of the case."

"Who is 'we'?" The lightness in his voice was replaced by suspicion.

Abbie explained the CD and Clarke. Her dad peppered her with questions about the recording. At first he didn't believe it. Then he wondered if it could have been doctored. Finally, when she mentioned Brother McConkie and Dr. Steiner, he accepted that the CD was exactly what Abbie said it was. He rubbed his temples.

"I'm going to try my best not to cause any trouble. I really am." A promise she would try to keep.

Her dad was struggling to process the facts. He was a critical thinker, a man who liked to analyze. Here the facts pointed in a direction he didn't want to look. It was easier, at that moment at least, to doubt the facts rather than accept them.

"Dad," Abbie said, "you need to be prepared for the possibility that Heber may have been killed by someone at that meeting."

Her dad clenched his jaw and straightened his spine.

"The idea that someone murdered an Apostle—let alone the idea that an Apostle was murdered by someone in the Church—is preposterous."

"Okay, Dad." There was no sense in arguing. "May I

take your notebook then? The one you kept for Heber? You won't be needing it."

"I don't know what use it can possibly be." But that wasn't a no.

Abbie opened the top drawer of a small chest in the corner of the cluttered study. Recently graded papers were stacked, rather precariously, on top. The notebook wasn't there.

"It would be here, wouldn't it?"

Her dad came over to cabinet. "That's odd. I'm sure I put it back." He opened all the drawers and lifted the stack of papers.

"I must've misplaced it," he said, sitting back down at his desk.

Abbie didn't think so. Her dad's office certainly looked like a disaster, piled high with stacks of paper that rose from the floor like stalagmites, but he always knew exactly where everything was.

He stared at his computer screen. Then started typing.

"Dad? You okay?"

"I'm fine, Abish. I have a lot of work to do. I'm sorry that I've misplaced that notebook, but it seems I have."

Abbie saw irritation in his face.

"Do you want to talk about it?

"Not really." Her dad leaned forward in his chair. "Abish Taylor, I know this Church is true. I believe our Prophet guides with revelations from our Heavenly Father. Our leaders have chosen a path—thus far—that does not include the practice of plural marriage. In 1978, President Kimball restored the priesthood to black men. Could our current president or some president in the future restore the practice of plural marriage? Yes. Absolutely."

He was telling her the truth, his truth, anyway.

"I know you think this meeting the night Heber passed away is some kind of smoking gun. I don't think so at all. What it sounds like is thoughtful deliberation about a sensitive subject. The fact that Port and Heber disagreed can hardly surprise you. They had very different approaches to most things in life. This was certainly not the first time they'd been at loggerheads."

"But it was the last," Abbie pointed out.

Her dad flashed her a look that could slice through frozen meat, but she went on.

"If Heber suspected plural marriage was already being practiced . . ."

"Abbie, I listened to Brittany Thompson. I saw her children and I saw her pregnant belly. I have no reason to suspect her of lying, but I haven't spoken to President Bragg. There may be a perfectly reasonable explanation—"

"A perfectly reasonable explanation?" Her voice was rising, in volume and register. Breathe in. Breathe out.

"Dad, I'll let you get back to work." Abbie walked around the desk, leaned over, and kissed her dad's cheek. "I'm glad you're doing well."

"Thank you, Abish. Promise me you won't jump to hasty conclusions."

"I promise."

★ ★ ★

By the time Abbie got back to Pleasant View, Clarke had settled in the conference room with all the evidence from both crime scenes.

He looked up from the table, holding Heber's cell phone, when Abbie walked in. "I've got confirmed alibis for everyone except Port, Bowen, and Caleb Monson. The way I see it, if we can figure out which one of these men could have been at the top of the cliff when Bryce Strong was killed, we'll have our man." Clarke's productive morning had sparked some much-needed optimism.

"That's if we think the same person killed both Heber and Bryce Strong." Abbie hated to be a wet blanket.

"You think it may be different people?" Clarke asked.

"I don't think we can rule it out at this point. We need an accurate timeline for what happened between when that camera in the boardroom was turned off and when Heber veered off the road. How long does it take to drive from Salt Lake that time of night? Was it possible for Port, Bowen, or Caleb to have raced ahead of Heber?"

"If you take I-15 from the Church Administration Building to Huntsville, it will take about just over fifty minutes. You take 89, it'll take closer to an hour."

"That's less than a ten-minute difference," Abbie said, pointing out the obvious. If one of the men whose names were circled in red on the whiteboard had killed Heber, he hadn't left himself a lot of time. He would have been rushed.

Abbie's mind drifted back to images of that horrible night, that moment when she'd realized the dead drunk driver wasn't a drunk driver at all. She thought about the story only she had heard from Bryce Strong. She thought about the ME report and the fact that a simple rock had been used to kill a man.

"Is that phone still charged?" Abbie asked.

"It is." Clarke handed Heber's phone to Abbie. The last time she'd held it, she had been trying to verify what Eliza had told her. Eliza's incoming calls still weren't there. Abbie then scrolled through the outgoing calls. The last call Heber had made before his death was to his wife. It had lasted nearly fifteen minutes. The second-to-last call was to PORT. It had lasted twenty-four minutes.

"What do you think?" Abbie faced the phone to Clarke. He looked at the call history.

"We need to find out about those calls. Let's talk to Sister Bentsen first. It'll be simpler."

Clarke was right. There was good reason to speak with Port, but Abbie had learned the hard way that in this state it was wise to play nice with Church leaders. Abbie had another reason for agreeing with Clarke's practical approach. She didn't want to tip her hand. The longer she could keep Port from knowing she knew about the meeting, the better.

THIRTY-THREE

"Abish, what a delightful surprise!" Eliza Bentsen opened the front door of her Huntsville home. "Please, come in."

Clarke and Abbie followed Eliza Bentsen into the living room. Floor-to-ceiling windows looked out over Pineview, shimmering in the sun. The darkness of the last time Abbie had been there seemed distant, like a memory from a movie. Eliza took Abbie's hand in her own and squeezed it, before they all sat down, Abbie next to Eliza on the sofa. Clarke sat across from them on a love seat.

"We're trying to get an accurate timeline for the night of the accident." Abbie touched Eliza's arm. "I know this might be hard."

Eliza patted Abbie's hand. "You don't need to worry about me. What do you need to know?"

"Well, first, the night I came to tell you about the accident, you said you'd been calling Heber all night and he hadn't picked up. We can't find any evidence of those calls on his phone."

Eliza put her hand to her chin. "Did I say that? Oh my, I must have been confused. So much of that night is a blur."

"That's okay. Let's walk through it now. You said it wasn't uncommon for Heber to have late meetings in Salt Lake."

"That's correct. I've been an Apostle's wife for a long time, dear Abish. I know the sacrifice that comes with serving the Lord."

"And the night of the accident was just like other nights when Heber had meetings in Salt Lake?"

"Yes."

"Nothing unusual?" Abbie asked. "Heber didn't mention any concerns he might have had about that particular meeting?"

Eliza coughed. She then pulled a cough drop from her pocket, unwrapped it, and put it in her mouth. "I'm sorry about this terrible cough. It doesn't seem to want to leave."

Abbie waited for Eliza to answer her question, then after a few beats repeated, "Heber didn't say anything to you about this meeting?"

"You know their work is sacred. Heber wouldn't discuss it with me."

In another state, in another religion, the idea that a husband and wife would keep such important parts of their lives from each other might seem strange, but Abbie knew of couples who didn't even talk about shared trips to the temple once they left the walls of the Lord's house. Secrecy in the name of what was sacred was a well-established practice.

"You're sure?" Abbie asked.

"I am," Eliza responded. She coughed gently again. "Abish, is there something about the meeting in Salt Lake I should know?"

"We have reason to believe it was contentious." Even though Eliza was like family, Abbie's professionalism kept her from telling Eliza everything about the investigation.

"Contentious?" Eliza's eyes were wide.

"There may have been some impassioned debate," Clarke said.

Eliza turned to Clarke. "How could that be? The Brethren don't argue, and if they did, they certainly would have good reason. And they would never discuss their reasons or their disagreements with any of us."

"Well, the recording is pretty clear," Clarke answered.

Abbie's stomach clenched. Clarke shouldn't have mentioned the recording, even to Eliza Bentsen.

She jumped in to change the subject. "The last call Heber made was to you. It looks like you spoke for about fifteen minutes. Do you remember that conversation?"

Eliza Bentsen studied her hands for a moment, then looked up at Abbie. Her eyes were misty. "I've thought a lot about that night and the last time I saw Heber alive. I made him whole-wheat toast and a soft-boiled egg that morning for breakfast. I had an early meeting with the sisters from Relief Society, so I left him in the kitchen, eating his breakfast and reading. On my way out, I kissed him on his head. By the time I got back, he'd left for Salt Lake."

Eliza coughed, then patted Abbie's forearm. "I know I'm rambling on. To answer your question, I don't remember the substance of the call. Heber always called me before he left Salt Lake. He's done that for over thirty years. We chat about our day, and he tells me what time he'll be home. Whatever we talked about the night of the accident was just like all the other calls. I wish I could remember something that would have set it apart, but I can't."

"That's okay," Abbie said. Eliza Bentsen lived in a world where wives weren't supposed to ask too many questions. "Maybe you can provide some insight into something else. Do you know if there were any unresolved issues between Heber and Port?"

Eliza Bentsen, like the Taylor family, called President Hinckley by his nickname. Abbie had tried to sound neutral, friendly even, but when she looked at Eliza's reaction, she knew she hadn't succeeded.

"Issues?" Eliza said the word as though it were a swear word. "No. None that I know of."

"Okay." Abbie nodded. "One last thing, have you heard of a man called Caleb Monson?"

"No. I can't say that I have. I know a lot of Monsons and a number of men named Caleb, but not a Caleb Monson."

Abbie pulled her phone out her pocket and scrolled through to a photo of Caleb Monson. She handed the phone to Eliza.

The older woman looked at the image. "I don't recognize him, but I'm not very good with faces. For all I know, he could be in our stake." She shook her head. "I'm sorry, Abish. I wish I could help you more."

"You've been great, Eliza. Thank you." The three of

them stood. Abbie turned and gave Eliza Bentsen another hug. "We've got to get going."

"Of course. May I send you away with some lemon bars? I made a full batch yesterday, and there's no way I can finish all of them before they get stale."

"With pleasure," Abbie said. "I love lemon bars."

"I know you do." Eliza smiled and disappeared from the living room. When she returned with a plastic container, Abbie and Clarke were at the door. Abbie took the bright-yellow pastries. "Thank you, Eliza. Please call me if you remember anything about that call. Anything. No detail is too small."

"I will, Abish. I will."

THIRTY-FOUR

Abbie and Clarke had spread out in the conference room looking through anything they might have missed. Most of the lemon bars were gone. Abbie had eaten two and Clarke had inhaled at least five. Abbie's phone beeped.

"Oh, darn it. I have to go," she said.

Abbie had completely forgotten that it was the day of her disciplinary council hearing. She would have forgotten it entirely had she not set a reminder on her phone.

Abbie rushed to her house to change into something appropriate for church. If she could forget how despondent her father had been when he was disfellowshipped, she might have skipped the disciplinary council altogether. She worried if she didn't go, though, it would reflect badly on her dad. Oh, how she hated the power Port had over her family.

Church-convened councils to sanction members was a tradition stretching back to the tumultuous years in the 1840s. Originally, they were meant to "save the souls of transgressors, protect the innocent, and safeguard the purity, integrity, and good name of the Church." Abbie felt fairly confident her transgressing soul was beyond saving, but she could pretend otherwise for her dad.

Abbie entered a church building she'd never set foot in before to meet, for the first time, a Stake President and Bishop who would be passing judgment on her life. She knocked on the Bishop's door and was told to enter.

Abbie opened it and did her best to not let her jaw drop. Two men she had never met before were sitting next to someone familiar—Elder Kevin Bowen.

The Stake President and Bishop introduced themselves. Both men were pompous in a way unique to those who peaked in middle management. Bowen, though, wasn't pompous, but then again, he hadn't peaked in middle management.

Abish watched the two men who didn't know her size her up.

She stretched out her hand to the man who'd identified himself as the Stake President. "Hello, Abish Taylor. I believe you're expecting me."

"Please have a seat." The Stake President waved at the metal folding chair.

It was not lost on Abbie that the men sat in comfortably padded chairs while Abbie was relegated to cold metal.

"How are you?" the Stake President asked.

"I'm well, thank you," she said. "And you?"

"Uh, I'm . . . we're all . . . uh . . . good," the Stake President stammered. "I'm sure you know who Elder Kevin Bowen is."

"Yes." Abish looked directly at Bowen. "We've met."

Abbie sat with her knees together, her hands resting in her lap. Her lips were turned up ever so slightly at the corners. She waited in silence.

Beads of sweat were beginning to form on the Stake President's upper lip.

"Do you mind if we start with a word of prayer?" the Bishop piped in.

"Not at all," Abbie said.

Everyone in the room bowed their heads.

"Our dear Father in Heaven," the Bishop prayed, "we are very grateful for this evening and for the many blessings that we enjoy in our lives. We are grateful that we can meet together now. We pray for Thy spirit to be here to guide us in this disciplinary council. We are grateful for the restored Gospel and for the Church. We say these things in the name of Thy son, Jesus Christ. Amen."

After everyone but Abish said "Amen," the Stake President spoke. "You understand why you are here?"

"Actually, I do not," Abish said. "The letter, which bears your signature, merely informed me that a disciplinary council would be convened tonight, and I was welcome to attend and make a statement concerning apostasy and conduct unbecoming a member. Would you be so kind as to clarify?"

"Uh, well," the Stake President said, "It's a weighty responsibility to be the Stake President. You are given keys, priesthood keys. You are responsible for the spiritual life of all members who reside in your stake. It is a large responsibility.

It would be much easier if a member of the Quorum of the Twelve told me what I should do, but I am guided solely by the spirit to serve the Lord." The Stake President shifted in his chair.

Abish said nothing.

"Are you, uh . . . would you like to, uh, make a statement?" he asked.

"Well," Abbie responded. "I'd like to understand what prompted you to convene this council before I weigh in. Unless I'm mistaken, we've never met. I also don't believe I have ever met the gentleman who is the Bishop of the Twelfth Ward. If you were prompted to convene this council, surely you can help me better understand why—"

The Stake President interrupted Abish before she could finish her question. He seemed to have found his footing. "Are you a member of the Church of Jesus Christ of Latter-day Saints?"

"Yes, I suppose technically I am, in that I was baptized and confirmed as a child, and I haven't asked to have my name removed from Church records."

"Then you are a member of my stake and a member of the Twelfth Ward. We are your immediate church leaders. You know why you're here. We have the authority—the responsibility—to do everything to help you return to our Heavenly Father. That is what this council is about; it's about things you've done, things you are doing, that a member of the Church should not be doing. Things you must stop doing."

A hint of a smile played on Abbie's lips. Watching the

Stake President and the Bishop was turning out to be sort of fun.

"May I say a few words?" Bowen turned to the Stake President whom he was about to rescue from his own bungling, self-important Church talk.

The man nodded his head with vigor. "Of course, Elder Bowen."

"Sister Taylor, perhaps you have a point that the letter you received was vague. We can remedy that now. We have convened tonight to perform a disciplinary council in your behalf, which may end in a few different ways: no action, formal probation, disfellowshipment, or excommunication. Do you understand?"

"Yes, I do." Abbie understood what Bowen was saying, although she'd never understand why the Church used the phrase *in your behalf* instead of *on your behalf*. Perhaps some linguist at BYU could explain it.

"The reason for this council is that you are reported to be in apostasy and, in your capacity as a police officer, you might act in ways that could discredit and harm the Church. Your actions may have temporal and eternal consequences not only for you, but for your family members as well."

The mention of Abbie's family hit the mark. While the Stake President and Bishop sat in bewilderment, Abbie understood. Bowen had done what Port had sent him to do. He didn't need to say anything else. She understood her father's membership in the Church depended on her.

"Do you understand?" Bowen asked.

"You've made yourself clear," Abbie said.

"You understand that if we see evidence that your behavior has not changed, there will be consequences."

"I understand."

The Stake President, eager to reassert his authority, started in again. "I want to share my testimony. I know the Gospel is true. I know Jesus is the Christ and He is the head of His one true Church restored through the Prophet Joseph Smith, who saw God the father and His son and brought forth the Book of Mormon by the power of God. I know the Church is guided by our Prophet through direct revelation. I know families can be eternal, and the only way to find joy and happiness is by living Gospel principles. I say these things in the name of Jesus Christ. Amen."

Bowen and the Bishop said "Amen." Abbie did not.

THIRTY-FIVE

SECURITY UP AND RUNNING AT YOUR PLACE.

Flynn's was the first text Abbie read when she climbed into her Rover in the church parking lot.

THANKS! YOU THERE?

Abbie stared at the screen of her phone, waiting for him to respond.

NOPE. AT THE RIVERDALE HOUSE.

Abbie started the engine and drove to Flynn's.

When she walked through the front door without knocking, she startled Flynn in the kitchen, shirtless in his boxers. She should have knocked. What was she thinking?

"I didn't know you were coming," he said. He wasn't embarrassed; he was simply stating a fact.

"I'm sorry. I should have told you. I can leave. I wasn't thinking." Abbie was gripped with the thought that someone was upstairs in Flynn's bedroom. A toxic mixture of nausea and jealousy bubbled in her stomach. Then she chastised herself. She had no claim on Flynn.

Flynn smiled, a slow delicious smile. He walked over to Abbie and wrapped his arms around her.

"You look like you could use a drink."

He took her hand, kissed it, and guided her to the library. He poured her a single finger of Scotch and handed her the glass. Then he said, "Let me put on some clothes."

The words *if you must* drifted into Abbie's head. She let them pass without verbalizing them and drank her medicine.

When Flynn reappeared, he was wearing jeans and a T-shirt.

"Was the council everything you hoped?" He poured himself two fingers.

"Bowen was there."

Flynn raised an eyebrow. "I guess the Taylor family warrants special treatment."

"Emphasis on the 'family' bit. The message was back off."

"Or else what? Excommunication?" he asked. "No one can really think that's a threat."

"Not for me. For Dad."

"Oh." Flynn's tone changed from playful to somber. "They're not pulling punches."

"No, they're not," Abbie said. "Bowen mentioned apostasy."

Flynn grinned, "Well, you are an apostate, my darling."

"Then he said I was there because as a member of the Church and a police officer, I might act in ways that could discredit and harm the Church."

"Well, that's true. You have that CD. Can you even imagine if that got out?"

"That's just it. Nobody knows about the CD but you, Clarke, my dad, and me. You didn't tell anyone and my dad wouldn't dare even admit he knows about it, not after his disfellowshipment scare."

"Your boss, Henderson, he's old friends with Bowen, right?" Flynn asked.

"Yeah, old missionary companions, but Henderson is out for a few days. I just barely told Clarke about it. I don't think there's any way Henderson found out."

"You sure about that?"

"No, I'm not." Henderson could easily have talked to Clarke without Abbie knowing about it; it could've just slipped out without Clarke even meaning to say anything.

Abbie set down her empty glass on the coffee table. "Eliza Bentsen may know, too."

"Heber's wife?"

Abbie leaned back on the couch.

"Clarke let it slip that there was a recording. Eliza didn't seem to care. She didn't ask about it, but if she talked to someone after we met with her this morning and she just happened to mention that the police had a recording . . ." Abbie sighed. "The people Eliza Bentsen talks to are people Port talks to. If Port thought there was any risk that we had a recording of that meeting, he wouldn't think twice about sending Bowen to make sure I know to color inside the lines."

"Are you going to?" Flynn asked.

"I've never been good at staying inside the lines."

Flynn set his glass next to Abbie's. He leaned over and kissed her. "I know."

Whatever worries Abbie had about the murders, about her dad, about the fact that Port knew about the CD receded to the farthest recesses in her mind. Her breathing quickened. She kissed him back. She slipped her hand under his T-shirt and dragged her fingers along the top of his jeans, resting it finally on the top button.

"Can you stay tonight?" Flynn asked. "The house is empty."

She wanted to, but she was torn. Part of her felt the professional push to finish her work, part of her questioned whether she was ready to move on from Phillip, and there were probably a whole slew of things in her subconscious that were making her feel like she needed to go.

Abbie sat up, ran her fingers through her hair, and stood. "I've got work."

"And?"

"I need to go home and do it," she said.

"You can stay here," he said, and then added, "I can be a good boy."

"It's not you I'm worried about."

"As you wish." Flynn stood up next to her. Close. His hand touched the back of her neck. He kissed her again, sliding his fingers down her spine and resting his hand in the small of her back. It took every ounce of discipline for Abbie to extricate her body from a situation it so desperately wanted.

He had to quote *The Princess Bride*.

★ ★ ★

Abbie breathed in the warm summer night as she quietly closed Flynn's front door behind her. Sparkles of light punctured the navy sky. She climbed into the Rover and reminded herself that she was making the responsible decision. Her mind needed rest to work. She knew she was missing something, but what?

As she drove the mostly abandoned roads between Riverdale and Huntsville, she tried to force her mind into a disciplined review of the facts. This case was straining her because, like everyone else who had grown up Mormon in Utah, Abbie had an aversion to polygamy the same way ex-smokers despised even a whiff of tobacco. Something deep in her pioneer DNA caused a visceral reaction against the very idea of it. Was Abbie not putting facts together because she was blinded by her own prejudice against the practice of polygamy?

Abbie didn't know the answer. When she climbed under her own covers, she knew only two things: her brain needed sleep and her body wanted Flynn.

THIRTY-SIX

It took Abbie a moment to orient herself when she heard the buzzing. Her hand instinctively reached for the button on the top of her bedside clock, but as her eyes focused in the gray light, she realized it was her phone, not her clock, making the sound. Abbie squinted to read the name: CLARKE.

"Bad news. I got a call from a friend who's an officer in Midway," Clarke said as soon as she answered. "President Bragg has a second home up there."

Abbie's heart started pounding too hard. Please, please, let it not be Brittany.

The silence before Clarke spoke again lasted only a fraction of a second, but it seemed like an eternity. "Brittany Thompson died last night. Anaphylactic shock."

Abbie felt dizzy.

"Were there kids at Bragg's house? Mary, Jacob, Moroni?"

"Who?" Clarke asked.

"A little girl, a boy, and a baby?"

"No. I think my friend would've mentioned something

like that, but I can double-check. President Bragg said the young woman was a family friend who had been struggling. He was counseling her."

Abbie couldn't believe Brittany Thompson was dead.

"Taylor, you okay?"

"Yes." Abbie said the word deliberately, the lie heavy on her tongue. She wasn't okay. She was anything but okay. Bryce Strong's death was already on her watch, and now so was Brittany Thompson's. It was worse with Brittany. Abbie had delivered Brittany Thompson to the house where she died.

"Do you know where Brittany's body is?" Abbie asked. If protocol had been followed, Brittany Thompson should be at the Office of the Medical Examiner by now.

"I imagine it's in Taylorsville."

Abbie winced. She had said the same thing, hundreds of times, *it* when referring to the body of a human being. Images flashed in Abbie's head of Brittany drinking chocolate milk in her dad's kitchen, of her playing with her kids, of her holding her new baby. Brittany was not an *it*.

"I'm heading there now." Abbie showered and dressed. This terrible feeling in the pit of her stomach was what it felt like to know someone had died because of you. If Abbie had only tried a little harder to talk the young mother out of going back, if she had refused to drive her, if she had done one of a thousand things, those three missing kids would still have had a mother. They were alive, Abbie told herself. As she drove to Taylorsville, guilt and regret swirled in her stomach, but there was one little spot of peace. The kids were fine. She was certain. Their existence was the whole reason for this strange experiment.

★ ★ ★

Abbie knocked on the door of Dr. Eriksen's office.

"Come in!"

Abbie wasn't surprised the ME was in already. Between the opioid and suicide crisis, there were too many deaths.

"Good morning. Do you have a few moments?"

"Detective Taylor? Sure." Dr. Eriksen was wearing thin-framed rectangular glasses that gave him a more intellectual look than the last time Abbie had seen him. He looked more like a ski instructor than one of the top MEs in the state. His tan and lack of a belly hinted that when he wasn't working, he was outside.

"I'm looking into the Brittany Thompson death."

"Thompson?" He typed something on his keyboard. "Oh. Here it is. Last night. I wasn't here when the body came it. Looks straightforward. Woman. Mid to late twenties. Anaphylactic shock."

Eriksen looked back at his screen. "There's a note that Dallin Bragg, the man who called the ambulance, told us he had no idea what caused it."

"Could someone her age not know she was at risk for this kind of reaction?" Abbie asked.

"It's possible, but unlikely."

"Is there any way for you to tell if she had a prescription or something to indicate that she knew she had allergies?"

Eriksen typed something on his keyboard and stared at

234 | D. A. Bartley

the screen in silence a beat longer than was comfortable. "This isn't such a straightforward case, is it?"

"I have a sinking feeling it's not." Abbie had much more than a feeling that this death wasn't straightforward.

"These records go back ten years. It looks like Brittany has had an ongoing prescription for an epinephrine auto-injector, an EpiPen, since she was a teenager. She has a severe allergy to fish and seafood."

He studied the screen again. "She wasn't wearing a medical alert bracelet when she came in."

"Would you expect her to be?" Abbie asked.

"Yeah, I would. It's pretty standard now." Abbie kicked herself. She couldn't recall if Brittany had worn a medical bracelet. How could Abbie have completely missed notic-ing something like that?

Eriksen scrolled through his screen while Abbie waited. When he finally looked up, he asked, "What's going on?"

"What do you mean?"

"Detective Taylor, you've had three deaths in a span of less than two weeks. Granted, different manners of deaths, different demographic profiles for each victim, but all looked accidental at first blush. Heber Bentsen and Bryce Strong weren't accidents, though. Now I'm beginning to wonder if Brittany Thompson was either."

The printer in the corner of Eriksen's office whirred to life, then started spitting out sheets of paper. When the printer was silent, Eriksen stood and picked up the stack of papers. He handed it to Abbie.

"This is everything we have on Bentsen, Strong, and

Thompson. I'll call if anything strange turns up." He scrawled a telephone number on the upper corner of the top page in the stack. "This is my personal number. Call me if you need help. I'm serious."

"Thank you."

Abbie sat in her car for a few minutes, flipping through the pages. Nothing jumped out except for the fact that the deaths had been meant to look accidental, but they weren't. It was like someone had thought far enough ahead to come up with a plan, but not far enough ahead to make it a good one.

There was no evidence yet that Brittany's death wasn't a tragic accident. Still, Abbie needed to see where it happened. She needed to understand. She pulled out of the parking lot at the ME's office and headed to Bragg's house in Midway.

She knocked.

"Come in." Bragg had seen better days. It was past eleven in the morning when Abbie arrived. He was in pajamas. What was left of his white hair was matted on one side of his head and sticking straight up on the other. His eyes were puffy and bloodshot.

"Thank you," Abbie said. "Are you here by yourself?"

"Yes. My wife's visiting her sister in St. George." Bragg walked into the living room and sat down on the couch. There was a pillow at one end and a rumpled blanket near the other end, half of it pooled on the floor. Bragg sat down in the middle. Abbie sat across from him in a matching love seat.

"You're here because you want to talk about Brittany," Bragg said.

Abbie nodded.

"I don't have much to say. We were eating dinner. We'd just started with our soup course when she started choking. Or I thought she was choking. It was awful." The words came out of his mouth like the voice of a virtual assistant. The words were correct, but the intonation was wrong.

"Did you know she had allergies?" Abbie asked.

Bragg stared past her, his gaze unfocused. He didn't respond for a few moments, and then something jerked him back into the present. "What?"

"Did you know she had allergies?"

"I knew she asked about ingredients sometimes. We really didn't spend that much time together . . ."

Abbie waited for him to say something else, explain himself, but he just stared into space. He wasn't telling her the entire truth, but she wasn't sure if that was because he felt guilty because he hadn't known one of his wives had a possibly fatal food allergy or because he felt guilty because he did know.

"What happened then?"

"We ate dinner." Bragg waved his hand toward the open French doors. The table was set; a bouquet of yellow roses filled a crystal vase. The silver breadbasket still had rolls in it. The water goblets were mostly full.

"We had soup first . . . and then, then . . . her face just started swelling up. She started gasping for air. I tried to give her some water, but she couldn't swallow. I called 911, but by the time they arrived, she had already passed. It happened so quickly."

Bragg seemed genuinely shaken. He was sad, but that authentic sadness was layered over something else, some other emotion.

"Where are the kids?" Abbie asked.

"Children?"

"Where are they?" Abbie asked again.

"I don't know what you're talking about. I'm talking to you despite my misgivings because I have the greatest admiration for your father. I cannot—will not—say any more than I have. Brittany's death is a burden I alone must carry. It weighs heavily on my heart, but I assure you that you will find nothing here but a tragic accident. If I were in your position, I would leave this alone."

Was that a threat?

Yes, it was. Despite his red-rimmed watery eyes, Bragg wasn't broken. He was not about to slip up. Abbie's questions wouldn't be answered. He had told her the story he'd told the police. That story wasn't going to change. Abbie had very little hope of finding anything useful, but the fact that Bragg hadn't cleared the table gave Abbie an idea.

"Could you point me to the powder room?" she asked.

"Down the hall. First door on the right." Bragg stared blankly out the window.

The door across the hallway from the powder room was closed. Abbie opened it. It looked like a guest room with all the charm you'd expect of a midrange hotel. Brittany's handbag was sitting on the corner of the bed and the suitcases were on the ground. No car seats. No baby bags. Abbie heard footsteps behind her. She grabbed Brittany's handbag and slung it over her shoulder before stepping back into the hallway and running right into Bragg.

"I thought you said left," Abbie lied. "You said right, didn't you?"

"Yes." Bragg's eyes narrowed. They didn't look sad anymore.

Abbie opened the door to the powder room. She closed it behind her as quickly as she could. She sat down on the closed toilet seat and opened Brittany's handbag. A wallet, some mints, lip gloss, keys, and a bright-yellow EpiPen.

★ ★ ★

"You are not responsible for what happened to Brittany. You know that, right?" The sound of Flynn's voice made Abbie feel a little better, but not much. Abbie was alone in her office at the station with Brittany's bag.

"I don't know that. I could've tried to dissuade her, asked her to wait a few more days. I don't know. Something. Anything."

"She was an intelligent, adult woman. She was following her own principles and beliefs."

"Flynn, she didn't ask to die."

Flynn's voice softened. "No, she didn't, but you couldn't have stopped her."

Maybe not, Abbie thought, but she should have been able to stop the killer. If she'd done her job better, the person responsible for the deaths of Heber and Bryce Strong would be in custody, and Abbie had a sick feeling in her stomach that Brittany Thompson would still be alive.

THIRTY-SEVEN

Abbie opened the top drawer of her desk and took out Brittany's pastel box of tampons, the one she'd brought back from Colonia Juárez. She studied the wedding photo. When she'd first seen it, Abbie had focused on Brittany, the happy bride. It didn't look like coercion, at least not coercion the way most people thought of the word. Then Abbie thought of the Church's eschatology, its focus on marriage and family in the afterlife. The only way for a young woman to reach the highest levels of exaltation in the Celestial Kingdom was through marriage.

Heber had been smart to come to her dad. Professor Taylor's graduate students were among the most devout unmarried LDS women there were: certain of their beliefs and committed to living according to the principles of the restored Gospel. They would not question a Church leader.

Abbie held Brittany's diary, reverently. Before the young mother had died, it hadn't seemed important. Abbie had read the mostly adolescent G-rated musings about sex, pregnancy, and motherhood with a jaundiced eye. But

Brittany adored her two children. She wrote in excruciating detail about their milestones and their personality quirks. She was deeply in love with the man she'd been sealed to in the temple, and she was frustrated with how infrequently she saw him. Instead of blaming him, Brittany blamed herself and her own lack of faith in the face of adversity.

Instead of reading the diary for insight into why a woman would choose this life, Abbie now read each daily entry in search of some clue, some statement that would directly link Port to the Mexican experiment.

I was feeling so alone. I wanted to go back to Utah and live with Dallin. I didn't want my children to be with another family. Then TSC visited. He was sealing another woman to Dallin. He told me not to let my faith waver. TSC reminded me of my covenant and of the glories that awaited me in the Celestial Kingdom. He gave me a blessing and my heart felt light again. I'm so grateful for the gospel, for the Restoration.

TSC. In the nineteenth century, when the members of the Church had first practiced plural marriage, women had used code when referring to their husbands in journal entries. Not without reason. Plenty of LDS men had been jailed for practicing polygamy. Abbie's own ancestor, the third President of the Church, John Taylor, had spent the last years of his life in hiding to avoid prison.

Abbie tapped on her keyboard. She gazed at the page of General Authorities and General Officers, the leadership of the Church. Dozens and dozens of nearly identical looking stamp-sized photos of men stared back at her. All of them were dressed in dark jackets, white shirts, and conservative ties. All but a few were white. Her eyes carefully scanned each row of men from left to right. There must be someone named Theodore Stanley Clayton? Thomas Steven Clark? Tad Samuel Callister? By the time Abbie got to the bottom of the page, where nine women beamed back at her—the leadership of the Relief Society, Young Women and Primary—it was clear that there would be no such easy answer.

"Taylor?" Abbie looked over her computer to see Clarke standing in the doorway.

"Yes?"

Clarke looked like someone had run over his dog. "Chief Henderson, well, there was a POST meeting." POST was the acronym for Peace Officer Standards and Training, the body authorized to discipline police officers. Abbie inhaled and held her breath.

Clarke continued, "It just happened. I wasn't there, but Henderson made some accusations about professional misconduct against you. Word is there'll be an investigation. You're being put on unpaid leave of absence until the matter is resolved."

Abbie slumped in her chair.

"I'm supposed to escort you out of the building," Clarke said with the enthusiasm of a child heading to the dentist.

"Okay. May I grab a few things before I leave?" Abbie asked.

"I'm not supposed to let you take any official police property." Clarke cleared his throat. "Oh! I think I hear my phone ringing. I'll be back in a few minutes to see you out."

Thank you, Clarke.

Abbie inserted a thumb drive into her computer, and then went to the conference room and took pictures of everything on the tables. Finally, she put the box of tampons into Brittany's bag and slung it over her shoulder. Anyone who knew Abbie well would have immediately known she would never own a handbag like Brittany's. Luckily, it didn't seem that anyone knew her that well.

Clarke waited while Abbie asked Hazel to look after her plants until she got back.

"This isn't right," he said once they were standing by her car and no one could hear.

Abbie forced a smile to her lips. "Thanks, Jim." That was the first time she had called him by his first name. He smiled back, but his eyes were sad.

She climbed into her Rover. It was nice that Clarke wanted to help, but if all it took was an unhappy phone call from Bragg to get her kicked off her job, she wasn't very confident that he, or anyone for that matter, would be able to fight for her.

THIRTY-EIGHT

Abbie drove out of the parking lot of the Pleasant View City Police Department. She started toward home, but when she got to the mouth of Ogden Canyon, she decided against it. She pulled into a space in front of Rainbow Gardens to think. Her thoughts were jumbled, like someone had dumped the contents of her head onto the floor, where they shattered into pieces.

Port liked playing puppeteer. He had to be behind this, right? Bragg must have called him after her visit. What did he expect her to do next? Did he think she'd sit this one out and let someone get away with two, possibly three, murders? Was someone watching her place? Was someone watching her dad?

Abbie stared up the canyon, watching the color drain from the sky. Shadows from the trees stretched long. She wasn't sure how long she'd been sitting there, but it was long enough to garner a few stares from people coming and going for dinner at the Greenery.

Abbie's phone vibrated.

She reached for it. "Flynn?"

She explained the day. It sounded worse when she said it all out loud.

"Come over here. I'll cook. You can put your feet up for a few minutes, catch your breath, and figure out what you want to do next," he offered.

She wanted to say yes, but she heard Bragg's voice echoing in her head, from that day when they'd discussed her father's restoration to fellowship: "I expect you'll hear before you get back to your house in Riverdale."

"We can't stay at your place," she said. "Bragg knows where you live."

"No worries." Flynn's cheerfully casual response gave Abbie a glimmer of hope. Maybe things wouldn't only get worse and evil wouldn't triumph. "We can stay in Deer Valley. I've got a place there." *Of course you do,* thought Abbie.

Abbie let herself dream. Flynn could whisk her away to some fabulous cabin overlooking the slopes. This time of year, the aspen leaves would flicker in faint breezes, the ski runs would be shaved swaths of green, and the dark pines would spike toward the sky. Abbie loved the Wasatch Mountains in the summer.

"Abs? You still there? I'm serious. My place is gated within gates. There's no place anyone can get in or out without security knowing about it." A breath. "Plus, we could have dinner at Grappa."

He was pulling out the big guns now. Abbie loved Grappa, as much for the wonderful outdoor tables set among the trees as for its Italian food.

She looked at the time.

"I need to make sure my dad is okay."

"Sure." There was just a hint of disappointment in Flynn's voice. "I'll meet you at your dad's, if that's all right with you?" Under any other circumstances, Abbie would have been aware of the undercurrent. She was giving every indication that she was rejecting him, but under any other circumstances, she wouldn't be. They would already be at Grappa sharing a nice Barolo.

★ ★ ★

"Abish, I wasn't expecting you."

Flynn and Abbie walked into the Taylor living room in all its shabby elegance. The room had once exuded the happiness of lovingly polished wood and vases of freshly cut flowers. It was dusty and unused now. Except for tonight. Her dad had a visitor.

Sitting on the love seat her mother had sanded, stained, and reupholstered was Eliza. Heber's widow smiled at Abbie.

"Your dad and I were just catching up. You must come up to Huntsville for a day. I'm not so good with the grilling, but I'm sure one of your brothers could handle that. Do you remember the camping trips we used to take when you were all little?"

"Of course," Abbie said. "Those were some of the best days of the summer."

Abbie's mind traveled back to those lazy, long weekends at Bear Lake. Those stolen days in the summer were one of the few times when both the Apostle and the professor weren't focused on work. Everyone spent the days swimming, boating, and picking the famous Bear Lake raspberries. When the sun grazed the mountaintops, the dads would grill burgers and hotdogs. There were stories around the campfire and s'mores before the kids all dropped into sleeping bags, exhausted from water and sun.

Abbie's dad stepped in where Abbie's own manners had failed. "Eliza, this is Flynn Paulsen. He's been John's best friend since Scouts. Flynn, this is our dear family friend Eliza Bentsen."

The two exchanged smiles and nice-to-meet-yous.

"I was just leaving." Eliza gave Abbie a hug. "Please stop by the house in Huntsville soon. I'm spending most of my time there now. I know you're busy, but even a short visit would brighten my day."

"Of course," Abbie said. "I'll give you a call as soon as I have some time."

Eliza turned to Professor Taylor. The two embraced like the old friends they were. The thought of there being a new dimension to their friendship flitted across Abbie's mind. After all, her dad was a widower and Eliza was now a widow.

Once Eliza had pulled out of the driveway, Abbie turned to her dad.

"I know you want to put what happened behind you, but I can't. I don't really think you can either. There's a difference between following Church leaders just because they're leaders and following them because they embody principles of decency and virtue. You can't do the former at the cost of the latter."

Abbie kicked herself for her word choice. Had she really just uttered the phrase *principles of decency and virtue*?

"Dad, I don't want anything to happen to you."

Abbie's dad didn't respond. Was he ignoring her on purpose?

"Professor Taylor," Flynn said. "Someone was willing to kill President Bentsen and probably at least two other people connected to your students. It's not unreasonable to think you need to be careful."

"Actually," her dad said to Flynn, "it is." Abbie knew that tone, that tone where her dad shifted from human being to priesthood holder. "If there is anyone we should be worried about, it's Abish. I talked to Brittany. I know what she was doing. As I told my Stake President at my council, I know our leaders may call upon any of us to follow a higher calling, a calling others may not understand." He paused for air, and then said, "Abish has demonstrated an inability to obey and follow the revelations of her elders."

Abbie felt her blood pressure rising. She was here because she cared about her dad, and he was going to lecture her on her lack of faith? Her angrier self wanted to take over and let her dad have it. That version of Abbie would have raised her voice, gone toe-to-toe with her dad in an argument about the authority of priesthood holders to receive revelation for others. Hell, she would have taken on the very notion of ongoing revelation from God. She would have told him she didn't believe in a God at all. She absolutely would have said that the ends almost never justified the means.

She didn't. That Abbie was still part of who she was, but she had moved beyond anger. She understood that while this religion, which had dictated the first two decades of her life, was not for her, it was important to her dad. He wanted to be part of it. Whether he supported all of what the Church did, she wasn't sure, but he was willing to count himself among the number who did. Abbie was not.

Before she could open her mouth, Flynn said, "You make a good point."

Her dad's jaw unclenched.

"It's late," Flynn went on. "Would it be too much of an inconvenience for the two of us to spend the night?"

"Uh, I guess that would be fine," her dad answered.

"Linen closet is still at the end of the hallway upstairs?" Flynn asked.

"Yes."

"I'll go get the beds made up." Flynn left the room and headed upstairs, leaving Abbie and her dad alone.

"Dad, have you found the notebook?"

Abbie's dad rubbed his hands down the front of his trousers. It was an unconscious habit he'd done for as long as Abbie could remember. He did it whenever he had something uncomfortable to say.

"I haven't," he said. "I think I must have lost it."

"Is anything else missing?"

Her dad turned to face her. "Yes, but only research I haven't looked at in a long time."

"Research on what?" Abbie asked.

"Early research on plural marriage, notes from graduate school and my very early career. Well before I was tenured. I did a lot of research from primary sources that even now aren't available online. I spent a summer traveling in Illinois, Ohio, and Missouri. The RLDS let me look through some of the diaries and records they had, ones they won't give to the Church."

RLDS, the Reorganized Church of Jesus Christ of Latter Day Saints, was the church founded after Joseph Smith had been murdered. Emma, Joseph's first wife, did not go west with Brigham Young. She stayed in the Midwest and became a member of the church led by her son, Joseph Smith III.

"What exactly is missing?" Abbie asked.

"I'm not sure. The papers aren't in proper order. It's possible I just moved things and forgot."

Her dad was absent-minded, but not about his research.

He sat down on the love seat. He leaned forward and rested his elbows on his knees, his head in his hands. Abbie wanted to give him a hug, but she knew her dad. He would not appreciate having his emotions acknowledged.

So instead she watched in silence as Professor Taylor choked back whatever he was feeling. Finally, he straightened up. His eyes were watery.

"I love your mom. I want to—I must—be with her again in the Celestial Kingdom. I know she had some unorthodox views of the Church, but she didn't express them to anyone. I have no doubt she is worthy of the highest degree of glory. I want to be, too. If I'm excommunicated and I die before I could repent, before I could be rebaptized . . ."

He couldn't finish his sentence, but Abbie felt the weight of what he was trying to say. Abbie didn't believe in an afterlife, certainly not one with degrees of glory where only the worthy members of the Church could dwell. A promise of exaltation in exchange for paying tithing, going to the temple, not drinking coffee, and following the rules set out by a group of old men who said they talked to God.

Abbie's dad, though—he believed. He believed in temple work; he believed in the degrees of glory sketched out by Joseph Smith; he believed in the Restoration; he believed there was only one true church and the Church of Jesus Christ of Latter-day Saints was it.

A single tear made its way down her dad's cheek. "Abbie, I can't go through another disciplinary council. I know I can't force you to believe, but please hear me. If our Heavenly Father has revealed to the First Presidency that we must practice plural marriage, I will support our leaders."

"Dad." The word came out of her mouth quietly, softly. Abbie used every ounce of discipline to channel her wiser, calmer self. She wanted to yell and storm out of the room, but instead she said, "I believe every adult should be able to create whatever family structure works for them so long as no one gets hurt. I'm not opposed to polygamy. I am, however, opposed to murder."

THIRTY-NINE

Flynn came back downstairs. "I smell cookies," he said, breaking the tension between Abbie and her dad. Flynn led the way to the kitchen at the back of the house, where Eliza had left a plate of chocolate macadamia nut cookies. Flynn sat at the table, and her dad sat across from him. Each took a cookie.

Abbie warmed up some milk, with a little brown sugar and vanilla, and poured three mugs. The three of them sat, eating the cookies and drinking the milk, pretending they had not just had a heated discussion about faith and polygamy.

Her dad finished his milk and a second cookie. He yawned and stood up.

"It's been a long day. I'll see you both in the morning."

Abbie hugged her dad. He drove her absolutely crazy most of the time, especially right now, but he still was her dad. It didn't matter what he believed, as long as he was safe and happy, or as happy as he could be.

She listened as his footsteps receded upstairs and she heard the soft thud of him closing his bedroom door.

Flynn asked, "No chance of a nightcap in this house, is there?"

Abbie couldn't help but smile. She shook her head.

"Is there even a liquor store in Provo?" he asked.

"There must be, but the last time you and I lived in this neighborhood, we wouldn't have been looking for one."

"Nope, we wouldn't have." Flynn chuckled.

They had both been such active members of the Church. Abbie had been the president of all her young women's classes—Beehive, Mia Maid, and Laurel—and finished her personal progress in record time. She'd worn her complete value bracelet for almost all of high school, proud of each colored bead representing different principles: faith, divine nature, individual worth, knowledge, choice and account-ability, good works, integrity, and virtue. All these years later, she still felt the glow of her teachers' praise.

Flynn, like her brother John, had been an Eagle Scout. He had also been the seminary president in high school. He'd served a mission and gotten married in the temple. He had been called to be a Bishop and to serve in the Stake Presidency. Now here he was, wondering whether there was a liquor store in Provo.

"What happened to us?" she asked with a wry laugh.

★ ★ ★

Abbie changed into pink ruffles. It was the only item of clothing in the house, of hers, that she could sleep in.

There had been a time when she thought this fluffy night-gown was inconceivably beautiful. Pale-pink cotton with a pattern of deep-pink strawberries and white flowers. It went without saying that it was modest. The ruffles around the neck nearly reached her chin. It had long puffy sleeves to cover her arms and it hit just above her ankle. She'd spent an entire afternoon with her grandma choosing the fabric and the pattern. Under her grandmother's expert eye, Abbie had cut and fit the pattern; then cut, fit, and basted the muslin; and finally cut, fit, and sewn the nightgown.

She walked to her window. A window she'd never climbed out of after curfew because that would never have occurred to her. She was pulling the curtains closed when a glimmer of light caught her eye. The street was abandoned except for a few parked cars. Without sidewalks, there was nowhere to stroll, not that anyone would be out this time of night anyway. She searched for the light she had seen, but it was gone. Instead of closing the curtains completely, she left them slightly open. She switched off the overhead light, then walked back through the darkness to the window. She waited.

There was the light again. Inside one of the cars parked across the street was a man looking at something on his phone. Abbie squinted. She was always skeptical, even of her own eyes, but the man looked an awful lot like Caleb Monson. Her stomach lurched.

Abbie yanked the curtains closed so that not a single sliver of light could get in or out. She slumped onto her bed. Was Caleb Monson there because of her or because of her dad? Neither answer made her feel very good.

Her thoughts were interrupted by someone tapping on her door with the pads of his fingers. She could barely hear it.

"Flynn?" Abbie whispered through the door.

"Who else?" was the quiet response.

Abbie turned the knob slowly so it wouldn't make a sound. Flynn slipped inside the room and closed the door silently behind him. He stood with his back right against the door. His expression was strange; then Abbie realized he was nervous. Full-on nail-biting scared. She wasn't sure if she'd ever seen him anxious.

"Did you see Caleb outside, too?" Abbie asked.

"What? Caleb Monson? Uh, no," Flynn said. He took a deep breath. "This is about something else. I didn't think I'd be saying this here," he whispered, "but I have to."

Abbie's eyes had adjusted to the dark. She could see just enough of Flynn's face to know something was unsettling him, but she had no clue what it was.

"I love you, Abish Taylor. I've been in love with you in some way or other since we were kids. We have complicated lives. I know that. I have an ex-wife I don't love and five kids I do. You're a widow who still loves the man she married."

Abbie had not been expecting this. She didn't know what to say.

Flynn went on, "None of that makes it impossible for us to have a future together in whatever unorthodox way we choose." He stopped and then, in a voice Abbie could only describe as foreboding, he added, "Whatever we want to do depends upon there being a future. Abs, I don't want you to get hurt or . . . or worse."

Flynn took her hand, and they sat on the side of the bed together, facing the closed curtains.

"I know Heber meant a lot to you, but it's not a given that you have to pursue this case. If Caleb Monson sitting outside isn't a clear enough warning, I don't know what is. In fact, if you want to keep this job as much as you say you do, I think you should lay low until the decision from the POST council meeting. Let Clarke handle things."

Abbie couldn't stop. Someone had killed Heber Bentsen, possibly the kindest man Abbie had ever known.

"I don't think I can live with myself if I don't follow this through," she said. "I know it sounds cliché—shoot, it *is* cliché—but I want justice for Heber. I loved him." Her love for Heber was matched by her guilt about Bryce Strong and Brittany Thompson. They shouldn't be dead.

They sat without saying a word. Even their breathing was silent.

Then Abbie turned to face Flynn. "I love you, too."

Flynn's body relaxed. He stretched his hand toward Abbie, facing up. She slid her hand onto his palm, and he closed his fingers around it.

For one more moment, they enjoyed this simple pleasure. But Caleb haunted the edges of Abbie's brain. She didn't like the fact that a trained soldier with a penchant for cruelty was parked across the street from her dad's house.

"Do you have a gun?"

"I do," Flynn said.

★ ★ ★

"Abish, I have class in an hour. You're not really going to walk with me to campus and wait outside the door, are you?" Professor Taylor asked.

"Nope," Abbie said. "Flynn is."

"You do know you're both being ridiculous."

"That's okay. I'd rather be ridiculous and have you safe than be reasonable and you get hurt."

"Abs, lock the door behind us when we leave," Flynn said. His tone sounded lighthearted, but there was no smile in his eyes.

She snapped, "You do know I'm a cop, right?"

She liked that Flynn worried about her, but too many years of having men think she was incompetent because she was a woman hit a nerve. She exhaled and said, in a distinctly friendlier tone, "Yes, I will lock the door." Abbie turned the deadbolt after two men she loved left for BYU's campus.

Abbie set up in the dining room. She spread out the ME reports Eriksen had given her, set out Brittany's diary, and then opened up her laptop.

The POST council meeting was tonight. She wasn't at all prepared. She wouldn't be. She had hoped—unrealistically—that she'd have something concrete in this case. As it was, she'd probably sit in a hallway while her professional future was decided by a handful of men who'd never liked her to start with.

She started rereading Brittany's diary. She'd been through it, carefully, at least three times since the young mom had died. She stared at Brittany's description of her first meeting with Bragg. It wasn't less stomach churning to read about that encounter for the fourth time. If anything, it seemed worse. All those exclamation points, as if enthusiasm reflected value. There was that damn *TSC* again. Abbie knew TSC had to be Port. It had to be, but there was nothing in Brittany's diary that made any reference to President Hinckley, Port's name in real life. Abbie read through the entry again.

She looked at the initials again. Then it hit her. She understood. How could she have missed it? She grabbed a Post-it and pressed the bright-yellow paper against the top of the page.

None of it made sense if you stepped out of a universe that rewarded unquestioning obedience, but it was clear now.

She had focused too much on *TSC*. Brittany had written about *SB* early on; Abbie had read it, but she'd glossed over it. Now, everything made sense in a deeply disturbing way.

She circled the letters and wrote the word TITLES on the sticky piece of yellow paper. She was so relieved to have finally figured out Brittany's references that she didn't process the cracking. It took a moment to realize what it was. The back door was old and made of wood. Someone had kicked through the locks. In an instant, Abbie was hyperaware of every sound around her. Her mind raced through every possibility. She was ready to fight. She waited for footsteps, but none came. Her gun and phone were in her bag on the sideboard, just a few feet away. Silence. Still no footsteps.

Abbie lunged for her bag. That's when she felt the hand around her neck. It was a big hand attached to an arm of solid muscle. The other hand grabbed her arm and pinned it behind her.

"If you care about your dad," a voice said, "you won't give me any trouble. For some reason, he has friends in high places. You don't."

Abbie twisted her body so she could see the face attached to the voice. Caleb Monson was smiling. He enjoyed watching pain.

Abbie said nothing and let herself be pushed out the back door. A dark-silver BMW SUV was waiting. As she got closer to the car, she recognized the driver. Bowen.

Caleb shoved her into the back seat. She felt his knee at the center of her back. He pushed her to the other side of the car. Her face hit the side of the door before she managed to get herself upright. He climbed in behind her. Before Caleb shut the door, Bowen started the car. He didn't speed off. Instead, he pulled slowly away from the curb and onto the quiet, tree-lined street. Most of the houses still belonged to people from Abbie's parents' generation. Behind the well-maintained lawns were older women sitting in their living rooms doing needlepoint while their husbands read the paper or busied themselves with woodworking in their shops out back. No one was outside.

Bowen didn't say a word. His eyes darted between the road in front of him and his rearview mirror.

Caleb Monson's knee bobbed up and down next to hers. He kept looking out the window to his left, turning as far back as his neck would let him. Something must have caught his eye, because instead of jerking his face back to check on Abbie, he continued to stare out the window.

Abbie had been trained for this, but it was hypothetical. In all her years as a police officer, she'd never been kidnapped. Taking a police officer was a risky proposition. Most criminals preferred to stay as far away from the police as possible, but Abbie wasn't dealing with most criminals. She was dealing with people who didn't think of themselves as criminals at all. That made this situation much more dangerous.

Abbie reached for her door, opened it, and threw herself onto the asphalt. It didn't hurt as much as she'd thought it would, but that might have just been the adrenaline. She stood up only to realize that Bowen had stopped the car and Caleb had jumped out. Caleb grabbed her forearm with such force she thought he might have crushed a bone and hauled her back into the SUV. The sheer pain almost made her scream, but something deep inside her kept her from giving him the satisfaction of knowing he had hurt her.

Abbie was torn about how to act. She didn't know Caleb, but she had read the redacted reports.

"Don't get clever, you bi . . ." Caleb stopped himself before he finished the word. He knew better than to swear in front of Bowen.

Bowen still hadn't spoken. As they kept driving, he was gripping the steering wheel so hard that the tendons inside his wrists were taut. Bowen didn't care that she knew he was driving the car. Bowen, the telegenic poster child for the Church who explained away inconvenient truths in friendly, easy-to-digest sound bites. He smoothed over PR disasters, like Proposition 8, Rob Porter, Bear Ears, conversion therapy, and on and on the list went. Was he making a novice mistake by not caring that she knew he was involved, or did he already know she'd never be able to tell anyone about it anyway?

Bowen turned up Big Cottonwood Canyon. How long had they been driving? Were Flynn and her dad home yet? Her gun and phone were sitting on her dad's dusty sideboard. They'd know she was gone, but there'd be no way to know how to find her.

Abbie forced her mind to stay in the present. She breathed in slowly and watched the beauty of the canyon pass by. Most tourists knew Big Cottonwood in the winter because it was where Brighton and Solitude were. Because of the lake effect, some of the best snow in the world fell here. In the summer it was a beautiful place to hike. Fall was the season Abbie liked best. The aspen turned gold, and depending on how dry the summer had been, there'd be shades of red and copper dabbed throughout the mountainside among deep-green spires of pine trees.

Abbie focused on markers, anything that would give her an indication of where they were going. Bowen turned off Route 190 onto a poorly maintained dirt road. This shiny SUV was going to take some damage. Caleb's attention wandered. They had established he was stronger than she was, and unfortunately, he was at least as well trained. Abbie could hold her own against a man with no professional combat background—someone like Bowen, who even with his daily exercise routine couldn't handle himself in a fight—but when it came to fighting a guy who knew what he was doing, well, that was not a thought Abbie relished. She was in no position to do anything at the moment, and she had a sinking feeling that her prospects were only going to get worse.

FORTY

Abbie tried her best to keep track of how long they'd been driving on this bumpy dirt road, but she'd stopped wearing a watch ages ago when her phone had taken over all her timekeeping needs. It was a long drive, at least fifteen minutes before Bowen slowed down. He parked the car in front of a two-story, red-brick house. The home looked like it had been built in the late nineteenth century. It was strangely familiar. It looked a lot like Brigham Young's winter house in St. George, except for the fact that it stood alone miles off Route 190 in the middle of nowhere. Someone had taken care with the gardening. Mature lacebark elms provided reliable shade in the front yard. Under different circumstances, the house would have seemed charming.

"Out," Caleb ordered.

Abbie did as instructed. She squinted in the bright sunlight. There wasn't a cloud to be seen. There was no sense in running. Caleb was well rested and would be able to tackle her without exerting much effort. She was worried what he might do if Bowen weren't there. Bowen emerged from the car wearing sunglasses. His jaw was clenched so tightly she could see muscles bulging on either side of the face that was usually so camera-ready cheerful.

Bowen walked up the herringbone red-brick path to the wraparound porch. A porch swing swayed in the breeze. It was painted sage green to match the trim on the doors and windows. Even the entry mat coordinated with the color scheme. Every perfect detail oozed menace.

Bowen opened the old-fashioned screen door with its scroll-like corner brackets. It didn't make a sound, which was unnerving. Abbie had grown up in an old house. One of her favorite sounds was the squeak of a screen door: in the summer it was the only thing between you and the outside. Once it got warm, Abbie's mom opened the front and back doors, along with all the screened windows, so that the house would stay cool with cross-breezes and the shade of the old trees that had been planted when the house had been built. The doors would not be closed again until the nighttime temperatures dipped below fifty-five degrees.

Caleb pushed Abbie through the door.

Just like the outside of the picturesque house, the inside was the epitome of late-nineteenth-century elegance. Dozens of pale-yellow roses had been carefully arranged in a large cut-crystal vase sitting on a handmade lace doily in the center of a round mahogany entry table. Bowen walked through open French doors into the formal sitting room. Abbie followed. Caleb stayed behind, his broad shoulders and barrel-shaped chest blocking the screen door.

"Elder Bowen, hello!" A blandly pretty young woman

with hair the color of wheat smiled at Bowen. "I just finished making some limeade. Would you and your guests like some?" The young woman was wearing a shirt tucked into the waist of a skirt that reached just below the knee. If a black name tag with THE CHURCH OF JESUS CHRIST OF LATTER-DAY SAINTS and SISTER WHATEVER emblazoned on it had been pinned to her blouse, she would have been a picture-perfect image of a female missionary. As it was, the only thing going through Abbie's mind was whether this young woman was one of the names on her dad's list. She and Flynn had found pictures for most of them, but because so many Utah Mormons had descended from the same group of predominantly British and Scandinavian converts in the mid-1800s, it was hard to distinguish one blue-eyed blonde from another.

"Thank you. Limeade sounds great," Bowen said. The words sounded forced to Abbie's ears.

The missionary girl disappeared down a hallway toward the back of the house. Bowen sat down on an antique love seat upholstered in pale-yellow chintz with ivory-and-blue flowers. Abbie sat on a matching chair on the other side of the coffee table. Caleb did not move from his post in front of the screen door.

"Here you go." The young woman set a silver tray with a patina indicating it was older than she was on the coffee table. Three glasses and a pitcher of limeade were arranged on the tray along with a plate of raspberry thumbprint cookies. The porcelain plate had a chintz pattern that almost matched the fabric covering the chairs, love seat, and drapes hanging on either side of the windows overlooking the front lawn. Bowen poured the limeade into the three glasses.

"Let me know if you need anything else. I'll be in the kitchen." The young woman walked back to where she had come from. Caleb stayed motionless at the door.

Bowen handed a glass to Abbie. She took it, but set it down immediately on a silver coaster. The air in Utah was dry. Condensation was not the problem for wooden surfaces that it was in more humid climates, but the formality of the room and years of being trained to behave appropriately triggered Abbie's instinct not to place a cold drink directly on wood.

This whole scene was surreal. Everyone was acting as though it was the most natural thing in the world for a General Authority to sip a soft drink with a kidnapped woman while a strong man guarded the door of a beautiful Victorian home hidden off the main road up Big Cottonwood Canyon.

Bowen took a sip, then placed his glass on the coaster in front of him. That's when Abbie heard heavy footsteps descend the stairs. Abbie had her back to whoever it was who was coming in. Emotions flickered across Bowen's face. The most prominent was dread. Then, disgust? Revulsion?

A raspy voice addressed her before she could see who it was.

"Detective Abish Taylor, so glad you could join us."

Port lowered himself slowly into the seat across from Abbie.

"Mr. Hinckley, let's not pretend that my presence is

voluntary. Your young ex-soldier over there isn't exactly an engraved invitation."

Bowen shifted in his seat.

Port smirked. Abbie had hit her mark. She knew he liked being called "President," which is what made calling him "Mister" so satisfying.

"Feisty as ever. I remember as a girl you had a rebellious streak. I warned your father about indulging that too much, but your mother had a strong hand in your upbringing. Oh, what did she call you kids? 'Independent thinkers'? Yes, that was her term. There wasn't much thinking going on in your sisters' heads, but you, Abish, the Lord blessed with intellectual gifts. Unfortunately, you were not likewise blessed with the common sense to know your place. And now, see where that has brought us?"

The old man shook his head in mock sadness. He leaned forward as far as he could toward the coffee table to reach his glass of limeade. Bowen had taken two sips, but he didn't seem to have an appetite for the cookies. Abbie didn't either. Port took his time leaning back into his chair, the glass of pale-green liquid shaking slightly from a tremor in his hand. He raised the glass to his lips and swallowed.

Port turned to Abbie. "Would you like to start this conversation or shall I?"

Bowen looked like he would rather have his wisdom teeth pulled without painkillers than be where he was at that moment.

Abbie said nothing.

"If you insist." Port reached for a cookie. Watching him

move was like watching a movie in slow motion. Abbie knew he was only a few years older than her own father, but he seemed to be in far worse health, which was saying something. "I don't know how much you've pieced together, but I'm certainly not going to fill you in on any details you don't know, so you can set that whodunit conclusion aside. I've tolerated your meddling since you decided to move back to Utah. I'm not an aggressive man. Generally, I believe violence is reserved for very special occasions. You've put me in a bind. I can't trust you, even if I can trust your dad, which I do, by the way. The hope of celestial union with your mother is enough to keep him in line for eternity. I have to give the old professor credit on that; he married well out of his league. Your mother was a beauty until the day she died. You're lucky you take after her."

As long as Abbie could remember, someone had been telling her how pretty her mom was. People would stop and comment on her mom's skin or her hair. Abbie had hated it when she was little. It was embarrassing—and annoying— to have your friends think your mom looked like some actress. Now that Abbie was older, she felt bad about all the times she'd been angry with her mom for something her mother couldn't possibly control. She wished she could go back in time and erase that teenage resentment.

Abbie kept her mouth closed. Did Port know he'd hit a nerve? Did he sense how much her mother's looks had irritated her as a child and especially as a teenager? She was not going to give him the pleasure of knowing his offhand comment had raised painful memories. Memories that hurt because they brought up her petulant unkindness as a child and her regret about never having had the chance to make amends as an adult. She let silence settle in the room until it became uncomfortable.

"Ah, I appreciate a person who can patiently sit without speaking." Port smiled. "Abish Taylor, I have all the time in the world. It is you, I'm afraid, whose time is in limited supply."

The panic that had motivated her to throw herself onto the street in Provo outside her parents' house returned in a gust. Abbie consciously slowed her breathing to counteract its effect.

"Are you trying to keep yourself calm?" Port smirked. He knew he hit a nerve that time. "The problem is this: I can't come up with any scenario in which détente works. There simply is no trust between us. There is nothing that would make you trust me, and nothing that would make me trust you. That leaves us very few options. Isn't that right, Elder Bowen?" Port's words seemed to startle Bowen, whose complexion had turned the color of the sage wall behind him.

"I'm . . . I'm not sure," Bowen said. If he was trying not to look both nauseated and terrified, his efforts were failing. Port's face turned a deep shade of burgundy. Bowen's stammering response had enraged him.

"Brother Monson." Port turned to Caleb, who was still standing in front of the door. "Take our guest to my study. I need to speak to Brother Bowen for a moment."

FORTY-ONE

Caleb yanked Abbie to her feet. His eyes twinkled as he pulled her across the hall to what in another era would have been called the smoking room. The heavy velvet drapes were drawn so that only a slice of sunlight managed to sneak in through the window. The walls, covered in a silk the color of pine, matched the long curtains. Joseph Smith and Brigham Young stared down, unsmiling, from gilded frames.

Caleb pulled the pocket doors closed behind him and pushed Abbie to the ground.

"Get up," he snarled, his voice no louder than a whisper. Only Abbie could hear him. She did as instructed.

He grabbed her jaw in one hand and pulled her face to his. "Don't give me a reason."

Abbie tried to pull away, but couldn't. Caleb Monson was a man of physical strength. He released her jaw and, in one swift blow, struck Abbie's cheek with the back of his hand. She stumbled, but remained standing.

The last thing she heard before the second blow was Caleb whispering, "Bitch." Then the room went black.

★ ★ ★

When Abbie opened her eyes, she was alone. Her wrists and ankles were tied together with duct tape. She was lying on the leather sofa in the dark-green room with the portraits of the first two Prophets looking down on her. She had no idea how long she'd been out. It was bright outside, so either she hadn't been out for long, or it was tomorrow.

Voices were coming from across the hallway. Abbie swung her bound legs to the ground and sat upright. She stood and hopped on the thick Turkish carpet to the pocket doors. She pressed her ear against the wood.

Port was midsentence. ". . . since the Mormon War. I was able to persuade a few old friends to let our dear Brother Monson be honorably discharged despite a well-established pattern of theft, torture, and murder. Our devout brother has come back home to Tooele to start a new life working for me. Most of the time he takes care of video recordings for our more sensitive meetings, but from time to time, I need his special skill set."

Bowen must have said something, but Abbie had a hard time making it out.

Port responded, "Not a concern. Brother Monson does not want the details of his former life to be disclosed. He has a wife and a baby on the way." Port coughed, then continued, "Remind me, what is her current status at the police department?"

This time, Abbie could hear Bowen's voice clearly. "She's been suspended without pay. The Peace Officer

Standards and Training council is set for tonight. They will determine what action, if any, is warranted."

"Have we managed to find anything particularly helpful for that meeting?"

"I expected there to be a lot more obvious infractions, but there aren't," Bowen answered. "I don't think we want to mention the recording of the last meeting of the Quorum."

"No, we certainly do not."

There was a brief moment of silence, and then Bowen spoke again. "May I speak frankly, President?"

"Yes," Port said. "You have earned that privilege."

"I'm worried that what we're doing—what we've done—that it isn't good for the Church. I don't think an objective observer would look kindly on what has happened. I mean to say—"

"Ah." Port exhaled the word slowly. "Now I understand why you have such a heavy heart. Don't worry. Surely you know by now that there is no such thing as an 'objective observer.' We have members of the Church. They've already made up their minds about what is true. Facts don't concern them. We don't need to persuade them. They live according to what we—the leaders of the Church—tell them. If we say doubt is bad, they work on their faith. If we say dissent is bad, they stay silent. We've told them to only believe information that affirms their faith. And that's what they do."

Abbie didn't know what Bowen's reaction was. He didn't speak. Port added, "You know, Brittany Thompson

272 | D. A. Bartley

didn't even ask who her husband would be. It didn't matter to her because she knew I was revealing our Heavenly Father's truth. Her testimony was strong. The Lord will forgive her momentary lapse in judgment."

Abbie pulled her ear away from the door. A chill settled around her in the dark room.

FORTY-TWO

Abbie watched a few dust motes dance in a long line of bright light that stretched from the top of the heavy curtains to the floor. It must be early afternoon by now. Her dad and Flynn must have come home. They must have seen the broken back door and her gun and her phone left on the sideboard in the dining room. They would know something was wrong. Really wrong.

Abbie took stock of the room. Although she could hop from one place to another, there were no obvious sharp edges she could use to cut through the duct tape. Her eyes moved methodically from floor to ceiling, starting at the left side of the pocket doors.

Abbie hopped to the fireplace. The mantel looked like marble from where she was sitting. That could work. As she got closer, though, she saw that it was wood painted to look like stone. Just like the Tabernacle. Still, the edges were straight.

"What do you think you're doing?"

Caleb's voice boomed behind her. She jumped around to face him as he grabbed her by the upper arm.

"Just when we're going to give you lunch, you go and do this." He hit her across the face with the back of his hand again. Hard enough to make her lip bleed, but nothing more.

"There's no need for the restraints," Port was standing behind Caleb.

Caleb pulled a knife from his belt and sliced through the thick silver tape. Abbie circled her wrists and stretched her fingers. Slowly, circulation returned. As Caleb leaned down to cut through the tape binding her ankles together, Abbie was tempted to push her knee into his nose.

"Don't think about being cute," he growled, and ushered her into the dining room.

Port took his place at the head of the table. "Please, have a seat."

The damask tablecloth was snow white. Two silver bowls, overflowing with yellow roses tinged with peach, flanked an elaborate candelabrum at the center. The table was set for six.

Three young ladies with round bellies of different sizes bustled through the room, arranging rolls, roast beef, green beans, a salad, and potatoes on a long sideboard. Abbie's stomach rumbled loudly enough that she knew Caleb heard it. He pushed her toward the head of the table, to Port's right. Abbie sat down. The pretty sister missionary who brought them limeade sat across from Abbie. Port took the young woman's hand and kissed it. Caleb sat next to Abbie.

Bowen sat next to the sister missionary. The place setting at the other end of the table remained empty.

Port folded his arms and bowed his head. "Our Father in Heaven . . ."

After everyone but Abbie had said "Amen," the pregnant trio plated food from the sideboard. The most pregnant of the three placed a porcelain dish with an embossed gold beehive in front of Abbie. Port was already chewing roast beef from his plate piled high with everything but green vegetables.

Abbie cut into a slice of perfect pink roast beef. It was as good as it smelled. She focused on the food. The water had a minerality that made Abbie think it must have come from a deep well. She looked out the window and saw long stretches of solar panels. This house had been retrofitted to survive off the grid.

No one at the table spoke until Port had eaten everything on his plate. While others were still eating, one of the pregnant young ladies swept in through the swinging door that separated the kitchen from the dining room. She silently whisked Port's plate away and refilled it, this time with slightly less food. Still, nothing green.

Port cleared his throat. "Our circumstances now are exactly as described in Genesis chapter sixteen and in Jacob book two. The Church depends upon our young women bearing children. What we're doing is no different than when Sara gave Hagar to Abraham."

Bowen bowed his head so low over his food that Abbie could see only the top of his head

Port smiled. "Now is the time for us to bring those last souls from the preexistence here for the final battle. These children must be born from our strongest leaders and our most devout young women. Some members, even the Prophet, are not ready for this part of the Restoration, but we can't risk the success of the restored Gospel because of one rogue apostate detective from Pleasant View."

Abbie looked around the table. The young women all smiled at Port with unadulterated admiration. Caleb Monson sported a satisfied sneer. Bowen looked queasy.

Bowen stood up. "President? I believe I told you I have an appointment with Brother Nielson to discuss our progress on the new Sunday schedule, as well as some possible changes to the temple ceremony." The Church had been on a campaign to make itself more user-friendly. There were rumors that the three-hour sessions every Sunday Abbie had known as a girl were being shortened to a mere two-hour commitment. A host of other changes were under way, too, changes to burnish the shiny veneer of the Church. Abbie hadn't heard about possible changes to the temple ceremony, but then again, she wouldn't have.

"Did you mention that?" Port responded. He spoke each word as if it were a sentence of its own. "It must have slipped my mind." He took a bite of potato and chewed. "Well, if you must leave us, Brother, then you must."

Bowen was halfway to the door when Port added, "We must not share sacred information with those who are untrained in the ways of the Lord. The untrained cannot think clearly for themselves."

Bowen tilted his chin toward his chest. Abbie saw him clench his jaw. He said nothing and let the door close behind him.

The air in the room felt heavy even with cheerful young women scurrying about, clearing plates and bringing in silver platters of brownies, cookies, and tiny pink cupcakes. The women placed glasses of milk in front of the four remaining at the table. Caleb reached for the brownies. The young sister missionary sipped her milk.

"You're eating for two now," Port said as he reached over and placed his hand on her flat stomach.

The young missionary took a tiny pink cupcake and slowly peeled back the pleated paper cup. She set the confection back down on her small porcelain plate. Port glanced at her. She picked up the cupcake again and started eating.

"And now to you, Abish. I must admit you are proving to be quite a challenge, but, fear not, I have the faith of Abraham on Moriah."

"If you recall, that parable ends with Isaac walking away."

"So it does." Port's lips curled toward his ears, showing off teeth yellow from age. "Are you waiting for the angel of the Lord to save you?"

"As it turns out," Abbie said, "I am not."

Abbie was on her feet before Caleb knew what had happened. He knocked over his milk and grabbed her arm.

"You're not going anywhere until the President says so." He tried to yank her back toward him, but she did the only thing she could think to do. She bit down on his hand. Caleb screamed and let go. She could taste blood on her teeth and it wasn't hers. She had dashed toward the front door when she saw a rectangle of light shimmering on the entryway table. There was a cell phone beside the vase of roses. Abbie grabbed it, stuffed it into her back pocket, and darted onto the porch. She made a decision in less than a heartbeat: up the mountain instead of down. Her stamina would be worth more on tougher terrain. She had barely scrambled up the mountainside into the trees when she heard the screen door slam.

Not much of a head start.

* * *

It would have been tough hiking under the best of circumstances, and Abbie was not going to have anything near the best circumstances. The worst heat of the day was beginning. It would be hours before the unrelenting sunshine would allow cool air to breeze through the canyon. Abbie scrambled up the rocky slope toward a copse of pine trees. Some spots on the mountain were so steep she had to grip dry earth and hope it wouldn't give way as she pulled herself upward. Caleb was somewhere below. She heard grunting and the occasional swear word, but she didn't dare take the time to glance behind her.

The ground was parched from the normal string of cloudless, rainless skies that stretched over Utah from May to September. Caleb was solid muscle and big. The dry dirt that withstood Abbie's grasping disintegrated under his weight.

By the time Abbie reached the pine trees, her hands and arms were covered with cuts and what would soon be bruises. Something had ripped through the fabric on her left leg. Blood mixed with dirt ran down her shin, making her leg look like something out of a low-budget horror film. It wasn't until she scratched her forehead that she realized she was bleeding on her face, too. She wiped her forehead with the bottom of her T-shirt, but blood kept dripping into her eyes.

The omnipresent buzz of grasshoppers filled her ears. A single screech of a hawk echoed above the treetops. Abbie looked at the phone. The words No Signal stood where bars indicating reception strength would be. It was a risk, keeping it with her. Without a signal, the phone was of no use to her or Port. And the moment she could use the phone, Port could track her.

Abbie's instincts told her to look back. Caleb was still scrambling at the outcropping of rock. Abbie kept up her pace as the ground beneath her evened out. She made it to the aspen, the ground covered in ferns enjoying the shade. It looked like a postcard showing off the alpine beauty of Big Cottonwood canyon.

Abbie crouched into the splay of ferns and waited. She watched through the columns of paper-white trunks. Caleb had lost track of her. He was turning around in circles, squinting in the bright sunlight.

About a hundred feet in front of her, the mountain got really rough. It would be a hard climb, but if she could make it, she had a chance.

Abbie wished she'd spent more time hiking this area as a kid. She knew the canyons near Provo pretty well, but here she was moving from place to place on instinct that came from childhood memory, which was hardly the most reliable source of information.

Her head was bleeding, but she convinced herself it was no big deal. So far, her strategy of running up the mountain was working. Abbie could run for a long time, and Caleb, while fit, was more a weight-bench kind of guy. His body was not built for long-distance speed.

Abbie kept running upward. The trees around her were no longer aspen. They were tall narrow pines. The air was still warm, but cooler than at the house. Abbie slowed her pace when she came to an alpine meadow. The full bloom of spring flowers was gone, but a few clusters of pinks and purples still dotted the field.

She stepped out of the shade from the pines. She pulled out the phone. One bar.

She dialed. One ring, two rings, and then the blessed voice of a woman on the other end of the line.

"Hello, this is Detective Abish Taylor of the Pleasant View City Police. I've been kidnapped. I don't know my exact location, but it's somewhere in Big Cottonwood Canyon near a two-story, red-brick house a few miles off Route 190. My kidnappers are armed and dangerous. This phone is not my own and I'll be destroying it so that it can't be used to track me. Please send help immediately."

The woman tried to keep Abbie on the line, which was indeed her job. But Abbie couldn't afford to keep talking.

"Contact Officer Jim Clarke, too, please," she finished, and then she took the SIM card out of the phone and smashed it between two rocks. She threw the rest of the phone as far as she could. She hated littering, but not as much as she hated the idea of seeing Caleb Monson again.

The 911 call had given her new hope. She tore a long strip of fabric from the hem of her T-shirt and tied it tightly around her head. The blood stopped dripping over her eyebrows. She was ready to make the dash across the open field to the rocks on the other side.

That's when she felt thick fingers pressing into her neck. She turned to see Caleb holding a rock. Then came the first blow.

It knocked her to the ground. Abbie tried to stand. Caleb let her struggle for a bit before his boot made contact with her ribs. She tasted dirt. Then came another blow. Sparks of light danced in front of her eyes, but Abbie blinked her way back to seeing. She reached for a rock. Caleb grabbed her outstretched arm and yanked her to standing. Her knees crumpled beneath her. Caleb watched her sway.

"This one?" He pointed at the rock Abbie had tried to reach. He smiled and picked it up. As she slipped toward the ground, Caleb struck the side of her head with it. Everything went black.

FORTY-THREE

Each heartbeat pulsed agony into her temples. The rest of her body felt bad, but the searing pain in her head had an intensity that made Abbie want to cry. She wouldn't, of course. She was not about to give Caleb the satisfaction. He was somewhere in the darkness watching her. Waiting. She knew it.

She blinked her eyes a few times before she grew accustomed to the darkness. She was in a room that was too large for her to be able to see its exact dimensions. There was no discernible source of natural light. The only way Abbie could see anything was from the bluish glow of night-lights placed at regular intervals along the floor. Abbie saw shelves. The ones directly in front of her were filled from floor to ceiling with jars. Gleaming rows of glass cylinders reflected what little light there was. Each jar neatly marked with a white label: PICKLED BEANS, TOMATOES, PICKLED CUCUMBERS, STRAWBERRY PRESERVES. The shelves to her right were stacked with white plastic buckets. These were full of grain, flour, and sugar.

Abbie was in a storage basement. This was familiar. She'd grown up helping her parents rotate and maintain their own provisions. The Church encouraged all members to be prepared to survive the apocalyptic upheaval preceding the Second Coming of Christ. Everyone should store at least three months' worth of food, water, medicine, and other necessities. Many people stored provisions to last far longer than a mere three months. Mormons had been preppers long before it became a thing.

This cellar had been built to withstand years of turmoil. Even if Abbie could figure out how to escape the duct tape binding her wrists, ankles, and mouth, whatever door led down the stairs to this bunker was certainly heavy and securely locked. She tried to stand, but felt faint.

"Don't even try." Caleb's voice echoed from somewhere behind her. Then he was directly in front of her. In one swift, violent movement, he yanked the tape from her mouth. "We've got all the time in the world. Might as well get to know each other."

Caleb had a pair of scissors in his right hand. He bent down and cut the tape around her ankles.

"You know, I've seen a lot of storage cellars in my life. This one's pretty cool. There's actually a full bathroom with like, I don't know, six stalls and showers. There's a schoolroom with desks, a room for medical and dental emergencies full of all kinds of equipment. There's an enormous kitchen like the ones at church, and then there's a huge sleeping area with at least twenty bunk beds. While you were napping, I found a chapel, a baptismal font, and an endowment room. Whoever planned this place really thought things through."

Nausea joined the pain-party in Abbie's head.

"Get up," Caleb ordered.

Caleb pushed her down a dimly lit hallway. At the end was a small-scale version of the standard Mormon chapel. A large, framed painting of Jesus and another of Joseph Smith hung at the entrance. Caleb kneed Abbie in back to make her move up the aisle toward the front of the chapel. It was dark, but there was light coming from a slightly open door to the left of the piano. Caleb kicked the door open, then pushed Abbie through.

This was the endowment room. It looked like an autocrat's version of Versailles or the Winter Palace. The walls were covered in white satin and the baseboards and crown moldings were gold. The chairs and love seats matched the molding. In the center of the ceiling, which was painted pale blue with cottony white clouds, hung an oversized chandelier dripping with crystals. The Hall of Mirrors might have been the inspiration; the reality was closer to Las Vegas.

"Time for you to repent."

Abbie's mind weighed the likelihood of her succeeding in kicking him hard enough to disable him versus just making him really mad. The odds weren't in her favor.

"If I'm going to pray, I'd like to be able to bow my head and fold my arms," Abbie said, hoping her apparent desire to pray wouldn't set him off.

"That bite hurt. You think I'm gonna trust you with your hands free?"

"I get that. I'm sorry. I wasn't thinking . . . maybe you could just take the tape off and then move my hands in front so that I can fold my arms?"

"I gotta get some more tape. I'll be right back. Don't move. Not. Even. One. Inch."

Abbie didn't move. She tried to get a sense of the room and where it might be in relation to the house upstairs. The house was legitimately old, although it was beautifully maintained. This underground bunker, though, was new and state-of-the-art. Abbie wouldn't have been surprised if it could house the entire First Presidency and their families for the duration of the final battle before the Second Coming.

Caleb's footsteps returned. He slammed the door once he was inside.

"So you can follow directions after all."

When he came into Abbie's field of vision, she could see he was carrying a pair of black-handled scissors and a roll of duct tape. He cut the tape between her wrists and ripped it off.

She moved her arms in front of her, grateful for the pins and needles in her hands. At least they still worked. She made circles with her wrists.

"Hey!" Caleb yelled. He lifted his hand to hit her.

Abbie said, "Please let me just get the blood flow back."

Caleb agreed for reasons Abbie would never know. He watched her move her hands until they no longer hurt.

"Thank you," she said.

"I'm not your Bishop, but you need to ask for forgiveness. Under such circumstances, our Heavenly Father would authorize me to stand in. I do hold the priesthood."

She had no idea why Caleb thought she needed forgiveness, but was happy to play along. "Thank you, Brother Monson. May I pray in silence to prepare?" Abbie wasn't sure if this statement would be met with violence or agreement. She exhaled when Caleb agreed.

Gathering every ounce of docility she could muster, which wasn't much, she gave Caleb a shy smile and bowed her head. How long could she pretend to pray? With her eyes closed, she reconstructed the layout of this basement bunker. Where were the stairs?

The door to the subterranean endowment room opened. Abbie kept her head bowed. She couldn't see who had come in.

"What exactly are you doing?" Port asked, anger radiating from each word. Then there was a quiet cough. A woman asked, "Brother Monson, can you explain to us why you are in this holy space?"

Abbie lifted her head and turned to look into the eyes of Eliza Bentsen.

★ ★ ★

Abbie was returned upstairs to the sitting room. No limeade this time. There was, however, a gun pointed directly at her chest. Caleb did not seem happy that Port and Eliza had unceremoniously kicked him out of the endowment room. He was, however, a good soldier. He followed orders. Eliza Bentsen, apparently, outranked him. Even without holding the priesthood.

Eliza and Port had retired to the smoking room. Eliza

had pulled the pocket doors closed behind them. Still, Abbie and Caleb heard each syllable of Port's diatribe.

"I don't care how long you've known her—don't forget, I've known her since birth, too—we can't let this work be compromised. You and I both know these are the last days. We must bring as many spirits from the preexistence as we can, as quickly as we can. This is the only way. If we wait until the general membership of the Church is ready, we'll lose valuable time. It took at least five years for Joseph Smith to share his revelation about plural marriage. Just think if he had to deal with social media. We can't risk this backfiring. If it comes out now, without proper preparation, it will be disastrous. It has taken decades for the Church to gain acceptance as a mainstream Christian church. This would ruin all that."

Abbie couldn't hear Eliza's response because her voice was soft. It always was.

When Abbie had figured out Brittany's diary, she had hoped she was wrong. Abbie's initial mistake was thinking Brittany had written someone's initials. The acronyms, though, were not names. Brittany had been referring to a Church title: The Second Counselor. TSC. Port. Once Abbie realized that, the reference to SB had become clear: Sister Bentsen. What Abbie had overheard in Mexico was right. The "Sister Bentsen" those sisters at the orphanage were talking about was Eliza.

Abbie strained to hear what Eliza was saying when Port erupted again.

"If this gets out now, we'll have to scrap everything.

We'll be worse off than where we are now. We can't risk that. I don't want to make changes to the temple ceremony for all those feminists. If this goes wrong, I may have no choice. The life of one person must not outweigh the future of the Restoration."

The house went quiet. Caleb stared at Abbie with empty eyes, his finger toying with the trigger.

The pocket doors slid open. Eliza took a seat next to Abbie. Port sat next to Caleb.

"Abish." Eliza placed her hand gently on Abbie's. "Being outside of our Heavenly Father's presence is an unnatural state, but when you live your life in accordance with the principles of the restored Gospel, death is nothing to be feared. It is simply a transition."

Thoughts and emotions whirled through Abbie's brain. She loved Eliza. Eliza had sat with her at the hospital next to her mother's bed. She'd held her when she cried and screamed. She'd stood with her in silence when her mom's coffin was lowered into the dark, crumbly earth.

"Abish, you don't need to understand everything," Eliza said. "That's always been your problem. You want to understand. We cannot know everything. Only Heavenly Father has a full understanding."

Abbie didn't think it was possible for her to feel any more betrayed than she did at that moment. This justification, that only Heavenly Father had full knowledge, was used to absolve a host of sins without ever addressing them. From denying black members entrance to the temple to blood atonement and plural marriage, each dark spot in the history of the Church had been whitewashed with the broad brush of "Heavenly Father knows best." Any questioning of that was taken as dissent from the one true Gospel.

Beneath Eliza's frail hand, Abbie strained not to make a fist.

"What I'm asking of you," the old woman said, "is that you simply keep what you know to yourself. Every young woman who has chosen to enter the New and Everlasting Covenant has done so with clear knowledge and a strong testimony that what she is doing is according to divine revelation. Respect the wishes of these women and men who have been sealed for eternity in the temple. Let them practice their faith as they see fit. When the time is right, they will share what they have done with the world. That time will come. I know this is true as surely as I know Joseph Smith restored the fullness of the Gospel to this earth."

Eliza motioned for Caleb to put down the gun. He lowered his arm, but his finger stayed curled around the trigger.

Abbie was silent. What could she possibly say?

"What I need from you," Eliza said, "is an assurance that you will not speak about Mexico. The world is not ready. Most members of the Church are not ready. We need time. The Lord needs time."

"Heber didn't understand that, did he?" Abbie asked.

Eliza shook her head. "No, he didn't. He was like you. He was patient for a while, but he believed in being open and honest. He would say, 'If you're doing something you don't want anyone to know about, maybe it's a sign you shouldn't be doing it at all.' There was a time when I found his innocence refreshing."

"Heber didn't believe in plural marriage," Abbie said.

Eliza's eyes twinkled. "Oh, Abish, he didn't *believe*—he *knew* it was a requirement for exaltation." Eliza patted Abbie's hand, then turned her gaze to Port. "Do you have it?"

Port pressed his hands against the armrests and pushed himself to a stand. He walked to an ornate wooden desk, complete with inlaid images of beehives, shaking hands, and an all-seeing eye. Port removed a tiny key from his pocket and inserted it into the lock of a drawer. Abbie heard a click. Port opened it, then donned a pair of pristine white cotton gloves. He pulled out a sheet of paper.

Port made his way over to Abbie and held the fragile letter for her to read:

1886 Revelation Given to President John Taylor September 27, 1886

My son John, you have asked me concerning the New and Everlasting Covenant how far it is binding upon my people.

Abbie skimmed to the final words: *I have not revoked this law, nor will I, for it is everlasting, and those who will enter into my glory must obey the conditions thereof; even so, Amen.*

Abbie caught her breath. It was true. The 1886 Revelation existed. Since the 1930s, the official Church position had been that there was no such revelation. And yet, here it was, in Port's hands.

FORTY-FOUR

The clock ticked. Caleb kept shifting positions, his knee bobbing up and down. Eliza's hand rested on Abbie's. Port retook his seat.

"What about Bryce Strong? Brittany Thompson?" Abbie asked Eliza.

"Are these the young people who have passed?" Eliza turned to Port. He nodded.

"That is inconsequential," Eliza said.

"What do you mean?" Abbie tried to keep her tone as calm as Eliza's, but it was a challenge. Abbie was angry. How could it be possible to think this was okay? Even with her great-great-great-grandfather's revelation, decent people did not behave like this.

"Reasonable members can disagree about polygamy," Abbie said. "I know the Church is facing demographic pressures. Plural marriage makes as much sense today as it ever did. I understand the desire for women to be married and to become mothers. If they agree to whatever arrangement you've set up, who am I to judge?" Abbie paused and then asked, "But killing people?"

"That was not our original intent," Eliza said. Abbie wondered if, according to Eliza's moral code, that made a difference.

"Heber thought that going to the Prophet would clarify matters," Eliza explained. Her tone shifted from warm to icy. "He thought he could pray with the President of the Church and find peace."

The throbbing pain in her head and excruciating agony shooting throughout her body did not dull the icy chill that ran down Abbie's spine.

"For argument's sake," Eliza continued, "let's pretend the Prophet possessed the mental capacity to function. Perhaps Heber could have found peace if the one man nearer to God than he was told him to keep this revelation secret."

Eliza's clear blue eyes focused on Abbie. "But Heber would not have found the certainty he wanted, not by talking to the Prophet. Each of us in this room knows that the Prophet has not been able to engage fully for quite some time."

For several years now, the Prophet had made the rounds. He could smile. He could wave. But his trips were highly orchestrated. The slide into dementia had been slow at first, but then it had picked up speed. At the moment, the Prophet was not capable of caring for himself, let alone making decisions on behalf of fifteen million members of the Church.

"There is no easy way," Eliza said. "In the end, we must all choose between the one true path of the restored Gospel or all other paths. How certain can we be that our doubts aren't the work of Satan to pull us from righteousness? How certain are we that our questions aren't a test of faith? I believe in the authority of this restored Church. I do not need to question each step and ask if what I am doing is moral. If I follow my leaders, it is right."

Abbie shivered. Then Port cleared his throat. "Eliza," he said, "you tried to convince me that we could trust Abish to just walk away. I hope you see as clearly as I do that we simply cannot do that."

Port looked at Caleb and motioned with his chin toward the back of the house.

Caleb wrapped his hand around Abbie's bicep and walked her through the house, out the back door. With painful efficiency, he yanked Abbie onto the lawn and pushed her to the ground. He hit her across the cheek with the handle of the gun, then hit the back of her head so hard that Abbie couldn't see. When she finally blinked her vision back, Caleb was pointing the gun at her head.

"Been wanting to do this since I saw your house last year. It's incredible to me that you're the daughter of a true servant of the Lord. You were given so much and you threw it all away."

Abbie had underestimated Caleb Monson's animosity. She'd known he was a man quick to anger, but she hadn't realized he was angry with her in particular. If he hadn't been waiting for instructions, Abbie was certain she'd already be dead, and probably not in as nice a way as a gunshot to her head.

Abbie was looking up at her executioners from the ground. She pushed her arms against the grass. First she managed to get to her knees. With extraordinary effort, she put one foot on the ground. She used her knee to push herself to a standing position. If she was going to go, she was going to go with some dignity.

Caleb shoved the gun under her chin so hard Abbie could feel it with her tongue.

The well-oiled screen door opened. Eliza stepped out onto the porch first. Port followed. A single wisp of a white cloud drifted across the wide expanse of sky. Abbie could smell that the peaches were almost ripe. Eliza held the railing and descended three steps into the yard. She walked toward Abbie.

"Brother Monson," Eliza instructed, "will you please take your aim from the porch?"

Caleb looked none too pleased that he wouldn't have an up-close-and-personal view of what was about to happen, but he complied.

Eliza walked over to Abbie and kissed the bloody gash on Abbie's forehead. "It's not in your nature to run away from the inevitable."

Eliza stepped to the side, turned back toward Caleb, and said softly, "Fire."

Time stopped. Caleb's eyes twinkled as he aimed the gun. He pulled the trigger. If it hadn't been impossible, Abbie would have said she watched the bullet slice through the air. Then, reality shifted.

Eliza's body crumpled in front of her.

The sky turned lavender. In the distance, Abbie heard sirens and the rumble of engines and cars crunching on gravel. She touched the back of her head where Caleb had hit her with the gun. Her hand was wet with blood.

FORTY-FIVE

Beeping. It was faint, but persistent, and not too far from her head. Abbie tried to open her eyes, but her lids resisted. The first scent to touch her nostrils was aseptic. Then there was something floral, roses maybe. Something metallic. And coffee.

Abbie tried to move her hand. She was warm, cozy. The blankets were heavy. A little more sleep . . .

The beeping, again. Abbie lifted her eyelids just enough to tell that it was either dawn or dusk. Without moving her head, which didn't seem inclined to obey her brain's suggestion anyway, Abbie saw Flynn staring at her with at least a day's worth of stubble on his face.

"Hey, gorgeous."

Abbie smiled. She tried to move, but everything hurt.

"What—" Abbie wanted to tell Flynn everything. Ask him how they'd found her, but she couldn't get her mouth to work.

"You lost a lot of blood. You've been out for a bit."

"How long?" Two words. She could say two words.

Flynn looked at the clock, then returned his gaze to Abbie. "Thirty-four hours and twenty-two minutes."

She wanted to ask, "Did the 911 dispatcher contact Clarke?" but all she could say was her partner's name.

Flynn nodded.

"He was pretty amazing, I have to admit. You missed your POST hearing, by the way. Clarke managed to rally the troops. He had the entire Pleasant View Police Department with him and some local guys, too. Helicopters, dogs, the whole nine yards. It was rather too melodramatic for your taste. Good thing you slept through it."

Abbie smiled. She did hate a fuss. Although, at the moment, she was quite thankful for whatever fuss, melodramatic or otherwise, had brought her here to this hospital bed with a bedraggled Flynn by her side. She was grateful not to have the barrel of a gun anywhere near her face.

"It was tough on your dad, but we saw your notes in Brittany Thompson's diary. I was skeptical, but as soon as your dad saw what you had written, it was like the last tumbler in a lock clicked into place," Flynn explained. "He didn't even argue when I suggested we search properties belonging to either Eliza's or Port's families."

"The house?" Again, her brain was capable of more than her body.

"That charming Victorian? Port's family."

"Arrests?"

The glow in Flynn's eyes darkened, just a bit. He exhaled. "You're not going to like what's happened while you've been napping."

"Why?"

"They're saying it was all Caleb," Flynn said. "Clarke has been trying to shake them, but everyone is giving a version of the same story: Caleb was unhinged and threatening everyone. It was his idea to kidnap you and he came armed. He went after you and Eliza. Port managed to turn his employing Caleb into an example of how he—and the Church—is helping veterans. In public, Port is clutching his pearls, 'shocked, absolutely shocked' at the turn of events. Caleb, as befits his role, is saying nothing. He's going to take the rap on this."

Abbie wanted to nod her head to show she understood, but she still couldn't make it move. Once she was feeling better, she could set the record straight.

But if that was everything, Flynn didn't look as relieved as he should.

"More?" she asked.

"Your dad's been called in for another disciplinary council, tomorrow morning. One of those former Mormon podcasters tweeted about it. It's everywhere. John's with him at the house, because he's not getting out of bed. I'm worried Port is angry. Eliza was not the person he wanted to take that bullet."

Port was probably livid. Eliza had left him to deal with the aftermath alone. Of course, he did have her to thank for orchestrating everything so beautifully. Everything could be linked to Caleb. That poor guy had probably never even seen it coming.

Abbie watched Flynn's eyes droop. He reached for his coffee.

"Go. Eat. Sleep." She tried to smile.

He kissed her bandaged head, then her nose, then her lips. "Don't you ever scare me like that again." He kissed her mouth one more time. "I'll be back in a few hours. A shower would be good. I'm a little ripe." He blew her a kiss from the door, said something to the nurse outside, and walked out of Abbie's sight.

Was Port really going to play it like this?

Abbie tried to lift her head and immediately felt faint. She rested back on her pillow and closed her eyes. She waited; then she opened her eyes again. There was a nurse in her room.

"Ah, Ms. Taylor, it's so nice to see you awake. Would you like to sit up?"

"Yes." Abbie's voice sounded like a memory. It was faint and fading.

The nurse placed a controller in Abbie's hand. "You can move the bed with this." The nurse pressed a button with a triangle symbol with its apex facing away from Abbie. The bed glided into a semi-upright position. Abbie was sitting, sort of.

"Would you like some juice?"

Now that the nurse mentioned it, her throat hurt. Not just a little unpleasant scratchiness, but actual pain. The part of her that was feeling faint with a sore throat wanted the juice; the wave of nausea that washed over her when she tried to turn her head to face the kind nurse did not.

"Please."

The nurse strode out of the room. An instant later, she

returned with a small plastic cup of orange juice, a straw pierced through the aluminum foil covering.

"Here you go." The nurse held the cup in front of Abbie so that the straw leaned right in toward her mouth. Abbie opened her lips and then closed them around the plastic cylinder. She sipped. It was a little too sweet. She sipped some more.

"Good job!" the nurse exclaimed when Abbie finished the tiny cup of juice. From the woman's tone, you would have thought Abbie had just crossed the finish line of the New York City Marathon in under three hours. "Do you want more?"

Abbie thought for a moment. She knew this was not a difficult question, but her head felt fuzzy. After some consideration, she said, "Yes, please."

"Would you like to watch TV?"

"No, thank you."

The nurse pointed to the controller still lying in Abbie's right hand. "Just press this symbol, and one of us will be in here. Breakfast is in a few hours." The woman pulled a notepad and pen from one of her many pockets. "Let's put in your order." With an efficiency that all good healthcare workers seemed to share, the nurse confirmed Abbie's breakfast order, brought her another cup of orange juice, checked her vital signs, made a few notes on a clipboard hanging at the foot of her bed, and asked again if Abbie wanted to watch TV. Then she bustled from the room.

Abbie tried to move her head again. This time her neck and head agreed. She was alone in her room. The window faced east. Rays of sunlight created a halo above Mount Olympus. She was somewhere in Salt Lake, maybe Holladay. She hadn't even thought to ask. There were bouquets everywhere. Judging from the number and extravagance, Abbie must have been in pretty bad shape. These were not get-well-after-your-appendectomy flowers. These looked like we're-glad-you're-still-here-after-your-emergency-heart-surgery flowers.

She opened the card attached to the nearest arrangement within easy reach. It was all sunflowers. GET WELL SOON, ABS. LOVE, LUKE, HEATHER, MATTHEW, LILY AND JOHN. Had John sent this on his own, or were her other brothers and sisters actually involved? Abbie wanted to believe the latter.

Abbie turned her head away from the card. The orange juice and a straw sat on the bedside tray. Abbie reached for the cup. On the third try, she managed to push the straw through the foil lid. Nothing like reconstituted frozen orange juice to start your day.

Dad.

Abbie tried to move her legs. They didn't want to cooperate. Damn it. Just hours—days?—ago, with duct tape around her ankles and with her arms fastened behind her, she'd had no trouble swinging her legs off the couch in that creepy Victorian house and hopping across a room. Now she was struggling to flex her toes. She tried again. It certainly wasn't graceful, but Abbie managed to get her left leg out of the bed; then she pulled the right leg to meet it. She sat for a moment, feeling the cold tile beneath the fuzzy socks that had twisted around so that the rubber strips stretched over the bridge of her foot. Little fragments of light flitted across her field of vision. She waited for them to pass, then pressed her palms into the mattress and pushed herself to stand.

Another wave of faintness washed over her. She waited for it to pass. It was time to get going.

★ ★ ★

"The Second Counselor isn't seeing anyone this morning," said Sister Appleby, if the brass nameplate on her desk was to be believed. The portly woman with well-coiffed short hair all the same shade of lemon cake smiled at Abbie. "Perhaps I can help you make an appointment with some-one else who may be able to, uh, help."

The woman's eyes reflected concern, compassion, and a hint of distaste at the disheveled young woman standing in front of her. Abbie couldn't exactly blame her. Abbie prob-ably smelled even worse than she looked.

"Oh, I think the Second Counselor will see me." Abbie kept moving toward the office door. Sweet old Sister Appleby was not prepared for Abbie's appearance and her apparent lack of manners. In all her years guarding Port's door, Abbie guessed this was the first time anyone had ever behaved as rudely as Abbie was right then.

"Sister Appleby, it's all right." Port's voice carried through the closed door. "I know Abish Taylor." He added, "Please do not let anyone disturb us."

Sister Appleby nodded and returned to typing whatever it was she had been working on when Abbie first arrived.

Abbie walked into Port's office and shut the door behind her. She did her best not to collapse into one of the leather chairs in front of Port's big, shiny desk. She stood behind the chair on the left and leaned into it.

"You don't look very good. Would you like some coffee, perhaps, to perk you up?" Port lingered on the word *coffee*. The way he said it, you'd have thought he'd just swallowed sour milk.

"I'm fine." Abbie didn't want to waste any strength on unnecessary words.

"That's not what I've been told. The last I heard, you were unconscious until sometime very early this morning. Apparently, you sustained several concussions during your altercations with that terrible Caleb Monson. The doctors expect that your memory of the past few days or weeks is going to be unreliable or nonexistent."

Abbie finally gave in. She stepped in front of her support chair and slid down into its upholstered softness. The change in elevation made her feel faint. She waited for the moment to pass. *Breathe in, breathe out.* Yes, sitting was easier.

"I wouldn't count on my memory being fuzzy." Each word took effort. Port was eyeing her, watching to see just how diminished his adversary was. Abbie felt like the injured elk in one of those nature documentaries on wolves. The elk, though, was fueled only by fear. Abbie was past fear.

"You think you have a license to lie?" she asked.

"I serve a higher purpose than the truth." Port looked Abbie directly in both her swollen and unswollen eye, as though he was making an important point.

"And that makes it okay?"

"It most certainly does." Port leaned back in his chair. "You, of course, still pose a problem."

"You don't think I'll stay quiet?"

"No, I don't. I am, however, hopeful that a taste of your father's excommunication will give you time to mull over your options. It will take him years to be worthy of rebaptism, if he lives that long." Port paused. "Darling Abish Taylor, I know your father. I know him as well as anyone ever has."

Port's eyes glimmered. Abbie knew he was reminding her that it was on Port's orders that Abbie's dad had left her mom just days before she died. The Church had needed someone to authenticate documents in New York. Port had called Abbie's dad, and Abbie's dad had obeyed. Nausea came again, but this time Abbie knew her queasiness had nothing to do with any injuries she might have sustained.

Port continued with his threat. "Your father will do everything in his power to return to the Church, you know. There's nothing he wouldn't do to be with your mother in the Celestial Kingdom."

Port was right. Excommunication would destroy her dad.

"Of course, in the process of becoming worthy again, he would have to distance himself from all non-faith-affirming influences." Port's smile had all the warmth of an ice cube. "Including you."

Abbie took a deep breath, then returned a cold smile of her own.

"Oh, my dear Port—may I call you that?—perhaps my

account of the last few days or even few weeks will be questioned because of my injuries, but you know I have the recording of your meeting."

Whatever satisfied ruddiness had colored Port's cheeks when he'd threatened Abbie's dad drained from his face. For the first time since Abbie had opened her eyes in the hospital, she felt like she might be the stronger person in the room.

"You know the one I'm talking about, the one from the night you had Caleb murder Heber. There's a fellow named Steiner from a PR firm who tested the waters about how receptive people would be to the practice of plural marriage. Then, a Brother McConkie with a fascinating account of Supreme Court case law. Oh! And this fun little conversation at the end of the recording between you and Bowen about your little experiment in Colonia Juárez."

Abbie paused to let that bit of information settle.

Port had lost the capacity to respond as a human being long ago. He was, however, capable of calculating the needs of the organization he had dedicated himself to.

"If anything happens to my dad and his standing in the Church, anything at all, copies of that recording will be sent not only to MormonLeaks, but to every major media outlet and social media platform on this planet. Transcriptions will also be made available."

Port studied Abbie carefully.

"If you're wondering, dear Port, if killing me right now would prevent disclosure, I assure you, it would not."

Check. Mate.

FORTY-SIX

The colors on the mountain were washed in gray. The air was still warm, but it promised to cool when the last glow of sun disappeared behind the mountain. Aspen leaves shimmered in the breeze. This land was raw and intense, its beauty marred only by the manmade behemoths that clung to the mountainside. Houses trying to own what their existence had destroyed. Still, Abbie understood the desire to carve out a piece of nature's perfection. If Abbie died at that moment, with that view, she would've died happy.

Flynn had persuaded Abbie to spend a few days recuperating at his place in Deer Valley. The "place" was built off the side of a mountain where roads hadn't existed even a few decades ago. It was, one could say, rather nice. Flynn's eye for detail and appreciation of imperfection made what could have been just one more expensive ski lodge around Park City into a place anyone with sense would want to call home.

They stood on an outdoor deck that could easily fit a

cocktail party for seventy-five. Flynn held up the dark, olive-green bottle with its shield-shaped label the color of butcher paper. It was going to be Abbie's first real drink since before the kidnapping. Her doctors had been cautious—overly so, she thought—about monitoring her recovery. Finally, they'd given her the green light to imbibe. Flynn pulled the cork from the bottle, letting it pop just a bit, to mark the occasion. Abbie knew he preferred to open the bottle silently, as many a sommelier would recommend, but she loved the celebratory sound.

"To Detective Taylor," Flynn said, and she raised her glass of streaming gold bubbles. She took her first sip before setting down her glass on a teak table, next to a copy of the *Deseret News*. Just below the fold was a story about an ex-soldier, suffering from PTSD, who had gone on a murderous spree, killing the former First Counselor to the President of the Church of Jesus Christ of Latter-day Saints, a world-renowned rock climber from Ogden, and the First Counselor's wife.

There was an op-ed about the need for more mental health care assistance for veterans. Bowen's name was the byline.

"No mention of Brittany Thompson anywhere, or did I miss it?" Flynn asked, taking another sip.

"Nope, you didn't miss it." There was no mention of Brittany Thompson. Abbie doubted there ever would be. "Clarke went back to Bragg's to search for the medical ID bracelet, but came up with nothing. No sign of the kids either."

"You worried about them?"

Abbie leaned against the railing that separated her from a steep drop into pointed tops of pine trees. It felt great to stand. She took another long sip, then said, "That may be the only thing that doesn't concern me. Eliza would never let the kids be hurt, beyond losing their mother, of course. Those kids are valiant souls from the preexistence."

"Is there any chance of charges against Bragg?"

"I wish."

Abbie and Clarke had gone about Brittany Thompson's death every which way. There simply was no way to prove Bragg was lying. Abbie believed he was, but her belief was not enough, and there was nothing they could do without a willing witness to testify against Bragg. Even if they could track down any of his other wives, Abbie knew they would not cooperate. The promise of eternal marriage was a strong motivator. They would never sacrifice their eternal exaltation for a doomed bigamy case.

The entire polygamous experiment had melted into nothing.

Port and Eliza had been careful. They had also benefited from the brash preposterousness of their plan. Who would ever believe such a story? The answer, Abbie was forced to admit, was no one.

"I have to tip my hat to Port and Eliza," Abbie said. "No purporting to be married, no cohabitation, and nothing within the borders of the great state of Utah. Their legalism would make my great-great-great-grandfather proud."

She finished her glass, probably too quickly. The bubbles

were beginning to have an effect. She felt happy and warm. Flynn's fingers touched Abbie's as he poured more champagne.

"There's nothing to be done?" he asked.

Abbie shook her head.

"What about Caleb? Has he said anything?" Flynn asked.

"Nope. I don't think he will. My best guess is Port is paying Caleb's legal fees, keeping a roof over his wife's head, and paying for that white Mercedes in the garage. Caleb can keep it all as long as he toes the party line."

"No chance that anything will stick to Port or Eliza?" Flynn asked.

"Not unless Bowen speaks up." Abbie pointed at the op-ed about the need to help veterans like Caleb Monson. "I think that's highly unlikely."

Flynn's eyes flashed. "I still can't get over the fact that he just walked away. He knew everything, he was part of it all, and when he realized how ugly it was, he slunk away."

Abbie had shared Flynn's anger at first, but as time had put distance between her and the day with Caleb's gun in her throat, she'd understood that Bowen was doomed to live with his cowardice and shame. He had escaped that house in the canyon because he'd seen what it meant to ignore the basic tenets of decency in the name of some supposed higher purpose. He had been complicit in something beyond justification, beyond morality, beyond goodness. Now he would live as the camera-ready spokesman for the Church, knowing he was not a principled man but only played one on TV.

"Maybe we can give him the opposite of the Neville Longbottom award: ten points for lacking the bravery to stand up to his friends," Abbie suggested. Flynn chuckled. As a father of five, he was well acquainted with the world of Harry Potter.

"This can't be it, can it?" he asked.

"Yeah, I think it can. I don't know what it's going to do to my dad. But he's made it clear he does not want to talk about it. Keeping his faith is a full-time job."

Flynn was right that this was not how a case was supposed to end. Abbie was supposed to get all of the bad guys, not just one of them. Caleb was paying the price for Eliza, Port, Bowen, and probably Bragg, too. There was supposed to be justice. Here, there was simply an end.

Abbie leaned out over the railing again, gazing up at the first stars sparkling in the sky. Flynn wrapped his hands around her waist. "Don't lean over so far."

Mischief lit up Abbie's eyes. She leaned a little further back and held her hands out over the empty space above the treetops. "Nervous?" she teased.

Flynn inhaled sharply. "Please, don't do that. My heart can't take another scare like you gave me last week." He pulled her back from the ledge.

"I know this isn't the ending you wanted," he said.

"It's not a perfect ending." Abbie shrugged. "But I'm not sure perfect endings exist."

"They might." Flynn kissed her.

Yes, they might, Abbie thought. She kissed him back. They just might.

Acknowledgments

Thank you to my fabulous and sharp-eyed editor who helped turn what was a too-wordy, too-much manuscript into an actual story. Thank you to everyone at Crooked Lane, especially Matt Martz, for believing there's a place in this world for Detective Abish Taylor. Thank you to Paula Munier and Gina Panettieri, who are always looking out for me. Thank you to my fierce writing friends (Charlotte's tribe, you know who you are), who inspire me and take care of me. Thank you, Kirsten and Ty. You amaze me every day. And thank you, Tycho, for everything.